D1606009

"A stimulating and satisfying read..."

*"A very different and refreshing approach
to historical fiction..."*

*"Patricia Reynolds performs a minor miracle: she
illuminates a largely forgotten time..."*

"...completely enthralling from beginning to end..."

*"This book accomplishes the twin achievements
of great literature: it is both completely literate
while simultaneously truly magical..."*

Patricia Reynolds

Keeper
of the
Souls

SERIES

A SCATTERING OF CROWS
BOOK ONE

Copyright page

KEEPER OF THE SOULS SERIES
A SCATTERING OF CROWS
BOOK ONE
Published by Old Crow Publishing
WASHINGTON

Copyright © by Patricia Reynolds 2018
ISBN: 978-0999834800

Cover design by Damonza.com. Universe image by Jean-Charles Cuillandre, jcc@cfht.hawaii.edu used with permission of the artist. Edited by: Roberta Edgars

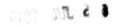

ACKNOWLEDGEMENTS

To Timothy—the magician and wizard and much more. My book could not be done without you. Words cannot express my gratitude.

William Jenner.. a magician of a different sort... thank you kind sir for all your help.

My sister Nancy Williams, who listened patiently to my story for years.

Norman "Dan" Weinstein... I know you are surrounded by mounds of chocolate and fairies, smiling while doing all kinds of amazing things... like, soaring wildly through the misty fjords. You are missed...

Foreword

In her debut novel, *Keeper of the Souls*, Patricia Reynolds introduces her bold new voice and her mastery of storytelling to the public. In the hands of a lesser writer, this tale would be moribund in facts, institutions, and "authenticity." But Reynolds eschews the obvious in this robust and riveting narrative. Instead, she aims for the human spirit, and hits the bullseye.

The linchpin of the story set near the end of the 19th Century is the forced removal of a group of Sioux children from their homes on reservations in the Dakotas to a boarding school across country in Western Pennsylvania. If that were all there were to the plot, we would simply say, "Ho-hum," and move on. But Reynolds's memorable characters and striking storyline quickly lures you into the scenario and holds you hostage throughout. The distant past becomes a personal experience as Reynolds recounts this shameful episode in our American history. So detailed is the description, the reader is made to feel the pain and suffering of these displaced children —ripped away from their beloved families and their ancient traditions.

Where did this idea for a mass abduction take place? The Bureau of Indian Affairs, founded in 1824, became convinced that the Sioux were on the brink of extinction as the country advanced into the Industrial Era. Influenced by the opinions set forth in James Fenimore Cooper's 1826 classic, *The Last of the Mohicans*, they were determined not to preside over the last of the Sioux, but rather take credit for their assimilation.

By now, the buffalo were extinct—the main source of the Sioux's food and shelter. The people were no longer free to roam and hunt on the Great Plains, their home for hundreds of years. Completely dependent upon the federal government, they had become wards of the State—essentially beggars. Exacerbating the problem, the U.S. Declaration of Independence referred to indigenous people as "savages" and Article I even excluded them from its protective laws.

We recognize the historic encounter of June 25, 1876 as Custer's Last Stand. More accurately, we might call it the Sioux's Last Stand, since, in the aftermath of the U.S. army's defeat, the Sioux were forbidden armed rebellion. Crazy Horse, a Lakota Sioux, who had led his people and the Cheyenne into the legendary battle, said, "When you defend your homeland, you are called patriots. When we defend our homeland, you call us savages."

As the century moved toward its conclusion, the Sioux people were being confined to small tracts of land the American government termed "reservations." That land was but a small fraction of what they had had been promised by an 1862 treaty— comparable in size to the Dakotas and Wyoming combined. (You will notice the term "Indian giver" takes on a new level of irony here.)

The prevailing view at the time, especially in the West was, "Kill them; kill them all. Every single Indian." There were groups, especially Christians, who believed that indigenous people were "the children of God, deserving of protection." But the Bureau of Indian Affairs saw the "Sioux problem" as the fault of the Sioux— the result of their clinging to the past and failure to adapt to the present—their refusal to become Jeffersonian citizen-farmers. The only solution, concluded the Bureau of Indian Affairs: "Take the Indian out of the Indian." But how?

In *Keeper of the Souls*, Reynolds creates a fictional, charismatic preacher she aptly names Preacher Jim. His vision is clear: unless these Sioux children accept Jesus Christ as their Savior, they will be damned to Hell. So schooling will be their path toward enlightenment. It is their souls in which he is interested, not their minds and bodies. Education is simply an adjunct to their Christianization.

As the story unfolds it is clear that Preacher Jim and his staff lack the requisite skills to effectively teach the children. So, without proper tools, they resort to harsh discipline—always a fallback position for the untrained.

"For Satan finds some mischief still, for idle hands to do."

-Isaac Walts,
Against Idleness and Mischief (1715)

"The past is a foreign country; they do things differently there!"

-Lesley P. Hartley,
The Go-Betweens, 1953

The trauma endured by these children is heartbreaking. Sequestered at a boarding school hundreds of miles from their home (the name of the school is fictionalized as well as the location), they are unloved, ill-fed, ill-clothed, and at the mercy of people with no understanding of the Sioux culture nor empathy for its adherents.

Preacher Jim's way of reacting to the trauma he and his staff have created is to completely ignore it. He makes no effort to change.

> *"Like all weak men he laid an exaggerated*
> *stress on not changing one's mind."*
>
> ~ William Somerset Maugham,
> *Of Human Bondage*

The flaw in Preacher Jim, Reynolds makes clear, is not in his religion, but his character. Instead of saying, "Lord, forgive me for the wrong I have committed in Your name," he chooses an apocalyptic ending—symbolic, rather than realistic.

Despite the horrendous damage they caused, including loss of lives, these boarding schools for indigenous children continued to operate into the 1930s, stopped not by moral indignation but by the economic reality of the Great Depression.

Underpinning the story is the eternal spark of hope in the indomitable human spirit. It is by no accident that the name of its mythic hero is Hidden Spirit.

In *Keeper of Souls*, Reynolds invites us on a hero's journey, as valiant as that of Homer's Odysseus in *The Odyssey*. This is not only the story of one group of Sioux children, most of whom survived their ordeal, but also of the survival of the entire Sioux nation—and of all indigenous people everywhere. With over 500 Native American tribes currently in existence, it is safe to say the Sioux managed to endure in spite of our best efforts to extinguish their culture.

On a plane where few American writers dare venture, Reynolds fuses historical fiction with magical realism. In effect, the reader is required to suspend disbelief in order to experience reality—the emotional truth that lies just beneath the facts and where every word jumps off the page and targets the heart.

In retrospect, the Bureau of Indian Affairs had not only misdiagnosed the problem, they also created the hair-brained solution they put into widespread practice. In this cautionary tale, essentially good men and women traumatized these children out of ignorance, not intolerance. Even today, well over a hundred years later, there has been no official acknowledgment of wrongdoing, let alone an apology.

From page one through to the end, this novel is filled in equal measure with illumination and heartbreak. The suffering of the children will haunt the reader forever—which is precisely what Reynolds had in mind.

If you read only one book this year, make it this one: ***Keeper of the Souls***.

William Jenner—Attorney, History Aficionado

A Black Hills expedition member James Calhoun wrote:

"For the hives of industry will take the place of dirty wigwams. Civilization will ere long reign supreme and throw heathen barbarism into oblivion;... Christian temples will elevate their lofty spires upwards towards the azure sky while places of heathen mythology will sink to rise no more."

1874 – POWDER RIVER, WYOMING

BOOK –1

DAY OF GREATNESS

MAGIC FILLED THE air on the warm summer day that Hidden Spirit was born. The sweet scent of blackberries and chokecherries was like an elixir, drifting throughout the camp on the soft summer breeze. Finally, the cries of a newborn broke the silence of the gathered crowd when a huge burst of icy droplets spilled from the sky, coating the newborn's tepee with a frosty glaze. A moment passed, then an explosion of fire shot from the sky, echoing a loud boom. Its reverberations melted the ice in a flash as a jagged bolt of lightning cut through the clouds—startling the onlookers. Someone hollered, "It's Broken Feather," and the people looked up, recognizing the outline of his magnanimous face as it disappeared into the heavens. Everyone was aghast. It had to be a sign from the Great Spirit, some explained. Others said it happened because someone extraordinary had entered the world—Broken Feather's grandson. Who could be more extraordinary?

Broken Feather was a mystical warrior, regal and bold, a wizard at medicine who foretold of the future. On the day that Hidden Spirit was born, Broken Feather departed to the Other World. Some whispered that Broken Feather was as old as the flowing rivers, while others claimed that he was as ancient as the towering trees that whispered their many secrets to those that could hear. But all agreed he was as wise and majestic as the Black Hills that called to him in his dreams. Shivers would float down the spines of the ones who remembered their beloved hero... but now a new hero had arrived—Hidden Spirit.

From the moment of his birth, Hidden Spirit was held in high esteem and adored by all. As the people neared the boy, they would gasp at the sight of his remarkable face and when they touched his tiny hand, a jolt of electricity would shoot straight up their arms, astounding the people. Hidden Spirit's childhood was filled with adventure and freedom as he ran carefree through valleys and creeks, mountains and meadows, searching for wonders as he fearlessly tromped along. His daring escapades captured the attention of his peers. He would jump into cavernous lakes—some claimed with no bottom—and dive deep into the abyss before coming up for air, declaring he could see far into the beyond. Hidden Spirit could navigate his way with ease through the mysterious, treacherous badlands and, just as mysteriously, blend into the shapes and shifting colors of the weather-beaten spirals. Sometimes he would emerge with a deer or wild antelope following behind... as if they sensed his greatness.

*

White Cloud, Hidden Spirit's father, and Limping Fox, his uncle, sat around a small fire smoking a pipe and talking.

Limping Fox thought Hidden Spirit, even at seven years old, had the same warrior spirit as his grandfather, Broken Feather. He crowed over the boy's accomplishments. "Your son is smart and wild and brave. Look how he stands—full of determination. He has the spark burning in his eyes." The old man paused as Hidden Spirit rode by. "And he rides as if he and the horse are one. There is no one better on horseback, except maybe for

Crazy Horse, who could ride like the wind." A hint of sadness surrounded the old man as he spoke of their beloved hero on bended knee, looking to the sky. "Your son will help us one day when the change comes for our people," the old man said softly. White Cloud nodded and the two men smoked in silence. Their faces filled with worry for their future as the whites encroached further onto their lands.

Hidden Spirit at eight years old was becoming more daring and brazen, even a little reckless. He loved showing off and receiving accolades. White Cloud was worried for his son, and warned him. "My son, do not become big-headed by your feats. That's when trouble begins." Hidden Spirit ignored his father. He was Broken Feather's grandson, after all.

When Hidden Spirit turned nine, his father gave him a white pony, a gift from a neighboring tribe. Delighted with the spirited animal, he hopped on its back and raced through the group of onlookers. Thundering past his father, he yelled. "Hey hey-hey-hoka-hey." He looked like a turbulent storm ready to erupt as the air around him crackled with electricity. Hidden Spirit loved the attention. He enjoyed the looks of awe and admiration from his friends as he stood atop his pony, bow and arrow in hand, and let off a mighty cry as if to say, "Look at me... am I not great." Cheers erupted from the crowd as he galloped off down the road and disappeared amidst the clouds of dust.

White Cloud looked on with concern, shaking his head as Hidden Spirit rode past. Limping Fox just smiled.

A couple of miles down the road, the sky darkened ominously as a large flock of crows huddled in the clouds overhead then swooped down like arrows, sharp and focused. They flapped their wings and cawed noisily as they soared around the boy. The pony swerved and Hidden Spirit faltered, barely managing to keep his balance. "Crazy crows... get away," he shouted. He was taken aback by their boldness as one darted close and pecked his arm, drawing blood. Crows were smart and crafty, but this? Hidden Spirit didn't know what to make of the crazy crows. He was determined to teach them a lesson so he reached for his bow and arrow, aimed carefully, and sent one hurtling through the air. As the crows scattered, he struck a silver-winged young crow through the heart. The injured bird screeched and floundered, as it flapped its broken wing and plummeted to the ground.

Hidden Spirit let off a war-cry and whooped, "Hoka-Hey!" He waved his bow in the air as his pony flew around a sharp bend in the road where a large oak tree had recently toppled from the rain. The pony came to an abrupt stop. Hidden Spirit lost his balance and, with a resounding jolt, tumbled head-first into the branches and stout limbs. A crushing wave of pain spread throughout his body. He arched back in agony, and cried out, unable to move. His leg was twisted in odd angles, and his bone protruded below the knee.

Hidden Spirit lay on the ground and moaned in pain. Through glazed eyes he saw the flock of crows swoop down in unison, squawking, and landing with a whoosh. The crows began frantically pulling out their feathers. Tufts of silky plumage filled the air in a whirling mass, circling the wounded bird. Then an exceptional-looking crow with giant wings, red scaly feet and eyes as bright as the sun sailed down. The crow skittered near the little bird, crying, "Koww-koww-koww," and in a flash it extracted the arrow with its stout, curved bill. It hovered a moment beside the bird, cawing softly, nudging it with its beak. The bird was barely breathing. Then the crow swiveled its big yellow eyes, and glared menacingly at Hidden Spirit before he flew off.

The group of crows gathered close to the dying bird, clucking, tapping, poking and pushing the soft feathers under its body. A cold wind billowed in from the north and sent a cloud of powdery ash from the red cedar tree that filled the air with its earthy fragrance. Then the winds of the west howled, sending mounds of cotton from the sacred cottonwood trees that scattered the ground with their soft, white balls. A scrawny looking crow out of the south brought twigs from the mountain birch, while another from the east brought leaves from the peach tree. A tiny crow with grey speckles, weighted down with sweet honeysuckle, landed in a heap of branches. The crows quickly and methodically began to stitch and sew, interlocking twigs, leaves and cotton, with their beaks, while weaving an intricate pattern. Once finished with the sturdy pallet, they carefully pulled the dying crow on top and covered the bird with the scented honeysuckle. In a flurry of caws and screeches the crows lifted the bird and off they went, soaring into the air.

One particularly fat crow stayed behind and waddled up to Hidden Spirit, its bluish feathers bristling on top of his head. He had an enormous black beak, long and sharp, that came dangerously close to Hidden Spirit's face. He screeched, "You have been taught better than to shoot the ones sent to help. Your grandfather, Broken Feather, feared you would not listen. You cannot meet this challenge by yourself, arrogant boy. The future holds peril. Be wary. Change is coming. Will you be ready?"

"I am not afraid." Hidden Spirit replied indignantly. "Ha," the crow snorted. "I see a boy who needs to be taught a lesson." Hidden Spirit gritted his teeth and moaned. "Crow, you know nothing about me." A single tear slipped down his cheek, and he quickly wiped it away, not wanting the crow to see him weep.

"I know more than even you, oh great one." The crow flapped his wings and his eyes darted back and forth, as he started to peck furiously at the boy's leg.

Hidden Spirit screamed, "Stop, stop, get away!" As the bird continued pecking, the boy's eyes grew wide with panic. He tried to shoo the crow away, but with no success and a few moments later, he abruptly blacked out.

The sun's rays caressed the early morning dew as it lay on a sprout of wildflowers sparkling like diamonds. A low chirp of pinion jays awakened Hidden Spirit. He slowly opened his eyes and looked around, warily, as thoughts of yesterday's events came flooding back. Bent on his elbows, he craned his neck as he looked to see if that fat crow was still lurking nearby. He wiggled his toes. There was no pain. He wrinkled his brow and wondered, *what happened*. He sat up further and whispered, "Was that you, fat crow? The one who scolded me?" He tentatively stood and touched his leg where the bone had once protruded, then placed his weight on the injured leg, and moved slowly. "I can walk," he gasped in astonishment, and looked around in the trees, squinting his eyes, hoping to see the crow to thank him. He hurried over to a clump of feathers on the ground, stained with blood, picked up a silver feather that fluttered atop the pile, and thought, *how unusual this is*. As he rubbed his cheek with the silky plumage a twinge of guilt filled him, and he was saddened. Hidden Spirit wondered if the crow had died.

A drifting breeze wafted across the valley. In the shallows of the wind he heard, "You have much to learn. "

Ever more changes were on the horizon for the Indians of the Plains. The white hunters and sharpshooters had all but eliminated the buffalo and were hailed as heroes. They were encouraged to "kill the beasts," for they hindered the railroads from passing through the Sioux hunting grounds. Now that the buffalo were almost extinct, some wasichu's—the white man—hoped that the Sioux would follow the same path, into oblivion.

1891- PINE RIDGE RESERVATION

H IDDEN SPIRIT'S DARK eyes smolder as he looks across the valley where his family had once lived. He marvels at the vast expanse of the prairies and soft mounds of rolling hills and tall sweet grass fluttering in the breeze. If he looked hard enough, he could envision the buffalo with their massive shoulders and long shaggy beards, thundering across the plains by the thousands and covering the land as far as the eye could see. Then in a flash, they would be gone. His people had roamed with the buffalo and winds of the seasons for eons. They would shelter in the hills to brace against the harsh winters, then move again when the spring winds blew. Shoots would pop open, leaves would bud, and grasses would sprout, bringing life. A new season would begin. Mother Nature's blessings.

Hidden Spirit was young when he killed his first buffalo. The memory was imprinted in his mind, as the scar on his left cheek still tingled to the touch.

Then his thoughts darkened as he remembered the day his grandmother was murdered.

It was a small gathering of mostly women and older men. They danced and prayed that the wasichu's would disappear from their lands. Leaves Dancing, Hidden Spirit's grandmother, yearned to join in the Ghost Dance, but her husband, Plenty

Feathers, said it would be dangerous to go. He worried that too many Blue Coats had come now that the dance had started. Leaves Dancing had no fear. She told him she could hear the Wankan Tanka better when the drums started. The drums pounded like her heart, giving her joy, and then her feet took on a life of their own. Leaves Dancing prayed for freedom to roam their lands as they once had. Her heart soared at the possibility. She hated to go against her husband's wishes, but the drums were calling—she could not resist. Sitting on her knees, she drew a handful of earth close to her heart and listened. Suddenly her heart pulsed wildly while gasping at the vision in her hands. She dropped the dirt and smothered a cry. The earth had turned a deep red, vivid with images of spilling blood. Her mind faltered at the sight, and she slowly pulled herself up to walk back home. Shaken, she was still resolved to go.

Early the next morning, Leaves Dancing hurried out the door, darkness engulfing the winter sky. Her breath looked like shards of mist as she hurried to the great gathering. She wrapped her green star blanket around her shoulders and shivered as the faint glow of the moon, slipping in and out of the clouds, flung shadows into her path. Nearing the group she felt a chill surge through her body, and she trembled with excitement. The image of yesterday was forgotten. The drums were beating a slow hypnotic sound, and she hurried even faster, waving to familiar faces as she ran. She called out to Yellow Dove, her friend since childhood. They clasped hands and started to join the circle when a sharp crack made Leaves Dancing jump and look around, nervously. The popping noise came closer and louder. Yellow Dove cried out, "The Blue Coats are shooting!" She grabbed Leaves Dancing's hand and started to run, but they froze as people were shot. Yellow Dove screamed out, "Please don't kill us!" and she fell to her knees pleading.

"We come in peace," another hollered. But his cries went unheard as a bullet shot through his chest, leaving the ground splattered with blood.

Leaves Dancing was faint from terror as she watched her vision play out. She whirled in circles, wanting to run, but which way? Bullets were flying from every direction. She was determined to get out alive and find her friend, from whom she had been separated in the chaos. When she found Yellow Dove, she was lying in a pool of blood, holding her daughter's limp body. Leaves Dancing bolted over, and pulled her to her feet. "We must run," she said. They only made it a few steps when Yellow Dove was shot in the back and fell to the ground. Leaves Dancing choked back her sobs, crying out to the Great Spirit as she witnessed her friend depart from the living. She felt numb as she stumbled through the maze of bullets and fallen bodies. When she heard her name called, she looked up to see if it was the Great Spirit. Then she heard her name repeated. Her eyes cleared, and then lit up at the sight of her grandson, Hidden Spirit, flying through the crowd on horseback, waving frantically. He was a few yards away when she heard a thunderous explosion and felt a jarring blow to her forehead. She stumbled backwards as Hidden Spirit scrambled off his horse and gathered her in his arms. She could feel his tears fall on her face. As she tried to speak, only a gurgle came out. Clinging to life for a brief moment, she gazed into Hidden Spirit's eyes before leaving this world.

Leaves Dancing floated off, feeling light and airy. Yellow Dove drifted nearby and joined her friend. The two held hands as they floated upwards and heard the Great Spirit whisper, "Iyehantu," as He guided them to the Other World.

Hidden Spirit carried his grandmother from the chaos to the hills, where he mourned her death. Plenty Feathers, his grandfather, followed behind and found a small cave to call home.

The day of the dance and the murder of his grandmother would always be etched in Hidden Spirit's mind. Sitting alone in the hills, he sharpened his arrows and ranted to the Great Spirit. A piercing cry rose from the hollows of his belly and he stomped forcefully on the ground. As the wind whipped around his body, he screamed about the fate of his people and paced back and forth, fuming. Anger filled him until he thought his head would burst. He was angry at his people who signed treaties believing the white eyes would keep their word. He was angry that his people didn't fight harder for their land, which would have been worth dying for. But now, his people were clinging to a shred of hope. Despair was closing in. Shoulders once proud, now stooped. It was hard to watch his once proud people of the plains become resigned to this life.

Hidden Spirit crawled into a cave to blot out his pain. He moaned of his despair. Then in the darkness, he heard Broken Feather speak from the winds. "I hear your despair, my grandson. You will survive. Our people will survive. We are strong. I will show you the way. But first you must listen. Your heart and your mind must be open. You are destined to become our Keeper of the Souls."

"Go away! I am not listening to you," Hidden Spirit shouted as he stomped off further into the hills, vowing revenge.

NEW RULES

THE GOVERNMENT DID not want another Indian uprising, especially after the Ghost Dance episode of 1890 in South Dakota, so they assigned Otis Reginald Peale, a Yale graduate, fluent in the Sioux language, now working for the Bureau of Indian Affairs, to the Sioux tribe. "Need to put new rules in place," they told him, "by whatever means." Otis Peale dutifully agreed and arrived on March 18, 1891.

Peale was a portly man with bowed legs and pallid features that melded into a thick neck. His head sprouted a few gray strands from an otherwise shiny scalp. Peale toured the grounds of the reservation, anxiously checking his pocket watch. He had seen a group of Indians congregate near the edge of town, huddled together speaking in hushed tones. Peale had instructed all the people to gather before him on this gloomy afternoon. As Peale stood on the platform he waved his arms to get their attention. The Indians slowly walked toward the man, eyeing him with distrust. "Thank you for coming," he called out. "As some of you already know, my name is Mr. Otis Peale, and I was sent by the Great White Father in Washington to help you Indians adjust to a new way of life." The crowd finally quiets and listens. "If you follow my rules, we'll get along just fine. There is no future in your past, so you must leave all that nonsense behind."

A blank look appears on the faces of the people as they stare back at him. Peale continues. "From this day forward, there will be no dances of any kind held on the reservation. Anyone caught disobeying orders will be severely disciplined. That sun dance of yours is now outlawed. It causes too much trouble and incites you people into rebellion.

Peale cleared his throat. "Like I said, if everyone obeys my orders, we'll get along just fine."

But his words were met with a stone-faced response. "Now that business is taken care of, I have more news. I want to introduce you to a fine fellow. His name is James Crumm—a preacher, a teacher, and a good friend. We met as soldiers in the Civil War, and have stayed in touch over the years. He left his church in Kentucky to bring his Good News to you."

Peale motions for James to come over. Crumm is a tall, lanky, six-foot-three man, skinny as a rail, sporting bushy eyebrows and thick salt and pepper hair. Crumm makes his way onto the platform in a few quick strides and vigorously shakes Otis Peale's hand. Then he raises both his hands to the sky, speaking English in a booming voice, he says: "My good people, with God willing, I will oversee the duties and operations of a boarding school opening in Pennsylvania. While there, the children will not only learn, but thrive as well. My mission is to bring Christ to the children and the children to Christ. There will be English taught and your language will be forgotten—Praise the Lord. My devotion to God inspires me every day, as it will the children." Preacher Jim bowed, clutching his Bible to his chest.

Otis Peale clapped, as he translated the words of Preacher Jim, encouraging the others to follow suit. All was silent. He cleared his throat, ignoring the silence and continued, "The school will be opening next month. All children ages five through eighteen will be required to attend. No exceptions. Upon completion of school, they will come home, forever changed." As the words penetrated, the people stood in shock—one more blow delivered to the proud people of the plains.

Hidden Spirit, only eighteen and already a strong-willed leader, looked directly at Crumm, vehemently shook his head no, and walked away. Crumm raised his eyebrows, and dismissed the boy.

As Preacher Jim and Otis Peale walked through the reservation towards Peale's house, Peale said, "I studied the Sioux, Jimmy. I learned their language, but I still don't know or understand them. They cling to their past and refuse to recognize any path that will save them from themselves."

"I'll tell you this," said the preacher ardently, "As I walk through the reservation, I see the Devil at work. There is idleness. There are houses that are nothing but shacks, unfit to live in, and half-naked children running around."

"Better than what they had," Peale said. "At Yale I had a professor tell our class that there would be no Christianity without the Devil. I say, hogwash!"

"The Devil is everywhere," said the preacher. "He haunts me constantly. He challenges me, testing my faith at every turn."

"I don't give a damn about the Devil. My boss in Washington says, 'In order to save the Indians, you have to take the Indian out of them.' Can you do that, Jimmy?" Peale asked with a trace of sarcasm.

"I seek nothing for myself, either now or in Heaven," Preacher Jim replied, looking upward. "I serve the children in the name of Jesus Christ." With clenched hands, he looked directly at Otis. "I will take the Indian out of the redskin Devils, and set them right. Just wait and see."

"Well, good luck, Jimmy. You will need it. In my class at Yale, I read something that goes something like this:

'I am as free as Nature first made,
Ere the base laws of servitude began,
When in the woods the noble savage ran.'"

Annoyed, the preacher responded, "I don't need any of your Yale books. The only book I need is the Holy Bible."

"I am trying to tell you that these Sioux are a stubborn lot. I can't figure out if they are noble or savage or just plain stupid. They will not change their behavior. One old man came up to me the other day and told me a strange thing. He said, 'Our children are different from the white children. The white man sees the child, but does not listen. We Sioux not only see our children, we hear what they have to say and listen with respect.' They believe that their children are blessed, even understand some nonsense about the spiritual world. They talk to their dead ancestors, to the animals, to the clouds and the trees."

Rubbing his brows, Preacher Jim said, "Devil talk. There will be no such talk at my school. Come and visit me at the school in Pennsylvania and you will see a transformation that will astonish you, and you will praise me, along with Jesus, for delivering these children from the clutches of evil."

"Well, that would be something. Say, I have a gift for you. It was given to me by one of the elders on the reservation. For the life of me, I don't know why."

Upon entering Peale's house, he dragged out a huge eagle-feather headdress and a buckskin shirt.

"This is for you, Jimmy. A parting gift."

PREACHER JIM

J AMES CRUMM WAS born on April 23, 1844 on a tobacco farm just outside of Bowling Green, Kentucky. He was the only son of a tobacco farmer who instilled in his son the love of hard work and religious piety. Every meal began and ended with a prayer of thanksgiving to Jesus. Six days of hard work were followed by a day of rest on Sunday, and church services were followed by a day of Bible reading. This farm was different than the surrounding farms in that the elder Crumm owned no slaves. He would say, "All souls are worthy of God's grace. Nothing in the Bible is for slavery. I say send the darkies back to Africa, where they belong." Instead of using slaves to work the fields, the Crumms would do the work themselves, and during harvest time they would hire out a few laborers.

When James Crumm was ten years old, he went to his father and asked him about a book he had just read: *The Last of the Mohicans*. He wanted to know if the Mohicans were going to Hell for all eternity since there was no mention of them being Christian in the book. His father assured him that they would surely go to Hell, but that he need not worry about a work of fiction. "Stick with the Bible, son, for that is the only truth."

When James turned seventeen, the Civil War broke out. He left his farm and joined the army, which is where he met his longtime friend, Otis Peale. Although they came from different backgrounds and religious beliefs, they remained good friends throughout their time in the military. During that period, both men witnessed a great deal of death and carnage, so, while Peale was not a devout Christian, he would gather with James as he prayed in the evenings for their survival and their souls. When all was quiet, he would read passages from the Bible in a soothing voice. That is how he got the nickname, Preacher Jim. He enjoyed the name, and it stayed with him after the war ended. He was now convinced that the reason he had survived was that God had a purpose for him. He went back home and started preaching the Gospel at a Church he created, no matter that it was an empty barn. When his father died soon thereafter, he took over the tobacco farm and continued preaching on Sundays.

He felt an inner peace doing God's work, but needed to do more. So, on a hot Sunday afternoon as he walked through his tobacco field, a vision came from the heavens saying, "Suffer the children unto me." James was dumfounded by the words, wondering what they meant. A few months later he received a letter from Otis Peale.

He knew then the meaning of God's message—his purpose in life—which was to save the Sioux children from an eternity in Hell. *Like in the book,* 'The Last of the Mohicans,' he thought, brimming with eagerness. *I can save them. My devotion to the Sioux will inspire all.*

VISION QUEST

WHEN HIDDEN SPIRIT was thirteen, his family, along with hundreds of other Sioux, had been forced to move, at gunpoint, to the reservation in South Dakota. Exchanging the freedom of the plains, valleys, and mountains for the confines of a reservation was unbearable for the people of the Plains—especially for Hidden Spirit. Even though the relocation was difficult, the Sioux people had not lost their spirit or their pride. They continued their rituals and prayers to the Great Spirit—but in secret. They also refused to give up their Wiwanke Wachipi… their sacred dance, the dance of the spirits, while asking for guidance as they stare at the sun and into the cosmic relation of the spirit realm, intimately connected to a time deep in the past seeking spiritual power and enlightenment.

Also in secret, they adhered to their vision quest—the journey that transitions young boys into manhood—a time spent alone in darkness, while awaiting the arrival of visions.

After they had been settled on the reservation for a few months, White Cloud told Hidden Spirit, "It is time, my son. It is time for you to be alone and commune with the spirits. It is time for your vision quest. We must do this in secret, now. Maybe you will talk to your grandfather. Let him guide you, my son… to become a man."

Hidden Spirit sat with arms crossed, and said nothing.

"I will take you," White Cloud, said, "to the special place where I have gone before you."

"No," Hidden Spirit said. "I will go alone."

"It would not be wise for you to go alone for your first time."

Hidden Spirit sat silent as White Cloud described the journey ahead. "We will head north, and climb the steep ravine by the falling water, then go toward the setting sun that leads to the cave surrounded by black pines."

Hidden Spirit felt he was old enough, almost a man now. "I am the grandson of the great Sioux warrior, Broken Feather."

"Yes. That you are, my son. That is why I must go with you."

Hidden Spirit pondered his father's words and, after a while, acquiesced to his wishes.

"You must begin with a three-day fast while praying to the Great Spirit. During that time ask Him for guidance. After that is completed, we will walk to the hills where the sacred cave is located and find the ancient lava stones that will be buried nearby."

The ancient stones were used to build a fire that would burn hot for hours on end. When the day of the vision quest arrived, White Cloud accompanied Hidden Spirit to the cave. He gathered the stones and wood for the sweat lodge and ignited a blazing fire. "It is time to purify your body before entering the darkness of the cave, my son. The heat will help clear your thoughts. Then you will begin your journey into manhood."

As Hidden Spirit walked into the searing heat of the sweat lodge, beads of perspiration poured down his face, and he felt his heart pound from the intensity of the fire. He sat for what seemed like hours in the scorching heat as all thoughts drifted away. After a while, he felt weak and drained, and just as he thought he might pass out, White Cloud opened the flap and announced, "Your body is cleansed. It is time. You are ready for the darkness."

White Cloud hesitated at the cave's entrance. Worried for his son, a brief look of concern filtered across his face, but he quickly brushed away his doubts. *Hidden Spirit will emerge much different,* and he said a silent prayer to the Great Spirit. He offered his son a subdued smile, as he handed him his grandmother's star blanket. Hidden Spirit shook his head no, and walked into the dusky light, wearing only a breach-cloth.

White Cloud covered the small opening of the cave with some branches and a thick hide. He said another prayer for his son, and then walked back home.

Alone now, Hidden Spirit carefully made his way inside the cave. The darkness was intense and surrounded him like a dense fog as he shuffled his feet on the gravelly floor. The damp, chilly air was unnerving. He rubbed his arms, and shivered. Now he regretted not taking his grandmother's blanket. He searched for a sign from the Great Spirit, but all he could see was a deep black vortex. The cave seemed mysterious in its silence and sent waves of fear rippling through him as he eased his way further within. He felt swallowed by the darkness except for a pinprick of light that seemed to stretch for miles. A trickle of water dripped behind him. It smelled musty, like slimy moss. He tried in vain to still his mind as fear rose and beads of sweat formed on his brows. He waited—but for what? He had heard numerous stories about vision quests that kept him up late at night, enthralled. *I must wait for the spirits to come,* he thought. *That's what the elders would say.* He wasn't so brave now. He was on edge and tried to focus. Plenty Feathers had told him before he left, "Once you enter the darkness, your sacred journey into soul and spirit begins. Concentrate." Hidden Spirit tried again, but was distracted by frightening thoughts. A strange noise caused him to jump. *It sounded like a moan,* he thought, and gulped, groping the floor. *Is someone in pain?* His body stiffened in suspense. He tried to see, but the darkness only grew deeper. He dropped to the floor and listened carefully. But this time there was an odd sound, like hundreds of leaves rustling, skittering in the breeze. Then he heard a piercing, bloodcurdling screech. He covered his ears. The noise was deafening. It reverberated in his head. His ears started to ring and his mind filled with frightful images that came from somewhere in the darkness. He ducked as eyes the size of turnips mocked him and floated past; a skeletal face followed—threatening, leering. He blinked and looked again. The images disappeared. Nothing was there. They seemed to have come from behind him—above him—he couldn't tell. He stood up and paced. *I must be calm.* He forced out a breath, but his hands were clammy and cold, and they shook. Out of the corner of his eyes he saw a flash of silver that seemed to dance, then waver. He scrunched his eyes. The silver sheen glimmered. Hidden Spirit sucked in his breath and recoiled as the silver shape moved toward him, slowly inching closer. Suddenly the ground was covered in a wiggling mass of silver threads that slowly uncoiled and stretched. He stared in disbelief and blinked furiously, unwilling to believe what he was seeing. Bending closer, trying to have a better look, he suddenly gasped and jerked back as thousands of pale green eyes stared at him, menacingly. His heart hammered and he tried to flee, but his legs quivered uncontrollably. Standing motionless and staring, he was rooted to the spot. There must have been hundreds of snakes on the ground next to him, hissing, laughing, writhing—their hypnotic pale green eyes fixed on him and mesmerized him. Then, weirdly, he started to dance—slinking, slithering like the snakes. He had no control over what was happening as he gyrated in circles until he found himself standing next to a grinning badger sharpening his teeth on a rock. The gritting sound was unbearable. As the badger's grin widened, his sharp teeth glistened and he let off a growl that was deep and low, and filled Hidden Spirit with its rumble. Then the badger reached up and bit off part of his ear. He felt himself quake as he pushed the animal away, grabbing his ear and sticking it back onto his head. If this was a dream, it was unlike any he had ever known. He was awake, wasn't he? He wasn't sure. A faint hiss roused him, came close, and whispered, "Oh, mystical one." The voice paused, mocking. "You come in here trying to prove you're so brave, and clever, and unafraid. How do you like your vision now, brave boy?" The snake slithered closer. "I hear you want to become a man. Hee-hee-hee," the snake hissed maliciously. "That'll take some doing. Ooooooh. You look scared. Are you ready to run yet?"

Hidden Spirit started to scream, but all he emitted was a faint "ehhhhh." The snakes began to shuffle and snap as they encircled Hidden Spirit's legs. Somewhere in the back of his mind, he knew this could not be real. Or could it? He could smell, no, taste the venom and he licked his lips, then spit. He shook his head, but his mind faltered. He could not think. He was dizzy and felt his knees buckle. The snakes continued to encircle Hidden Spirit as they hissed and lunged, and began to tumble over one another in frenzy. Huge fangs glinted in the shaft of light, ready to devour the quivering boy with their gaping mouths.

Hidden Spirit heard a commotion off in the distance. It sounded like a thunderous whirlwind. Another prickle of fear ran up his spine. "What, now?" he gasped as something roared over his head. A giant mass of whirling feathers and beaks and claws swooped down. He nearly fainted at the sight. Hundreds of wings seemed to propel him forward, nudging him, pushing him out of the cave. He felt light as air, as the hissing snakes slithered underneath him. *Do snakes have feet?* That was his last thought as he found himself outside the cave, lying in the dirt, slowly awakening from his stupor. He pulled himself up from the ground and looked around, rubbing his eyes. The opening of the cave was right in front of him, and nothing followed. "It had to be a dream," he mused. "Nothing more…" He touched his arm, which didn't hurt. Then he felt for his ear. It was there. In fact, he didn't feel any bites, anywhere. "So, what was it? It couldn't be…" Then his thoughts stopped. It had to be his imagination, to run out of the cave in fear of snakes and a badger? He was Broken Feather's grandson, after all. He could never speak of this incident to anyone. His friends would mock him. Ever since he could remember, the stories he heard of Broken Feather left him spellbound, anxious to hear more. They would always remain with him, locked in his memory.

Hidden Spirit lay on the ground, closed his eyes, and drifted off. He saw his grandfather running beside the buffalo, flying across the plains, waving at him—calling out to him. He tried to hear, but Grandfather's voice was drowned out by the thundering hooves. Next, he saw his grandfather bending over a wasichu. He reached into his sacred pouch filled with assorted herbs and rubbed a handful of salve over the man's wound, and in a blink, Broken Feather pulled a bullet from the belly of a dying man that the Blue Coats had shot, giving him life. Those events seemed to be happening right in front of him, like he was there. He sat up, shaken.

The realization was too much for Hidden Spirit, and in a panic he ran for miles, until his legs gave out and he was unable to go any further. He slipped into a nearby stream and doused his head beneath the cool rushing waterfall to clear away the images of the dancing snakes and the grinning badger. "Nooooo." He tried to push the images out of his mind. It couldn't have happened, and yet he knew he had felt them, even heard them talk. But still, the thought of being devoured by thousands of snakes or a badger was ludicrous. Nonetheless, his heart thumped at the memory. Exhausted and confused by the ordeal, he finally collapsed by a fallen willow tree and drifted into a deep sleep.

When Hidden Spirit awoke, it was dark, and the sky was ablaze with twinkling lights. He squinted when he saw the stars move, and looked up to see them gather into the shape of a snake and start to dance. He straightened up. Anything that looked like a dancing snake made him nervous, so he closed his eyes, hoping to wish them away. He stayed in the hills for the next three days and sat and pondered his vision quest. Now and then, he drifted off, recalling stories from the elders about their own vision quests, which were nothing like this. He shivered, pulled his arms around his legs, and pondered, wishing he had Broken Feather's powers. Just then, he lifted his arm and saw a feather follow his motions. He was so startled that he dropped his arm and, to his amazement, the feather dropped, as well. Caught off-guard by the strange event, he tried it again. The feather moved along with his fingers. Stunned, he looked up, and thought, *it has to be a sign from Broken Feather or maybe the Great Spirit.*

He bounced up from the ground, dizzy with excitement, and set off toward the reservation. When he got home he found his father was waiting with some jerky. "It must have been powerful in the cave of the ancients, with their secrets hidden in the walls." Hidden Spirit took the jerky, but stayed silent. White Cloud watched his son closely and noticed a smile had crept over his face.

ELUSIVE BOY-WHERE ART THOU

OTIS PEALE, THE BIA agent, sits alone in his office. He looks out the window at the Indians wandering by. He sees Will Wigley, a scrawny twenty year old, with a handlebar mustache walk past. Peale shouts, "Get in here, Wigley!"

Seconds later, Wigley stands in front of Peale. "Yes, sir."

"Wigley, we have a list of all the Indians going off to the school, except there's one sneaky son-of-a-bitch that refuses to go. His name is Hidden Spirit and he hides somewhere in the hills. He sneaks into town to see his parents on occasion. You go get him and bring him back. I want that son-of-a-bitch standing right in front of me. He's going off to that school."

Hidden Spirit, now eighteen, still has the freedom in his blood. To be confined to the reservation is like dying a slow death. Even though he has been hiding out in the hills for months now, his freedom to roam freely is lost. He knows Peale and Wigley are looking for him, but he is determined to remain unseen. "You will never find me, stupid white eyes," he says, boasting, as he pulls hard on his bowstring. Hidden Spirit knows it is dangerous to go into town, but he shrugs it off. He misses his family and, mostly, he misses his love, the light of his dreams, Morning Star. He can see her beauty from afar. *It is worth the risk*, he thinks.

He sets off down the hills, creeps unseen into town, and hides behind his father's house, where he hears people talking.

His handsome face streaks with anger as he overhears a couple of traders bartering with his father over hides and beadwork and other trinkets made by his mother. "I'll give ya two jugs of the finest whiskey this side of the Mississippi for yer string of bear claws and buffalo hide. Even throw in some…"

Before the grizzled man can finish his words, Hidden Spirit storms over to the men, eyes flashing dangerously, with bow and arrow in hand. "Go!" he commands.

The men are taken aback by the ferocity of Hidden Spirit's eyes. Their mouths drop, but they don't question the fierce boy. They simply gather their jugs and hustle off into town.

After they leave, Hidden Spirit demands answers. "How can you trade with those white men, Father? They are no good."

"You know, my son, we must now adapt to the white people's ways. The choice is no longer ours. Besides, the frog skins will be useful. It is good that you and your sister, Chasing Rabbit, know the white language."

Hidden Spirit is angry at his father's words and that he is trusting of the whites. The boy learned early on that the white eyes were not to be trusted, *especially the ones that smell of whiskey*. He knows their tongue is treacherous and filled with greed. With their lies comes more destruction and stolen lands. Hidden Spirit would only go so far listening to his father on that subject. "You are wrong to trust them," he says admonishingly, and heads back to the hills, forgetting about Morning Star.

That evening, Corporal Jenkins comes running up to Wigley, calling out. "Sir, these traders complained about some fierce-looking Indian boy threatening to kill them. Sounds like the one you've been looking for."

Wigley turns around and faces the men, unhappy for the

interruption. He was on his way to get a bottle of whiskey. The burly mountain man with a haggard red face blurts out, "That Injun came upon us out of the blue, looking ready to fight. We don't want trouble, so we left."

"Mean as snake oil, too," the other trader says, stroking his bulbous nose.

"I'll handle this matter," Wigley says, irritably. A couple days ago, Wigley had heard about this clever young Indian and that he would never be able to catch him. That made Wigley furious. He was a guy who hated to be outdone, especially by that low-life Indian.

*

The next day, a wealthy rancher and cattle baron, James Phillips, rides into town, livid. He tells Peale, "You best keep those heathens off my property. I spotted a wild one riding to beat the Devil across my lands—most likely after one of my prized longhorns. You'd better get him or I'll call my friend, Senator Williams, in Washington to fix this problem. I say we hang him."

Peale says, "You're not going to have to worry about that Indian boy anymore. He's going off to the boarding school. I guarantee it."

Phillips says, "I'm holding you to it," and gives Peale a warning look before riding off.

Peale is distraught by Phillips's anger. He is supposed to keep order on the reservation but has recoiled, wanting no trouble with these ranchers. Peale hustles off to find Wigley. "You need to do your job. Get that troublemaker, and be quick about it."

So Wigley rounds up a group of soldiers and they go thundering off in the hills after Hidden Spirit. One of the soldiers spots the Indian kid in the distance and fires, missing him by a mile. The others now open fire, seeing the kid zig-zag through the rocks and bramble as bullets whiz past. Hidden Spirit smiles, enjoying the chase. "Let them try to catch me," he says as he races up the steep, jagged hills with ease, mocking the soldiers as they fire their guns, hitting shadows. The soldiers follow in hot pursuit until, suddenly, the tracks disappear. They pull up on the reins, and curse, "Damn. Where'd he go to now?" The young Corporal, Jake Austin, scratches his head as he looks for more tracks. None is found. He had heard the recent rumors about the Indian kid having some kind of magical powers. "Maybe they're true," says Austin under his breath.

None of the soldiers had really ever seen him. A few think they caught a glimpse of him in town, and whisper about having seen odd things happen when he was there. One soldier says, "While I was on watch a couple nights ago, it was silent as a ghost. Then, right out of the blue, my gun went flying out of my holster, let off a blast, and fell to the ground." Another soldier speaks up. "Yeah, I saw feathers floating in the air... all by themselves. Spooky as hell, too."

Wigley doesn't believe the rumors, but still, everyone is cautious as they patrol the hills, looking for the boy.

In the distance someone is shouting. All of a sudden, one of the soldiers comes running around a tree and yelps, stumbling over his words in fright. Wigley flies over to see what all the commotion is about.

Corporal Jake Austin pants. "Something came up behind me and walloped me right on the back of my head. I turned just in time to see a stick float off, like it had wings... or some strange thing. No one was there, either. I don't get paid enough for this crazy stuff," he says nervously. "I'm getting out of here." The soldiers quickly mount their horses, looking around apprehensively, ready to leave as Will hollers, "Where the blazes you chicken-shits going?"

"It's your job, Wigley, not ours. You can find that Indian kid yourself!" Corporal Austin shouts, and the soldiers thunder off down the hill, back to town.

"Just wait. They're gonna pay for this," Wigley grumbles.

Agitated, he paces back and forth, as a feeling of unease surfaces. He looks around. His breath catches in his chest as he hears a rustle in the nearby rocks. He pulls his gun out, ready to shoot, and, before he can blink an eye, he finds himself face-first on the ground. Then he feels something bump his shoulder and he hears a low whisper that gives him the willies. "You'll pay with your life, if you come up here again." And silent as a ghost, the shadowy figure disappears.

Wigley looks around, wide-eyed. Seeing the coast is clear he hops onto his horse and skedaddles back to town. At his quarters, he bangs the coffee pot on the stove, then slams it down, deciding he needs something stronger to calm his nerves. "Charlatan, that's what that kid is."

Will pulls out a bottle of whiskey, takes a huge drink, and sits down, hands trembling. "Damn that kid." He recalls the time he went to White Cloud's house looking for that Hidden Spirit, or whatever that horseshit name is. White Cloud scared the crap outta him. "Bad as his kid," he mutters under his breath. "I hate that redskin bastard. I've gotta think what to tell Peale, and quick-like. He's gonna be madder than a hornet."

Will doesn't need any problems going on right now; he has some big plans about to hatch. "Oh," Wigley moans, "how I hate this stinkin' place."

He orders the soldiers not to speak of that Injun anymore. Gives him the willies, with all that talk. "Now, blast it, they're talking about him."

Hidden Spirit skirts the trees and bushes. He looks down at the town from the hillside, and smiles. "You will never catch me, white eyes." Then his thoughts brighten as he thinks of someone else—his love, Morning Star. He can feel his heart lift with her beauty, and believes she is filled with wonder. "Morning Star," he muses softly, "between darkness and light. I miss you."

WHITE BUFFALO CALF WOMAN

WATER SPLASHES OVER Morning Star's face, pulling her from a beautiful dream. Half asleep, she brushes away the water and dozes back off, once again finding herself with the buffalo—thousands of them are outlining the horizon as far as she could see. As the herd thunders toward her, the earth begins to shudder. She holds her breath, afraid to move, as the wild beasts come to a billowing stop a few feet away, sending thick clouds of dust into the air. As the dust settles, Morning Star hears a loud bellow erupt. A magnificent white buffalo ambles from the herd. It's so close she can feel its hot breath on her cheek. She reaches out and touches the magnificent animal, lightly brushing her hand against the quivering snout, then rubs the shaggy beard that feels like pine bristles. The buffalo looks at Morning Star, staring intently, with its huge dark eyes—so hypnotic that she cannot look away. She feels that if she stares any longer she will be swept away by the intensity, deep inside the abyss. Excitement and fear fills her body, and she trembles. "The stories are true," she says in awe. "I have always dreamed about seeing you, and now..." Morning Star is at a loss and twists her hands nervously. "I have heard stories about you since my youth," she whispers. "My father said you are sacred to us." She starts to weep, remembering the story.

The White Buffalo Calf Woman came to earth centuries ago and brought with her a beautiful peace pipe. Exquisite to look at, she told their people, "With this holy pipe, you will walk like a living prayer." She taught the Lakota how to use the pipe for rituals and prayers and spoke of the value of the buffalo. "For he is like your brother, sent as a gift," she said, imploring them to follow her words. Upon leaving the camp she sang, "With invisible breath I am walking." Upon reaching the crest of the hill, she looked back at the crowd with solemn eyes, and then continued walking. A moment later she turned into a mammoth white buffalo.

Morning Star shakes her head, remembering the story, and now—she can hardly believe her eyes. "Is this real?" she wonders aloud, holding her breath. Then without warning, the buffalo starts to cry. She watches in disbelief as huge tears splash down its shaggy, massive face. She wants to reach out and comfort the buffalo, but the animal backs away. It makes her so sad to watch the creature in despair that she starts to cry along with the buffalo. Suddenly, the water begins to rise, swirling at her feet, higher and higher. The buffalo's tears are now the size of boulders. Morning Star's eyes are peeled on the buffalo, as the water churns. Frightened, she backs away screaming. "Please. You must stop crying..." Before she can finish her words the buffalo is swept downstream, pawing frantically to stay afloat. The torrential water is relentless in its quest.

Morning Star hears an eerie whisper that sends chills up her spine, as the words float over the water. "Something is about to happen... your people will be..." The words diminish as the buffalo is swept further down the river. Morning Star strains to hear more and boldly steps into the water, but the relentless current pulls her back. She hollers frantically, "Don't drown... I beg you!" Morning Star falls onto the muddy bank and starts to weep. She sees through her tears that the water has now risen past the buffalo's head. She screams out in desperation and pleads again, "Don't cry anymore, I beg you." Through her grief and sorrow, all she can see is depthless eyes staring back at her from the raging river of tears. She hears the white buffalo softly bellow as a cloud of steam rises from its nostrils, looking like silky plumes of smoke fluttering in the air. Then the massive head slowly disappears under the water. Morning Star is hysterical and screams a loud piecing cry. "Come back! Please, come back!" All she can hear now is a soft ripple of water lapping gently on the bank's edge, where she falls to her knees watching helplessly. She feels like dying and thinks, *this is a bad omen for our people.*

Morning Star awakens, gasping for breath, as drips of water spill down from the flimsy roof. For a moment she thought she was drowning, but now she sits up, dazed, her mind whirling. She looks around, realizing she is in her bed, inside her ugly house. The dream haunts her. "I wish I could have saved the buffalo," she moans. *What was the buffalo trying to tell me? Maybe he was warning me of danger.* She frets nervously. *I should have done something. I wish I could remember the buffalo's words. But I fear it's too late.*" Trembling at the thought of her dream, she sinks into despair. "Please, let me go back to sleep," she pleads, shutting her eyes, trying to recapture the moment. "I must help." But it is useless. Morning Star sits up and brushes the water from her face. She notices the curtain next to her bed move, and she hears a sound. "Maybe it's the white buffalo," she says, frantic with hope, hopping out of bed. But to her disappointment, it was only the wind. "It seemed so real," she whispers, "like I was there." The thought sends her mind trembling as she lay back on the bed, still in awe, the scent of the buffalo still lingering. Then Morning Star looks over at her younger sister, Little Moon. She is grateful she finally fell asleep after crying for most of the night.

Her parents, Thunder Cloud and Swift Deer, did their best to console their little girl. They sang sweet songs to soothe her and eventually fell into a troubled sleep. Morning Star whispers, "I should have told the buffalo we needed help."

When her family was told that all the children would be leaving for a boarding school somewhere back east, Morning Star was devastated. Now, she looks around the musty house with its rotting wood, haphazardly put together, that sends the wind whipping through the small cracks in the winter. She feels imprisoned living inside this house with its drafty walls and longs for the warmth and coziness of the tepee, where she slept in peace so long ago, living freely on the plains.

The house is situated on a barren plot of land surrounded by patches of dirt, dotted with pine trees. But if you look closely, in the distance, you can see the faint outlines of the Black Hills with their snow-covered peaks. To the north lay the badlands— intricately carved into sharp spirals, pinnacles, and buttes. Their beautiful red and brown shades shift softly with the weather. At bedtime, riveting tales and mysterious legends of the lands keep the children spellbound. The Sioux know how to navigate through the ethereal peaks and meandering valleys with ease. But the white eyes fear the mysterious mountains.

Morning Star glances tearfully at her parents. *This day feels like a day of death. How will I survive? How will Little Moon survive? We have never been separated before.*

Overwhelmed by sadness, she slips quietly from her bed and feels a jagged piece of wood catch in her finger, causing her to cry out. She winces as she pulls out the sharp sliver, and quickly puts her finger to her lips. Relieved that no one has stirred, Morning Star tiptoes past her sleeping parents, where her white deerskin dress hangs by the door. The garment is adorned with yellow beads that fall around the neck and a shimmering blue sash that accents the waist. She puts the soft dress to her cheek and smiles sadly, remembering the many hours her mother had spent working on it. *I will treasure it forever,* she thinks. As Morning Star slips the dress over her delicate frame, she gasps as blood oozes down from her finger and onto her beautiful dress. A bright red stain mars the shimmering sash. "Oh no," she whispers nervously. "I hope this isn't another omen of…" She stops, puts her hands over her mouth to silence her fears, and quickly slips on her moccasins, pausing at the door. She looks at her family with longing. Even in their sleep, she can see their faces are full of sorrow. She wishes she could erase the sadness that fills their hearts and hurries outside as tears threaten. Making it just a few yards, she falls to her knees sobbing—no longer able to hold back her pain, her sorrow, her anguish.

The storm outside has ended, leaving in its wake voluminous gray clouds hanging heavily in the sky. A few bright patches of blue ease through the fluffy clouds, showing the promise of a clear day. The ground is still damp from the night's storm and fresh raindrops sparkle like jewels on the leaves, filling the air with its delicious earthy scent. Springtime has arrived.

Wiping her eyes, she looks to the Great Spirit and cries out. "Why have you sent the white eyes to our land?" Her voice quivers. "They are sending us away and I leave all that I know and love. I'm not sure, that I can bear the pain. I think I might die." She wipes her eyes and whispers, "I fear my bravery has departed along with the storm. What will happen to my family left behind and my beloved Hidden Spirit?" Her voice cracks as she says his name, and she quickly blinks back her tears. "Please forgive my weakness. I only ask that you hear my plea." A sudden breeze ruffles Morning Star's hair and a fluffy black feather drifts down, landing at her feet. She smiles sadly, takes the feather, puts it to her lips, and then fastens it to her hair as she runs down the path to sit by a nearby stream—her place of quiet and solitude. She pays no mind to the crisp morning breeze that brushes up against her cheek and she ignores the purple sage that fills her nostrils with its pungent scent. She is oblivious to her favorite time of year. Nearing the stream, raucous jays screech overhead, scolding her intrusion upon their morning. The water gurgles peacefully as she sits nearby.

Morning Star's father would always say, "When your heart is troubled, sit by the trees. They will feel your pain and understand. Amongst their beauty, you will be comforted." She leans against a gnarly black pine, and can feel its sturdy bark against her back as she breathes in deeply, inhaling the acrid air. Then a trickle of life flows back into her body. She moves closer to the gurgling water and lies on the ground, staring idly into its depth while looking at her reflection. As she runs her hands back and forth through the cool, silky water, she becomes lost in thought, recalling the day the missionaries arrived.

It was on a brisk March morning. Morning Star was out walking alone and heard a wagon rumbling down the road. Running over to investigate, she saw a large wagon carrying two prim ladies and a pile of luggage on top. Curious, Morning Star hid behind a strand of pine trees and silently stole a look at the two women, who stepped down from the carriage.

The taller, pear-shaped, woman's eyes bulged out, as she craned her neck to take in more of the surroundings. "I think the good Lord sent us to purgatory by mistake," she said, frowning.

Morning Star detected a hint of despair that echoed in her voice.

"Yes, indeed," the shorter woman sniffed with displeasure, as she surveyed the bleak environment.

These ladies must be the missionaries that Peale sent for, Morning Star thought. She closely observed every detail about the women as they stretched their limbs and walked stiffly, as if from a long journey. Their hair was pressed into a tight bun, stretching their pale skin taunt, making a striking contrast to their heavy black clothing that covered them from the neck on down. Morning Star believed these women were unwise to dress so oddly. "How can they possibly breathe?" Touching her own soft clothing, she felt a twinge of sorrow for the ladies, so uncomfortably dressed. "They don't look happy," she mused softly, continuing to stare.

"Why have you come? Are you here to bring more change for our people?" she whispered, "or more misery? I see no joy in your eyes—only your stern faces."

Morning Star followed the missionaries as they walked a short ways into town and stumbled upon an old, rundown building with boarded-up windows.

"Could this be our place of worship?" the shorter woman gasped, looking around. "This is the only building I can see."

"Must be," the taller woman replied with an air of indignation. "Our place of worship," she gestured. "We can worship anywhere the good Lord sends us, my dear —even in an outhouse, if necessary."

The shorter woman looked at the taller with raised brows and hesitantly climbed the steps, clinging to the rail. Staring at the slanted oak door with its rusted doorknob and corroded hinges, she paused on the porch as it sagged slightly, wondering if it would collapse.

"How on earth will we get inside?" the shorter woman asked, apprehensively.

"Knock it down, my girl. We have the Almighty's strength," the pear-shaped woman cried out. "Let's roll up our sleeves and give a hearty push. On the count of three, now—push."

The women grunted as they heaved their shoulders against the heavy door. The door groaned, then toppled over with a tremendous *bang*. A large cloud of dust billowed up, spewing dirt in every direction, covering the ladies from head to toe and causing them to cry out. They covered their noses with their bulky sleeves, and ran from the building in between shrieks and fits.

Morning Star watched the flustered ladies and almost burst out laughing at the sight of them brushing the dirt from their clothes. *The taller, pear-shaped lady seems to be the boss,* Morning Star thought. She slid behind the tree when she saw Otis Peale running down the road, sweating and huffing, waving his kerchief in the air to get the women's attention.

Mopping his brow, he shouted out, "Hello there ladies, yoo-hoo!" The two women turned around, eyeing the funny-looking man. "Good afternoon ladies," he panted, reaching out to shake their hands. "My name is Otis Peale."

The taller lady nodded her head at the man, watching him with curiosity. "My name is Mrs. Comford," she said, followed by a swooping curtsy. "How do you do, Mr. Peale?" Then she pivoted around on the balls of her feet and tipped her head at the shorter woman standing beside her. "This is Mrs. Green, a most righteous woman," she said, clearing her throat. "Just as myself." Mrs. Green curtsied and extended her hand to Peale.

"I must say," he said, enthusiastically, "how nice it is to finally meet you ladies. Praise the Lord you have arrived. Most grateful to you coming on such short notice in the middle of nowhere." Wiping the sweat from his brow, he panted, "Pardon me for rambling on so, as I'm sure you've had a most tedious trip. I'm afraid my manners are severely lacking. Haven't been around such fine ladies in a spell." Then he stopped and noticed the women were covered in dust. Observing the fallen door, he said, "Well now, I see the Lord sent not one, but two clever ladies, who have found our place of worship. I'll have this old building fixed up in no time at all. Ramshackle or not, the Lord knows it'll be just fine for the Indians. Would've had it done already, but I've been terribly busy overseeing this place. Got a bunch of unhappy Indians to contend with right now." Moving in closer to the ladies, he said in a hushed tone, "The government gives these Indians lodging. Plenty of food, too. But still, they walk around here resentful, like they wouldn't hesitate to scalp us. Look at all the land they have." He gestured with his kerchief.

The two women looked around at the barren landscape and saw nothing but sagebrush, rundown shacks, scraggly trees, and sprouts of grass rising up from the dirt.

Mrs. Comford said tentatively, "We've heard chilling things about the heathens from the newspaper." Bending closer to Otis Peale she states, "If you ask me, it looks like we've neared purgatory."

"So it seems." Peale said, clearing his throat and continued on, in a lower voice. "Rumors have it that the Indians are sulking over that Ghost Dance episode awhile back. Word was, they were carrying on, dancing up a storm in a frenzied state, the likes of which you've never seen." The look of horror on his face mirrored his tone. "Sinful they were, skewering themselves like stuck pigs dancing around a pole for days on end. Satan's dance," he said, chortling.

"Oh, how dreadful," the ladies said in tandem.

"Chilling stories began trickling in as hundreds of them gathered with war-whooping going on so loud it could chill your bones. And," he gestured, throwing his hands in the air, "there were smoke signals going up, calling for more sinners to join in the frenzy. They started dancing like the Devil himself and Lord knows what else —scaring people half to death."

The ladies gasped at his words and clutched each other's hand.

Otis puffed up his chest, reveling in his storytelling. "You know I had to come after hearing such news. Do my duty as an American. Thank goodness you ladies are here to save such this bunch that was headed straight for—ah," he said, clearing his throat. "The gates of Hell."

Morning Star listened closely, clenching her fists in anger. She wished she could spit on them—show them how much she despised their intrusion.

Otis continued on, enjoying the women's rapt attention. "That Ghost Dance was nasty business. Some crazy Indian spread the word that he saw the end of times for the white people. A few savages wore shirts painted with some sort of symbol to protect them from bullets. Most likely it was Satan's symbols. Well, anyhow, can't blame the soldiers. They got nervous and thought the Indians were planning some sort of an attack—maybe an uprising."

The ladies clung to each other, glued to Peale's every word.

A shiver of excitement ran down Mrs. Comford's arm as she whispered hoarsely. "We heard such awful stories bandied around about the heathens. Truly frightening, it was."

"Well," Peale clucked his tongue. "Luckily, our brave soldiers didn't hesitate and stepped in with guns-a-blazing. Didn't want another catastrophe like we had at Little Bighorn with General Custer."

"A ghastly incident that was," said Mrs. Comford, crying out. Mrs. Green nodded, vehemently.

"Now," Peale said, shaking his fist, getting riled. "The Indians are still all up in arms about a few meddling women and children and old men who were smack-dab in the middle of the ruckus and got themselves killed."

"Well, sorry to hear about that state of affairs," Mrs. Green said, chiming in. "But praying to the wrong sort and all will bring the Devil's doings and—well, people get what they deserve."

"Yes, yes, Mrs. Green. Sorry matter that was," Mrs. Comford said, nudging the woman aside. "Please continue, Mr. Peale," she stated, straightening her dress, and patting her hair. She encouraged the man with a stilted smile.

"These Indians, I tell you, are sneaky devils. But I have faith you can turn their lives around in… well, frankly, in no time at all, now that you ladies have arrived. Be careful of your belongings though, for they will steal you blind if given a chance."

Mrs. Comford's eyes swiveled sideways towards Mrs. Green. "Why, indeed we will. You are a brave man, coming out here, and all alone amongst the savages, braving the wilds. But still, how lonely it must be for you with no wife to tend to your needs." Mrs. Comford, preened—practically crowing at the man. "Bless your soul, a saint you are," she said, matter-of-factly, as she held her Bible close to her chest, her fingers trembling.

A native of Connecticut, Mrs. Comford had always pined for a husband, but was unsuccessful in that endeavor even though she was attentive to unattached men, sending them scrumptious meals, ever so eager to please. She could not fathom why men avoided her. She eventually gave up and immersed herself in the teachings of the Lord and His commands. But now here he was, a man of substance standing before her—and so dashing. She concluded the good Lord must have guided her to this place of misery for a reason.

Mrs. Comford blinked, lost in thought, as she heard Mrs. Green say, "We'll be hard-pressed to convert some of the heathens, I'm certain. But we both look forward to our work, no matter the danger." Raising her Bible in the air, she continued. "We'll save as many souls from Hell as possible. So, don't fret about the conversions, Mr. Peale. We'll get them all, one way or another. Bloodthirsty ones, included."

"Well, of course, of course, ladies," Otis Peale said, scratching his head, wondering about these women. He might have his hands full and wonders who'll be worse—these two or the heathens. "Yes indeed. Yes indeed. That's why the good Lord sent the two of you." He swallowed hard, clearing his throat. "Now let's go to my house for a little refreshment, and you can clean up. We can have a nice little chat about your trip and discuss the future of the Indians. Afterwards, I'll have my housekeeper, Mrs. Stover, show you your quarters."

*

As Peale and the missionaries walked down the road, Morning Star sat, staring after them, head in her hands. She felt more misery had just arrived. "I'm not sure what will become of us, Great Spirit, now that they have come."

Her mind drifted off to Hidden Spirit. She yearned for the sight of him. The thought of the handsome young man set her heart fluttering. She knew he was hiding out somewhere among the hills where his grandfather lived. The soldiers had figured some of the older Indians, not much for change, were hiding out there, but left them pretty much alone as long as they didn't cause any trouble. Besides, it was a dickens of a place to get to.

Hidden Spirit is lucky to be away from the white eyes and their rules, Morning Star thought. *At least he won't be forced to go to that boarding school.* Her parents didn't want any trouble, so she had to go. Besides, the soldiers would come and take them by force if they resisted, and Peale said he would set an example of Indians who didn't obey his rules.

Morning Star was in love with the brave and handsome Hidden Spirit. She loved to watch him ride. It seemed as if he was floating on the back of the animal while giving the appearance of a formidable warrior. His raven-black hair fell past his shoulders, free and wild, like his spirit—floating in the wind. Her heart would jump, remembering the sight of his glimmering body, bare from waist up. *Maybe if she hugged him tightly enough, some of his power would fill her,* she thought with longing. She could use some of his strength for what was to come. But Morning Star was shy when he was near. She could never get her words out without stumbling over them, blushing, and she would look away when his dark eyes wandered toward hers, leaving her breathless. When he wasn't looking, though, she would sneak a glance out of the corner of her eye, absorbing every detail of his muscular body. He had a scar about an inch long on his left cheekbone, which only enhanced his good looks. His lips were bold and powerful and his face was filled with intensity. She often wondered what it would be like to kiss him, but she quickly reddened at such thoughts, and sighed. It was rumored that Hidden Spirit held the magic inside. Morning Star knew it was true. She had seen it in his eyes. Some say they saw the magic in him the day he was born.

Morning Star reluctantly awakens from her daydream, startled that she had drifted off. She looks around to make certain Peale and the ladies are gone, then she takes off in a sprint into the hills, hoping to find Hidden Spirit. Maybe, his grandfather, Plenty Feathers, has seen him.

After a few miles of running up the steep terrain, she stops to catch her breath, and thinks she hears a noise in the distance. Her pulse quickens as she slips on the sharp rocks. She mustn't get caught in the hills with soldiers wandering about—or worse, that awful Will Wigley.

Barely into his twenties, Wigley already looks haggard, with lines deeply etched around his eyes. He sports a mustache far too big for his lean face, which he likes to stroke at the tips as he walks about the reservation, twirling his big gun. Once, it accidently fired as it twirled right out of his fingers and came within inches of hitting his foot. The people watching got a real good laugh at him, while most of them were disappointed the bullet had missed.

Morning Star knows there is something dark, even menacing, about him.

Ration day comes every other Tuesday. On one such Tuesday, Morning Star was standing in line with her father to wait for their supplies. As they neared the front of the line, Wigley remarked crudely to her father. "I'll give ya some extra rations fer that squaw of yers. I don't mind some red meat to warm my bed." Her father didn't need to fully understand the English language to know what he meant and he never let her go with him again. After that incident, her father was harassed each time he showed up. One time Will Wigley shoved him to the ground and tried to make him beg for his rations. He turned around and left empty-handed. He was a proud man. He told Morning Star's mother he was sorry, but he would not get on his hands and knees, and beg. "The one thing we must keep is our dignity," he said. "We have lost everything else to the white man, but this we must not lose." Then he would go off to the Great Spirit, and pray.

The thought of Wigley makes Morning Star run even faster into the hills. She scurries up the rugged terrain, dotted with ponderosa pines and junipers. Relieved to be near the top, she stops once again to catch her breath, and looks around at the beautiful countryside. She especially loves the hills when they are filled with budding flowers ready to bloom, making a stark contrast to the gray rocks and craggy ravines.

Up ahead she hears the sound of running water, and smiles. "I must be getting close," she whispers excitedly, and walks on. Then she stops. A noise in the brush causes her to jump. A bad feeling engulfs her. She looks frantically for Grandfather's cave, praying she was close. But it is hard to find in the dense shrubbery, trees, and brush, so she calls out, "Grandfather, where are...?" Someone, grabs her from behind, closing a callused hand over her mouth. A voice hisses, "Lookie by crookie what I just found—a sweet ripe squaw. One I been eyeballing for a spell." He whirls her around with such force that she falls hard on her knees to the ground and feels the trickle of blood down her leg. Grabbing her face, Wigley bores his sinister eyes into hers. Morning Star backs away, and smothers a cry. "Say, whatcha doing up here, anyways? Looking for that Indian kid?" He gives her a rough shake. "Why don't you take me to him an' I'll give ya a reward for yer help. Let's give him a big ole surprise. But, hey, before we get going, how's about a big sweet kiss for me?" he says with a meaningful grin. "Making me climb these big ole' hills and all..." Pulling her close, he mutters in her ear. "Yer sweeter than a bear in heat."

Morning Star freezes, then stumbles back. Every inch of her is shaking.

"When I find him, I'm gonna string him up for all the trouble he's caused." Will's eyes glide over Morning Star's long legs, noticing the blood. "Say," he says, stroking his mustache, "you gotta nasty cut there. Let me fix it for ya." His hand slips up her dress, revealing shapely legs, and he licks his lips in anticipation. Now he strokes his mustache faster, thinking about what he's going to do. "Could be dangerous fer you up here all by yer lonesome." A slow grin spreads across Will's scruffy face and he bends down on his knees. "I got something that'll perk ya right up," he says, wickedly. "My own special love potion. Fixed a passel full o' women with it." As he moves closer, his holster presses against Morning Star's thigh, and he groans, "Got yer dress all mussed up here." He starts to wipe the dirt off, and then in a flash he slides further up her legs, rubbing them with his calloused hands. Easing his way to her shoulder, he finds her breast and squeezes. Unable to contain his excitement, he shouts out. "Whoopee! Nice an' ripe… just as I like 'em. I bet you're one sweet whore," his says hoarsely.

Morning Star can't believe this is happening. Her eyes glaze over in shock, as Wigley hollers and moans, "I found me the mother-lode, little squaw. Get on closer now." He nuzzles the side of her neck, starting to lick it, forgetting about that Indian kid. Morning Star comes out of her shock, disgusted at the closeness of this vile man, touching her. She eases her hand to his side, as Will moans louder, and inches closer toward his holster. Feeling for the gun with trembling hands, she pulls it out and slides back the trigger. Before Will knows what is happening, Morning Star shoves him away and he feels something hard pressing against his side.

Morning Star swallows the lump in her throat and, as calmly as she can manage, threatens him. "Get off me before I shoot!" Her entire body is trembling, and her hand shakes like a leaf.

Will grins when he sees the girl pointing a gun at him and looking wild. *Just how I like 'em,* he thinks. But his grin quickly fades when he sees the hatred burning in her eyes. He starts to reach for his pistol, but realizes it's gone. That look of hers makes him cautious, and he backs away, thinking he'd better stick his hands up. *Never know what a nervous squaw with a gun will do, especially, when it's teetering in her hands, and aimed straight at him.*

"Whoa there, Nelly," Will chortles, trying to ease her fury. "Now just hold on a minute, little squaw. Don't want that gun going off now. Just havin' me a little fun was all. I like squaws. Like 'em just fine. Wanted to show ya how much was all." He adds a wink.

Morning Star finds her voice, and her nerve. "If you come

near me, I'll shoot," she threatens. She can barely manage to hold the gun still and clasps both hands together.

Will sputters in disbelief. "Well, you may be a sight pretty for a squaw, but yer meaner than a rattler. No wonder they call ya savages," he spurts out. Then he tries to take a different tactic, and tries to sound contrite, but instead whines. "Say, little squaw. Didn't mean to give you a fright. Ya hungry? Got some rations in my saddlebag. Nice can of beans. Ya like 'em?"

Morning Star says nothing and watches Wigley with wary eyes as she backs away, still pointing the gun.

"Was out looking for that savage kid, called Hidden Shits." Will let off a loud snort. "Bet you know who I'm talking 'bout, too. Heard he hides out 'round here somewhere. Gonna string that bastard up when I catch him." Wigley's face clouds as he eyes Morning Star. Getting no reaction, he inches his way toward her. Then, in a flash, he dives at her.

Morning Star gasps, as she falls backwards. The gun explodes and the bullet ricochets—sending Wigley and his hat flying to the ground.

"Dammit," he shouts. "Almost shot my darn head off."

Morning Star opens her eyes and, to her surprise, she sees Will on the ground. Fuming, he picks up his hat, which now has a smoldering hole in the center, and brushes off the dirt.

The shock on Wigley's face gives Morning Star a brief moment of satisfaction, but the image of his hands touching her comes flooding back. She clenches her teeth, emboldened, and shouts, "Get up! If you dare follow me again I'll shoot you dead."

Splotches of dark purple and red cover Wigley's face. "Mighty sorry yer gonna be, little squaw. Next time I won't be so nice to the likes of ya." Scowling, he hops on his horse, and yanks the reins. The horse whirls around and speeds off down the mountain.

Blood pounds in Morning Star's temples as she watches him leave. Her legs almost give out, and she fears she might faint. She prays Hidden Spirit will be at Grandfather's camp. After steadying herself, she takes off in a run, flying across the hillside. She pushes herself even harder, not caring that tree branches are catching her hair and snagging her clothes. Panic sets in. Realizing she is lost, she pleads in desperation, "Where are you, Grandfather?" As tears well up, she looks around. The hillside is full of trees and rocks and shrubs, and she forces herself to calm down so she can think clearly and breathe. She remembers an ancient oak tree with deep scars from its many years in the hills—it's near Grandfather's cave. And a small stream that runs in the back. She concentrates, trying to remember the way. She knows she has to be close now, and she moves on, concentrating. Looking ahead she sees a bright speck of red through the shroud of trees, and quickens her step. Her heart leaps in anticipation. She wonders what it is and, with great trepidation, pushes the branches aside and stops, mid-stride. Morning Star blinks, not believing what she sees in front of her. In the middle of the forest, surrounded by pines and cottonwoods, stands a beautiful tepee. She holds her breath wondering if this is a vision, or if she is in shock. Just to make certain, she puts her hand out and carefully touches the side of the tepee. Then, she stares at the drawings in wonder.

Grazing in the center stands a solitary white buffalo with deep piercing eyes that seem to come alive as she stares at the stunning creature. She thinks she sees it move, ever so slightly, and reaches out to touch it. When she feels the animal quiver, she jumps back, in awe. "Oooohh. This is special," she whispers. Then her eyes move to the smudges of red that cover the bottom and the black crow feathers that crown the top, with specks of red dripping down. Above the entrance, a single star glistens.

It's like a dream! How did the tepee get here? she wonders, walking around the side. The lovely scene brings back fond memories. *Is this Plenty Feather's tepee? It must be,* she thinks, and softly calls out, "Grandfather?"

A moment later, the old man peers out of the opening, and beams at the girl in delight.

"My dearest Morning Star, come in." He opens the bearskin flap, welcoming her inside.

The musty fragrance of sage and tobacco floats out, and she inhales the wondrous scent. It's comforting and peaceful. She hugs herself, knowing just a short while ago she was in grave peril, and now this. She smiles.

While observing his granddaughter, Plenty Feathers sits down against a willow backrest holding his long pipe, and fills it with tobacco from the bark of the red willow.

Morning Star looks around in astonishment. "This is wonderful, Grandfather." Turning in circles, she absorbs each and every detail. She closes her eyes for a moment and imagines living here, in this beautiful place with Grandfather and Hidden Spirit. When she opens them, she sees Grandfather's eyes watching her closely, sensing her wish. She smiles at him and wraps her arms around his leathery neck. His long gray hair is pulled into a loose braid with an eagle feather at the end. Deep lines, sunken like caverns, are etched into his face and his eyes look like small slits, lost in the folds of his sagging skin. *He looks like the craggy hills I just climbed,* she thinks, but his frail body still holds strength.

She murmurs softly, "It is good to see you. I wish I could stay here with you, forever, Grandfather. I hate living on the reservation. They treat us like we're of no importance. And, we have so many rules to follow." Morning Star forces out a smile, not wanting to worry him. *Besides, there is nothing he can do,* she thinks miserably.

Plenty Feathers motions for her to sit next to him on a thick buffalo hide. "I am glad you made it safely, my dear. The hills can be dangerous."

Morning Star lowers her eyes, looking at her torn dress, and says nothing.

"I see you speak white man's tongue well. It will be useful for the future."

"Yes, Grandfather, it will." Then she brightens. "When did you put up the tepee, Grandfather? It's so lovely... it makes me want to cry." She can find no other words, and stares in awe at its beauty.

"Hidden Spirit is a clever young man," Grandfather says, pleased. "It was Leaves Dancing's wish to live once again in the old way. I thought it was not possible until Hidden Spirit surprised me. He told me it was a gift from Leaves Dancing. She made it years ago and kept it well hidden." Plenty Feather's voice trails off as he thinks of his beloved wife who, not long ago, was killed at Wounded Knee.

Morning Star remarks softly. "It's beautiful. When was Hidden Spirit last here?" she asks, hopefully. "I worry and miss him, Grandfather."

"Not since he put up the tepee, child."

"Peale forbids us to live in tepees. He told us, 'your past is now gone. You must learn the new ways and live in proper houses, like it or not.'" Morning Star sighs. "The soldiers came and tore down any tepees they found still standing. We now live like the white men, in the drafty houses. I wish I could stay with you... and Hidden Spirit."

Plenty Feathers nods his head somberly. "I wish that, as well. I am saddened by the news you bring." He draws slowly on his pipe. "I am afraid that progress for the white man has not boded well for our people. The buffalo was our life, and is no longer with us. The white man came on the big roaring box that cut through our lands and killed our buffalo. They made heroes out of men who destroyed our way of life. Now, our lands we loved has been sold to the cattle people. There is little left for us. We must pray to the Great Spirit, and ask for strength to survive."

Morning Star fights back the tears, thinking he's right. Unable to speak, she stares silently into the glowing embers that fill the space with a soft glow. Breaking the silence, she says, "Grandfather, I saw two white missionaries arrive today. It was unsettling to watch them… I suppose they will try to convince us our ways are wrong… that our religion is evil."

"The white man, my child, does not understand our religion or our ways. They are set on changing us. They do not see that we do not need to pray inside in a walled house, or read from their big book. We know the Great Spirit can hear us better out in the open, where we marvel at all His wonders. We look to the trees standing tall and graceful, and thank them for being among us, giving us life. We thank the stones that lie beneath our feet. They also have power. We marvel at the mountains soaring beyond the clouds that seem to touch the stars, and make us yearn to discover their secrets. The Great Spirit is all around. If we cherish Mother Earth, she will in turn bless us with all we need. The white man does not see it that way. They scar the land and kill its creatures without cause. It will be difficult to convince the whites not to harm Mother Earth, for she is fragile."

"Yes, Grandfather," Morning Star says sadly. "We waste our time believing anything they say. They will never let us live how we choose." She falls silent once again, reflecting on Grandfather's words.

Morning Star looks around the tepee and asks Grandfather about the drawings.

Plenty Feathers answers with a hint of pride. "Hidden Spirit's grandmother said she saw the symbols from a vision in her dream before she died. A circle of light appeared around her and she heard Broken Feather's voice telling her what to draw. When she awoke, she found a single black feather lying by her side."

"Grandmother's presence is very strong in here. I can almost see her dancing and feel her love of the drums," she says, softly rubbing her arms.

Grandfather nods. "I feel her presence each day and it brings me great peace sitting in here, surrounded by her love. I know she is pleased I live here."

Morning Star's face glows as she looks up and stares with fascination at the circle of feathers. She swears the feathers are moving, swaying gently back and forth. She waits. Her heart flutters for an instant. She can feel Leaves Dancing smiling at her. Then, she feels Hidden Spirit's presence. *It's as if the feathers are speaking to me,* she thinks, as they whirl around her body, giving her a renewed sense of strength. Soon they stop, and the black feathers are back in place at top of the tepee.

Grandfather seems amused, watching Morning Star, saying nothing.

The two sit around the fire talking until the shadows grow long and it is time for Morning Star to leave.

Standing slowly, she clasps her hands together, hating to say goodbye. Her voice shakes with sadness, "Goodbye, Grandfather."

Plenty Feathers wipes a tear that fills the corner of his eye and slips down his withered cheek. He gazes at her with melancholy eyes. "Be careful at that white man's school, my dear. No good will come of that place. I will pray that the Great Spirit will protect you."

Morning Star hugs him tightly and can feel his bones quiver. She wants to tell him she will be fine at the school, but he would see her lie. She hugs the old man one more time. It takes all her strength to leave.

Outside, Morning Star looks back at the tepee with longing. She wishes times were different for her people. As she walks down the hillside she sees the moon casting flickering shadows on the surrounding trees and hillsides. She stays close to the shadows, not wanting to get caught by Wigley again.

EYES OF THE SOUL

CHASING RABBIT IS up early this morning. Normally, she would be talking about everything from the sky to the trees to the birds. How do they fly? How do the trees grow? She would pester her parents endlessly. At nine years old she is intuitive and inquisitive and always smiling, making her brown eyes sparkle with excitement.

Little Moon is also nine, and her best friend. They play outside every chance they get. When Chasing Rabbit comes upon a fragrant shrub or plant that she recognizes, she makes it a point to stop and tell Little Moon its name and what it is used for. Chasing Rabbit likes to impress her friend. She isn't at all interested in cooking or sewing—only exploring. Little Moon is more timid and shy, so Chasing Rabbit has to coax her along on her adventures.

One bright sunny day, Chasing Rabbit is out exploring with Little Moon when she discovers a pond full of cattails. "Come on, let's go swimming," she yells excitedly, diving into the murky water, giggling.

Little Moon is reluctant to join her in the muddy water, but little by little, she slides her toes in. A few feet out into the pond, her feet sink in the muck and she screams at the top of her lungs, "I'm going to drown, help!" Chasing Rabbit quickly swims over, and pulls her frantic friend to the shore. "I'm not going in there again," Little Moon says, sputtering. "It's dangerous! I can't even see the bottom." Sitting on the bank dangling her legs, Little Moon watches as Chasing Rabbit swims to the center, waving. Little Moon is fearful. "Be careful, Chasing Rabbit," she warns. "I can't save you if you drown." Chasing Rabbit only grins at Little Moon, as she deftly swims through the cattails. "I'll be fine." Then she hollers excitedly, splashing in the water. "I caught a frog," she says proudly, holding up a large green bullfrog that croaks in alarm. "Come back in. We'll catch dinner." The bullfrog slips out of Chasing Rabbit's hand, making her squeal, and smacks the water in delight. "Come on, Little Moon. Help me catch more. Our parents will think we're smart." But all the coaxing is of no use. Little Moon refuses to budge. Finally, after capturing only three small frogs, Chasing Rabbit gives up. "I would give you half of my frogs," she says, looking at her bag, "but there's not too many." Little Moon smiles and says, "That's okay, Chasing Rabbit. I'm just glad you didn't drown." On the way home, Chasing Rabbit stops, remembering to thank the Great Spirit for the frogs. Holding up her bag, they both yell, "Thank you, Great Spirit," and look up at the sky. The girls were taught the importance of thanking the Great Spirit for whatever they take, no matter the size.

After walking Little Moon home, Chasing Rabbit sprints into her house with her bag, and calls out. "Mother, look what I have." White Tail smiles at her daughter in amusement. "By the looks of your bag it might be enough for your father."

White Cloud walks in and sees Chasing Rabbit's face beam. "You're so resourceful, sweet girl. My mouth waters thinking about eating frog legs. I haven't had those in quite a spell." Chasing Rabbit runs into his arms, and gives him a big wet kiss.

Her mother cooks up the frog legs and Chasing Rabbit watches as her father devours his supper in a few bites.

In the evenings, Chasing Rabbit likes to run outside and catch fireflies. She is fascinated by their pretty shades of green as she carefully inspects them to see how they glow. Concluding they must have tiny lanterns inside their bellies, she sets them free. One night after tiring of her inspection, she thinks, *Little Moon and I need a real adventure.* The next day, she runs to Little Moon's house and gushes in excitement. "Let's go see the Badlands, the magical place my father talks about." But Little Moon is not interested. "It's a long ways, Chasing Rabbit. I don't think I can walk that far."

Determined, Chasing Rabbit says, "Well, let's go a ways. Maybe we can see the peaks." Little Moon reluctantly agrees. So the two girls set out and walk and walk—but still don't reach the Badlands. Chasing Rabbit finds a spot where they can look across the valley and see the jagged peaks.

"I'm so glad we can stop. I don't think my legs can take me any further," Little Moon says, moaning.

"Me, neither," says Chasing Rabbit. So the girls fall to the ground in relief. Nearby, prairie dogs climb out of their holes, watch the girls with interest, and chatter loudly about their intrusion. The girls giggle when they spot mule deer on the ridge, and point in delight as their large ears outline the horizon. They stay until the sun falls against the pinnacles and majestic hills—turning shades of yellow, then gold. Holding hands as the daylight fades into dusk, they start on their journey home. This is the last day the girls will be able to explore together. The next day they will be sent away from all they know and love.

On this particular morning, Chasing Rabbit is very quiet. White Tail tries to lift her daughter's spirits, but can't manage. Her own heart is heavy with sorrow. She goes to her daughter's side and puts her arms around her, kissing her round cheek. "This is an important day for you, my sweet daughter. Turn around, and I'll comb your beautiful hair and make it shine." White Tail's eye's well up as she brushes her daughter's long hair and braids the thick strands between her fingers. She fights to hold back the tears and begins singing an old song her mother had sung to her long ago. It's a melancholy tune, about a lone young wolf, lost in the wilds. She encourages Chasing Rabbit to sing along, but her daughter shakes her head vehemently. The girl's thoughts are on leaving, being without her parents. She has never been away from them before, and she is scared. Her big eyes fill with tears and she interrupts her Mother's singing. "What will happen to us at this school? How long will they make us stay?" Chasing Rabbit wipes her tears and then straightens. A look of defiance shows in her eyes, and she crosses her arms in resistance. "Why do we have to go?"

White Tail hugs Chasing Rabbit tightly. "My daughter, the church women came over the other day and explained the new school to us. One of the women even spoke a little of our language and told us it's a very nice place for the children to go. There will be lots of food to eat and a nice warm bed to sleep in. There they will teach you how to be farmers and grow vegetables, like they do," she adds softly. "That doesn't sound so bad, does it, my daughter? You will even learn more about the white tongue people."

"I don't like them," she said, pouting, "and I can speak like the white tongue. I don't want to go." She stomps her foot angrily.

White Tail normally would be amused, but on this day she is crestfallen. She reaches her arms toward Chasing Rabbit, and pulls her close. "They will teach you about their God. The women say he is more powerful than our Great Spirit, for they have a big book to prove what they say is true. Maybe if you pray to the white man's God, he will let you come home soon." She looks at her daughter, raising her brow. "That is, if you're good." She tugs her braid, chiding her. "Who knows? You might be happy and want to stay in your new place."

"I am happy here with you and Father," Chasing Rabbit says, stubbornly. "I don't want to go with them. Please don't let them take me." Her mother puts her arms around her daughter and tries to console her, but the girl breaks free. "I don't want to go with those ugly women to that school and eat their food. I don't want to pray to the white man's God, either. I am not white. I am Sioux. I will pray to our Great Spirit." She stomps her feet angrily. "I will run away and hide in the hills with Hidden Spirit."

Chasing Rabbit's father watches from the doorway, and picks up his little girl. She starts sobbing, clinging to his neck. Between tears, she says, "Oh, Father, please don't make me go. Tell them you need me here. Tell them you love me and can't let me go. I can learn all I need from you and Mother. I am happy here."

White Cloud rocks her softly in his arms and hugs her tightly against his chest. "We are happy with you here, my dear. And, yes, we do love you very much." He needs to stay strong for his daughter so he says, "My little girl is getting so tall now. You have grown as fast as the willows. I know you don't want to go, but all the other children are going, and you can play with your friends. I know you are too much like your brother, and as headstrong, but I am sorry you can't stay with us, my dear, or run away in the hills with Hidden Spirit. We will get into trouble if you do not go. You must be brave now and do as they tell you. Please, do not cause trouble at the new place, my little rabbit, for I'm not certain of the measures they will use for discipline." Trying to hide his worry, he walks around the room, holding her in his arms. "I am sure they will treat you fairly, for you are children and not warriors. I think you might even enjoy yourself," he adds with a wink, "once you get used to their ways. Let me hug you tightly, so you will feel better. But, whenever you're lonely, you can hold this for comfort."

Chasing Rabbit stops crying and opens her father's fist, screaming out in delight when she sees a beautiful round stone that looks like the color of glacial ice. There is a mystique to the stone, its golden center filled with fire. If she looks closely enough, she can see the outline of her face. Looking deeper, she peers into the center and sees an eye pop out and wink at her. She jumps in amazement. "Where did you find such a treasure?" she says, bubbling with delight, eyeing the mysterious stone.

White Cloud is grateful to change the subject about the school, and brushes away her lingering tears.

"Yesterday morning," her father says, "I was walking along a narrow path heading toward the large rock that juts out over the cliff to pray. I was getting close when I heard a whisper in my ear, coming from a distance. It sounded like a whoosh in the breeze. I looked. No one was around, so I continued on my way when, suddenly, a large bald eagle flew overhead, swooped down close to my head, and dropped a snowy white rabbit at my feet. The rabbit sat up, and, straightening his ears, told me, 'This is for our spirit sister that carries our name, Chasing Rabbit. She is very special; we know of her sadness, and her tears make us cry. We want to lighten her heart.' Then the rabbit wiggled its nose, pulled out a pouch, and handed me this stone. Its rays traveled high into the heavens and lit up the sky. When I looked for the rabbit to thank him, he had already scampered away. I think the Great Spirit knew of your dilemma and sent you a gift, my daughter."

"That's a wonderful story, Father. I'll thank the rabbits later." Chasing Rabbit scrambles from her father's arm and runs to her bed. Pulling out her small deerskin pouch from the mattress, she says happily, "I'll put it with my other treasures." She runs back to her father and kisses him on the cheek. Then she frowns, worried. "They won't take it from me at the new place, will they?"

"I'm sure they won't, my little rabbit, but keep it close, just in case. Show no one." White Cloud fights to keep control of his emotions as he holds on to his precious girl.

Wearing an elk-skin dress covered with little tufts of white feathers, Chasing Rabbit lies in his arms asking for more stories, so White Cloud tells her the story about the day she was born, her favorite. Leaning back in his chair smiling, he recalls, "When you were ready to come into this world, two rabbits ran in circles around and around and chased each other until they grew dizzy. Then when you appeared, they jumped high in the air, dancing together, feet thumping, and calling out for their friends. You were now surrounded by hundreds of rabbits, wiggling their noses as they hopped over each other and shyly inspected you. A few even nibbled your cheek, making you laugh. You cried out with such great enthusiasm, I knew you were glad to be among the rabbit family. You even wiggled your nose like the rabbits. Chasing Rabbit—they liked your name. I could only stare at your lovely face for hours and hours. I told you stories before you could even open your eyes. I knew you were a curious one, and the first word you spoke was, 'Why'?"

White Cloud grasps Chasing Rabbit's hand tightly, and says, "It is now time to go." His voice trembles slightly and he closes his eyes to block out his daughter's sadness. "We have waited as long as we can. We will be in trouble if we are late, my dear."

Chasing Rabbit takes one last look around their house. It is not much, but it is home. They walk out the door, each lost in their own thoughts. White Tail squeezes her hand, trying to give encouragement. White Cloud fights back his urge to flee with his little girl. She is his life. His grip makes her fingers numb, but Chasing Rabbit doesn't mind. Numb is how she feels.

As if in a dream, the three of them walk down the dirt path, silent, clinging to each other, hoping to give each other strength.

Chasing Rabbit wishes they could walk into the Badlands, hide out and never come back. She loves the craggy peaks and fills her thoughts of the mysterious place. Determined to keep her tears back, she can't imagine what is to come.

White Cloud keeps his thoughts empty as he walks, holding onto his daughter's hand. White Tail is afraid to speak, fearing she will break down and cry, and never be able to stop.

As they near the wagons, White Cloud holds his breath to keep from shouting out, "You can't take my daughter." One of the drivers looks at him contemptuously as they pass by, and spits tobacco juice on his foot. White Cloud ignores the man, holding his head high as he walks past.

Chasing Rabbit spots Little Moon sitting by herself in a wagon. Wondering where Morning Star is, she bites her tongue to control her fear—of all the commotion. The people seem flustered, not sure of what to do. Chasing Rabbit clings tightly to White Cloud as they run into Brown Dog, who seems dazed and lost. "My boy is gone," he laments, and stumbles on.

Otis Peale barks orders at the soldiers standing at attention. "I want you to oversee the children's departure. Make sure that it goes smoothly. Don't let anyone get away." So the soldiers walk among the crowd looking for signs of rebellion, eyeing the reluctant ones. Peale wants no trouble today. So far, he is pleased that everything is going off without a hitch.

Will Wigley struts among the crowd while yapping out orders. "Hurry up an' git on in the wagons." Annoyed that no one pays him any mind, he sniggers, pulls out his gun, and fires off a couple of shots. "That'll get yer attention." He grins at the people, cowering. "Come on, gitta movin'! We ain't got all day. Scoot yer skins in them damn wagons. I'm sick of all this whining an' sniveling." Just then, Will spots White Cloud, and struts over, smirking, "Hey, you think you came to some kinda picnic? Looks to me like yer lollygagging 'round. This ain't handout day, ya know." Will hates that White Cloud fellow. *Little too proud actin',* he thinks. Wigley gets close, nose to nose, and taunts him. "If you ain't careful, dirt-digger, I'll keep this young-un of yers for me an' the boys."

White Cloud's face is stoic, even serene, as he stares evenly at Wigley. "No wonder you Injuns got yer asses kicked. Bunch of chicken-shits," he says, snorting. "Looks like yer ready to bawl. Boo-hoo-hoo! Yer nothing but a bunch o' beggars now." Shoving White Cloud, Will says, "Git your squalling papoose in the wagon or I'll…" He doesn't wait as he grabs Chasing Rabbit by the back of her dress, carries her to the nearest wagon, and tosses her inside, like a sack of potatoes. She lands with a thud on the floorboard. "There, that's how it's done." Turning to White Cloud, he threatens, "Now get outta here before I shoot ya."

Chasing Rabbit's elbow stings from the force, and she clamps her jaw to keep from crying out. Wincing, she hobbles to her feet, slips out of the wagon, and sprints toward the wagon where Little Moon is sitting. But she trips on a rut, and falls headfirst into the belly of a fuzzy-haired soldier standing guard. He pushes her away, and swats at her head with the butt of his rifle. He misses. Chasing Rabbit kicks the surprised soldier in the shin, and keeps running.

Breathless, Chasing Rabbit nears the wagon and struggles to climb up on the buckboard. Little Moon reaches out and tugs and pulls until Chasing Rabbit tumbles inside. The girls hold onto each other, heaving a sigh. "I'm so glad you're here, Chasing Rabbit," Little Moon says, smoothing her friend's hair. Chasing Rabbit nods, unable to speak, and leans against the sideboards, catching her breath. Now she slides on her knees, peering over the side of the wagon, watching the uproar. Families mill about, lost, while clinging to their children. Frantic goodbyes are heard throughout the gathering. The soldiers, on high alert, walk among the throngs of people.

Morning Star is the last one to arrive, walking slowly in her beautiful white-fringed dress. Wigley's face pales upon seeing the girl, remembering the incident in the hills. He is livid that she got away and that she almost shot his head off, to boot. For quite a spell, he has been keeping his eye out for that squaw, waiting for his chance to nab her. He swore if he found her he wouldn't let her get away again. That didn't happen. Now, his eyes narrow and he simmers at the sight of her. "Hey, boys. Take a gander at this redskin bitch comin' down the road!"

Will struts up to Morning Star, and hisses, "Where ya been hidin', you little whore? I oughtta take you into the storage room an' give ya something to moan about—other than yer rations. Show ya what ya missed the other day. That'll set you right." Grabbing her hair, he pins her face against his. Morning Star smells the bacon grease on his moustache and tries to pull her face away. Wigley smirks, and is ready to take her away, but he suddenly loosens his grip when Otis Peale hurries by.

All in a dither, Peale hollers. "Get everyone in the wagon, Wigley. Gotta schedule to keep."

"Yes, sir."

Red-faced, Wigley watches him hurry past and grips Morning Star's arm as she tries to get away. "Not so fast," he says, wickedly, twisting her arm. He grins at the soldiers, thinking he's gonna show them who is what around this place. "This one here's a wildcat, boys," he says, pulling Morning Star along as he slips his hand inside her dress.

Morning Star gasps and squirms out of his clutches.

His eyes bore into hers. "I'd say she looks real sad about leaving. I'm gonna help her forget her troubles," he says, grinning like a jackal. "She's a fine lookin' gal, for a redskin, ain't she fellas?" His shrewd eyes stare. "Kinda hate to see her go," he says, squeezing hard on her arm. "I'm gonna teach her 'bout pleasing a man. A white one." He pulls Morning Star against his chest, and licks his lips and smiles. Then he yanks her hair back, and says hoarsely. "I'm gonna give ya a big ole kiss. One ya ain't likely to forget either."

The soldiers cheer him on and clap, enjoying the spectacle. Then, out of the blue, *thwack*. A stone knocks Wigley's hat to the ground. "Who the hell threw that?" He growls and whirls around, pulling out his pistol, glaring at the crowd.

Morning Star wrenches free of his grasp, and starts to run. Wigley starts after her when another stone, the size of a ball, hits him square on the head. He's stunned for a moment, then stumbles after Morning Star, grabbing her by the hair.

Bristling with fury, Morning Star turns around, balls up her fist, and socks Wigley as hard as she can in the jaw, with a force that surprises even her. Will reels back in indignation, losing his grip on her hair and his balance. Then his pale face begins a slow burn. He is furious at the turn of events. His temple throbs from that blasted stone and his jaw smarts. But what smarts even more is his humiliation as the soldiers howl in laughter, mocking him.

Will curses the fleeing girl, "damn Injuns," he says, spitting. "I hate 'em." He pulls out his gun, and shouts. "If'n I see which one of ya red devils threw that stone, I'll shoot ya deader'n a doorknob."

Grinning, Chasing Rabbit lowers herself into the wagon. She peers through a crack and sees Morning Star race toward them.

"Faster, Morning Star, faster." Little Moon says, squealing in fright.

Chasing Rabbit stands and waves, shouting, "Over here," she cries, holding out her hand. "Hurry." Morning Star bounds into the wagon, trembling, relieved to be out of Will's clutches.

The soldiers need to restrain Will, who is livid. He curses and threatens to kill them if they don't let him go. A scruffy soldier with hulking shoulders speaks in a threatening tone. "Leave the squaw alone, Will. There's plenty more around here you can get friendly with besides her."

Will shrugs off his grasp and stomps away, yelling angrily at the last of the children clinging to their parents. "Better hurry on into the wagon, 'fore I shoot ya." He shoves a young boy out of his way. "And I mean, pronto."

Finally, everyone is in the wagons except for a little girl named Otter, whose mother, Brown Hare, clings to her, stubbornly refusing to let her go. A soldier tries to take the child away, and Brown Hare fights like a warrior, kicking and punching ferociously. Finally, it takes two other soldiers to come over and help. They knock Brown Hare to the ground, and then hit her on the head with the butt of their rifles.

Morning Star sees Otter clinging to her mother as she lies in the dirt, bleeding profusely. Morning Star jumps from the wagon and grabs Otter before the soldiers take her and kill Brown Hare. She carries the girl into the wagon and sits her between Little Moon and Chasing Rabbit. Otter is hysterical, pleading for her mother, who still lies in the dirt with blood streaming down her face. Brown Hare can barely see as she picks herself up and runs to Otis Peale, begging for mercy.

Otis can't understand her words, but knows it's about her child and scowls at her display of emotions. "Here, now. You're behaving ill-mannered. Get ahold of yourself. Your daughter will be just fine. Going to a fine place. Now, run along." And he shoos her away with a wave of his kerchief. The missionaries start to sing, "When the Saints Go Marching In."

Desperate, Brown Hare runs to the wagon that has her baby girl inside. The driver cracks his whip, and the wagon starts to leave. Brown Hare hangs onto the side and wails, "Otter, my Otter."

A blond soldier runs up behind her, and pulls her back. "Get away from the wagon, you crazy squaw. You wanna get run over?"

Morning Star holds a crying Otter in her arms, trying her best to soothe the hysterical girl. She thinks this must be a surreal moment, and looks around at the surrounding chaos, families torn apart, lives lost, families in shock, and Brown Hare struggling to cope with the loss of her only child.

Will fires a gunshot into the crowd. People scream. The drivers crack their whips at the horses in a hurry to leave. They see the Indians getting worked up, and shout. "Giddy-up, now. Gee-haw." Everyone scrambles to get out of the way of the wagons as they hurtle on past.

Otis looks relieved, wiping his brow. He is glad that this ordeal is over. The heathens will be on Preacher Jim's shoulders now. He signals to the ladies to join him in verse. His baritone voice booms. "Glory, Glory, Hallelujah, the troops are marching on."

The families try to smother their grief the best they can. The men and women hold tight to whoever is near, and help the ones who collapse in grief. After the last of the dust settles and the haze lifts, a deathly pall descends. The people watch their lives and children disappear down the road into a cloud of dust. Death would have been kinder for these people of the Plains.

White Cloud chokes back his cries. The thought of losing his Chasing Rabbit sends his heart racing. He looks to the sky with outstretched hands, and cries out. "Please, Great Spirit. Help us."

HIDDEN SPIRIT

HIDDEN SPIRIT SPENDS several nights huddled under a ledge, trying to keep out the chilling drizzle, while hiding from the soldiers. Last night, he gathered boughs of pines to lie on, and he sleeps fitfully—his mind filled with bizarre dreams. A sharp, burning poke, poke, poke on his leg stirs him awake. Still groggy from the dream, he calls out, shivering. "Who's there?" A dark, raspy caw echoes in the stillness. "Coward!" Hidden Spirit cracks open his eyes. He swears he sees a crow step out of the shadows, fluttering its wings. "Look who's hiding in the hills like a coward." Hidden Spirit leans on his elbows and strains to see who is talking in the darkness, but the vision floats away.

His eyes fly open and he bolts up. Not seeing the crow, he shakes away the image of the strange dream, and paces back and forth. He feels guilty for staying in the hills, but what else can he do? If they capture him and send him away, he will be of no use to his people. His mind is full of torment. He feels the need to run and race among trees and feel the earth beneath his feet, to free himself from his torturous thoughts. He is no longer able to concentrate and needs something to do, or he will go mad. Knowing his family needs food, he decides to go hunting. In the early morning hours, he quickly gathers his freshly sharpened arrows, slings them across his back, and sets off. A sultry mist languishes over the valley, floating above the trees, like a soft velvety blanket. The dew drips on his face as he ducks under low-lying branches. In the east, a pink glow is inching its way upward as most of the stars disappear. Catching a glimpse of the morning star fading into the depths of the horizon, he stops and closes his eyes for a moment, thinking of his love. Then, from somewhere, arises an ominous warning against his ear. "Be swift on your hunt, for the white eyes will be watching. Be back before the moon rises." The hairs on his neck stand at attention.

Hidden Spirit sets off in a run down the mountain, past blooming dogwoods, thick with their sweet scent, and heads west with several miles to go. He is heading toward the rolling plains full with sweet grass, where the elk gather at this time of year and graze in the lush meadows. He knows it will be dangerous to go through the rancher's land as the soldiers are instructed to shoot anyone caught off the reservation. Hidden Spirit ignores the warning. *I follow my own set of rules*, he thinks, determinedly. He lowers his body and treads lightly through the rancher's land, watching carefully to see if the white eyes are out. It takes most of the morning to get there, since the grasses are high and the ground is wet. He travels past bubbling springs and bluebirds that are singing in shrill voices—loud enough to captivate a mate with their lovely tunes. The Black Hills pines dot the hilly landscape along with cottonwoods and willows. Hidden Spirit loves roaming the forbidden hills and the plains. It is in his blood. He cannot stop that. After hours of traversing the area he sees fresh elk tracks, and quickens his pace.

Up ahead, he spots a small group of elk and quickly drops to his knees, checking the wind's direction. After studying the elk for a time, he decides it is best to come toward the herd from the south, staying downwind. A young buck is grazing at the edge of the group and an older one tilts her nose, sniffing the air. Hidden Spirit calmly pulls an arrow from his pouch, and aims. The arrow glides through the air with exact precision, entering the young elk's heart, killing it instantly. The remaining herd thunders off in alarm. Hidden Spirit runs over to the stilled animal, and bends to his knees, marveling at the elk's beauty. He silently thanks the Great Spirit for guiding him to the herd, and then somberly thanks the gallant young buck for his life.

Pulling his knife from its sheath, he cuts a couple of young saplings, making a travois. Then he carefully skins the animal, and cuts it into quarters. Holding it up, he thinks the hide will make a nice present for his mother. In less than an hour, he finishes with his task, and places the meat on the travois.

The sun is now high overhead, and sweat is pouring down his back. He stands and stretches his muscles from the strenuous work, then freezes when he hears a twig snap and lowers himself to the ground. Muscles taunt, he peers through the tall grass. Suddenly, a loud crack goes off. A bullet whizzes just inches over his head. Without a second glance, he leaps up and flies across the meadows, zigzagging through the tall grass toward a gulley that lies over a half-mile away. He hopes he will make it in time. Hidden Spirit is fast. He could run for miles on end, barely breaking a sweat, but he is tired from the long walk here and prays his strength will hold out. Adrenaline soaring, his feet fly across the ground, his heart thudding from the exertion. He glances back over his shoulder and, seeing the rider on horseback closing in, he pushes himself to run even harder. He thinks his lungs might explode before he can make it to safety. As the grove of trees looms near, he gasps for air and feels his chest burn. Just a few more feet and he'll be there.

Sailing into the cover of the trees, and crashing through the thickets, Hidden Spirit dives headlong into a murky stream in the gulley, pulling branches and brush with him as he goes. Then, out of breath, he collapses. The water gurgles as he sinks into the muddied depths, leaving only his face exposed. Panting, he gulps in air that sends his chest heaving.

Wigley is right behind and reins in his mount as the horse snorts and whinnies. Wigley pulls out his gun and cocks it, aiming for the boy.

Hidden Spirit remains motionless.

Wigley calls out. "Come out, come out, wherever you are. Lousy Injun!" His horse's hooves slip on the rocks, inches away from the banks of the stream. "Whoa, there," Will says. Holding tight to the reins, he kicks the side of his horse.

Hidden Spirit catches a glimpse of his adversary as they maneuver down the banks and into the water.

Will gets off his horse, and, with gun poised, he steps into the water, looking around. A puzzled expression crosses his face as he scans the width of the stream, trying to figure out where the kid went. Water ripples as he walks further into the center, calling out, "I'm gonna git you, Injun!"

For a moment, Hidden Spirit's brain whirls. He thinks about running, and then everything stops. As Wigley nears, he holds his breath. The water covers his body up to his neck, and he slides silently, further into the depth of the bank, slipping into the brush. Just the tip of his nose rises slightly above the water. He stills his mind and asks the Great Spirit for help. A sense of peace begins to fill him as he continues to pray.

In the distance, a faint yip-yip is heard. Then hair-raising howls filter through the air—eerie sounds—growing louder by the minute. Just then a pack of wolves comes crashing through the trees and into the gully running, growling, and yipping ferociously. They splash through the water with ease, and stop within inches of Will—circling, snarling, snapping. Their long sharp fangs flash dangerously, as if daring Will to move.

His whole body shakes uncontrollably as the wolves inch closer, still baring their long, sharp fangs. He fumbles for his gun and, in his haste, he shoots wildly into the air. He makes a bold move and quickly scrambles up the side of the bank before the wolves can devour him. In the process, he drops his gun and fumbles frantically on the ground to find it. Meanwhile, his horse is getting nervous. It backs up and whinnies, shying away as the wolves edge close enough to nip at its legs. Will finally retrieves the fallen gun, and this time he steadies his hand and aims directly for the wolves. But his aim is off and the bullet hits a nearby tree, instead, sending branches and bark tumbling down. The horse starts bucking wildly, its eyes wild with fright. Then it bolts out of the trees—hooves and tail flying high in the air. Will goes scurrying after his horse and dives for the flapping reins. He is desperate to get away from the howling wolves and their sharp, treacherous teeth. All thoughts of capturing that Indian vanish as he manages to grab the saddle horn, hoist himself atop, and bounce along like a wet rag, hollering. "Whoa up."

Hidden Spirit raises his head slowly, wiping the debris from his eyes, looking for the wolves that saved his life. When he peers through the branches, he hears them howling in the distance, but they are nowhere to be seen. He pulls himself from the murky water and tries to stand, but his strength is gone, and he collapses into the gulley.

When he awakens, it is dark. He listens carefully, hearing only the sounds of insects humming, and his own raspy breathing. Climbing out of the gully, he crosses the stream and sets out, hoping to find the elk. To his delight, the carcass is still there. He quickly loads the meat onto the travois, and pulls it behind him. He walks most of the night, anxious to be off the rancher's land. With daylight nearing he gratefully comes upon an inviting looking pond filled with cattails and low-lying bushes. *A perfect place to rest*, he thinks then yawns, settling back. The pond is nestled amongst a group of willows and sparse pines. As the rising sun spans the horizon, butterflies spread their fragile wings to warm themselves, while sparrows chirp a faint song and nuthatchers squeak, all welcoming in the new day. Hidden Spirit sits down by the serene pond covered with bright green lily pads. Leaning against a willow, he starts to close his eyes when, out of the corner, he sees something jump out of the water. A large distinctive-looking bullfrog sits atop a broad lily pad, looking at him with protruding eyes the color of topaz. Its skin bears shiny yellow dots and its feet are a rusty orange—a most impressive sight. The frog sways lazily back and forth as its skin glistens from the rays of the sun. It appears completely at ease—unafraid of the stranger who has entered his kingdom.

Hidden Spirit hears a deep throaty *garummp*, and then sees the frog hop over to stretch out and sun itself in the muck beside the water's edge—never taking its eyes off the boy. The frog seems curious and in no hurry as it hops from the banks onto another lily pad and then another, croaking all the while. In a blink, the bullfrog is just a few feet away from Hidden Spirit and eyeing him cagily with its large speckled eyes. The frog hops to a nearby lily pad and lies back—its arms crossed under its neck. As it begins swaying in the breeze, kicking its rusty orange feet up and down, it hums a happy tune, enjoying the bright sunny day. Finally, the frog opens his bulging eyes and croaks a greeting. "Welcome my friend, the one who speaks to me in his dreams."

Hidden Spirit is taken aback, and simply stares at the frog with unease.

The frog continues. "Oh, the one destined for greatness is sulking in the hills, angry at life. Your bitterness will consume you, brave warrior, like a venomous snake, if you are not careful." He lets out a hoarse croak. "I hear you like snakes that slither in the darkness…"

Hidden Spirit is becoming angry as he listens to the frog. Then the frog changes its tone. "You, brave one, are going to embark on a dangerous journey. You had better do more than wiggle a few feathers around and hide in the shadows." He seems to be mocking the boy. "Heed my warning, great one… before it's too late."

Hidden Spirit cries out in frustration, "What would you know? You're a foolish frog who sits on a lily pad, like you haven't a care in the world…" Then, *wham*. A stick pelts across the water, knocking Hidden Spirit over. "This is a gift from the wise one. Learn how to use it." Then the frog winks!

Hidden Spirit opens his mouth as the frog jumps gracefully onto another floating lily pad and sits on its edge, watching the boy. His long legs turn to a pale shade of lavender, and swish up and down. Hidden Spirit looks at the mysterious object, and rubs it. It is as smooth as stone, light as a willow branch, yet hard as a rock. He is ready to throw it into the water, when his hand stops mid-air. Frustrated, Hidden Spirit jumps up, yelling at the frog, "I am not bitter. I have no love of the white eyes that talk with two tongues. They have stolen my life and leave me to fight a battle I cannot win." Then he throws the stick at the frog. It whirls around in the air, and flies back and smacks him between his eyes. The sound reverberates in his head. Letting out one long, loud croak, the frog splashes into the pond, disappearing before Hidden Spirit can say anything more. The boy runs to the water's edge and steps into the brackish water, sinking up to his waist. "Wait! Come back! What journey?" Shaking the stick in the air, he says, "What am I supposed to do with this?" The stick is unlike any wood that he has ever seen. It is not of their sacred cottonwood, or of the pliant willow or scraggly pine or oak. As he turns it over, it seems to have a permanent sheen. Looking closer, he notices the stick is adorned with drawings that shift with its movements.

Hidden Spirit looks around for the frog, waits for hours, hoping to learn more—but the frog never returns.

Later that evening, he arrives at Grandfather Plenty Feathers's camp, carrying the meat. The old man is sitting outside by a campfire and smiles when he sees the boy. "That was quite a strange encounter you had with the frog, my son," he said, taking Hidden Spirit by surprise, as he often does.

Hidden Spirit sits down and listens to Grandfather Plenty Feathers, telling him the story of long ago. "When I was a young man of eleven or so, I was told of a vision through a fish. It was a message about my mother leaving. She died the next day. One never dismisses the voices, no matter how strange. The Great Spirit holds many secrets and finds unusual ways to reveal them. His voice can whisper through the rustling of the trees and carry it in the wind. We just have to be still and listen."

TROUBLED CHILDREN – WOE'S BEGINNING

SIXTY BOYS AND girls head down the dusty road toward the unknown. It's now late afternoon, and the children are exhausted and frightened. They have been riding for hours with no sign of letting up. Chasing Rabbit wonders how much longer they will have to ride in this bumpy wagon. Her back hurts and her head aches. She is certain that their destination will not be much better than the ride, and holds her bear claw close, rubbing the smooth surface against her cheek—hoping to calm her worried thoughts.

Clouds of dirt roll into the wagons, coating the children from head to toe with the grime, and turning their shiny black hair into puffs of gray. Chasing Rabbit's throat is so parched she can barely swallow. She runs her tongue across her dry lips, making her grimace from the gritty taste. Then her stomach lets off a low rumble, reminding her how hungry and thirsty she is. As they bounce along, everyone is silent and seems to be in a daze. The drivers pay little heed to the children as they urge the horses on.

Chasing Rabbit's gaze falls over the rolling hills and prairies that she has loved for as long as she can remember, but now the beauty rushes by in a blur of tears. The wagon hits a large hole and Chasing Rabbit clenches her teeth to keep them from jarring. She is anxious to arrive at the train station, and hopes the iron horse will be more comfortable than this jostling wagon. It might even lift everyone's heart a little. She looks at the sorrow on Little Moon's face, and sits up, wanting to comfort her friend.

Nudging Little Moon, she says, "I hear the iron wagon is faster and goes without horses." Little Moon's head pops up from her shoulder. Curious, she wipes her swollen eyes, wanting to hear more.

So, Chasing Rabbit makes up a story about the train, fashioning sounds like, "*Whoooo-whooo... chug-chug...*"— anything to make Little Moon smile. It works for a moment, and then Chasing Rabbit tells her the story of how her father talked to the rabbit people. "They even left a gift for me—a stone that looks like magic. Would you like to see it?" Little Moon isn't certain she believes the story until Chasing Rabbit holds it high in the air and shows her its glimmering center and pretty colors. Kissing the bright stone, Chasing Rabbit places it in Little Moon's sweaty palm.

Eyes glistening with delight as she holds onto the magic stone, Little Moon cries as she watches it sparkle. "This is beautiful! I could stare at it for hours."

"Look in the center, and you'll see rabbits dance."

"Really?" To Little Moon's surprise, she sees the rabbits... *and they are dancing.* Wiping the dust from her eyes, she looks even closer, and beams brightly. "You are right. I see them."

"You're lucky to have the rabbit totem. It's very special," Little Moon says, wrinkling her brow. "I wish I had something like this."

"Well, I think you're special, Little Moon. The moon lights the night sky and I can see you, shining, whenever I look up, so we are both lucky." Chasing Rabbit touches her friend's cheek with tenderness.

Little Moon, with her petite frame and round baby face,

seems far younger than Chasing Rabbit, who always feels the need to protect her.

Otter, dozing off in Morning Star's arms, opens her eyes when she hears about the magic stone. She sits up and asks Chasing Rabbit, "Do you have anything I can look at?"

Smiling at the little girl, Chasing Rabbit squeezes her hand, still moist with tears, and whispers, "My brother gave this to me before I left." She opens her pouch to show Otter her treasure. "It's a bear claw. Hidden Spirit told me it holds big power, and if you hold it close and listen you might hear a roar. It will even protect you."

Otter is amazed by the story, and holds the bear claw close to her ear, and listens. "I can't hear anything, Chasing Rabbit. I listened real hard."

"Well, sometimes the bear claw is sleepy, and doesn't want to growl. Maybe later it will feel differently." Chasing Rabbit can't help herself and smiles wide, her dimples creasing her face.

Otter sits up, sniffling, eyes brimming with tears. She pulls a necklace from around her neck. "This is my treasure. Look what my mama made." She hands her necklace to Chasing Rabbit to inspect.

Chasing Rabbit holds the heart-shaped necklace up to the light, making the red beads sparkle. "Oh, Otter, your mama must love you very much to make you something this pretty. I bet she's very…" She stops abruptly when she sees Otter starting to cry. Then she puts the little girl's necklace back around her neck and holds her on her lap, wrapping her fingers tightly around the bear claw. Chasing Rabbit can't wait for this miserable day to end. She looks over at Morning Star, who is silently staring off into the distance, her face filled with longing. She knows Morning Star must be thinking of Hidden Spirit. Chasing Rabbit loves Morning Star and thinks she should have stayed in the hills with her brother, but her parents were afraid to disobey Otis Peale and his orders.

*

The children arrive at the train station later that evening. Everyone is glad to be off the wagon. As the children near the iron horse, ready to board, the train makes an ear-splitting noise. Everyone scrambles and falls to the ground, alarmed at the sight of the huge iron monster they are about to ride. Otter is hysterical, and the frenetic whirl of sounds has Little Moon cowering behind Chasing Rabbit. Morning Star gathers the girls close as the whistle screams once again. This time a large cloud of soot erupts from the smokestack and filters through the air, covering the children like a black web of death.

*

After four days of traveling, the children finally arrive at the boarding school, exhausted, hungry, and scared. The grounds they pass on the way are hilly, and full of oaks, maples, junipers, and streams. Chasing Rabbit's eyes widen when the wagon rounds the corner and catches sight of the austere buildings—gray and foreboding—seemingly out of place after passing such beautiful lands. Apprehension fills Chasing Rabbit. She lets off an involuntary shiver and feels her heart sink. She can't shake off the feeling of dread as they near their destination.

A tall boney lady wearing spectacles comes running over and greets the children as they step down from the wagons. "Welcome. This will be your school and your new home. My name is Mrs. Trimble. I will be the headmistress and overseer of your bountiful beginnings."

Mrs. Trimble is dressed in a loosely fitted gray dress with stiff white ruffles encasing her neck. A big feathery bonnet sits perched atop her head. It looks ready to take flight as streaks of black and gray hair slip out from underneath. Chasing Rabbit notices a brown leather strap at the woman's side, and whispers to Little Moon. "She looks like a scrawny crow with glasses." Giggling, they catch a warning glance from the headmistress.

"Rules and order," Mrs. Trimble says with authority. "That's what we will strive for at this school. No exceptions."

She motions for the boys to gather at her side and announces, "The boys will be staying in separate quarters," pointing to some buildings at the far end of the grounds. "The girls will be staying over here. Now gather in a circle by Miss Snodberry," she says, as the girls obey. She leans over to the plump woman next to her. "They're still half-wild, you know." The plump woman nods her head vigorously. "Mr. Darrell should be here momentarily to collect the boys himself. Mrs. Burns, please count the number of boys we have," she sighs, clearly agitated. "Children, I would like to take this opportunity to welcome you to our boarding school and..." Mrs. Trimble stops speaking and looks up as a man hurries over and mumbles something about being late. He's short and thick, with thinning black hair.

"Mr. Darrell, very glad you could make it. Please take charge of your wards. Tardiness does not set a good example at this school," she says, irked at the man, but trying to contain her anger. "We don't want the children to get the wrong impression on their first day." Mr. Darrell, looking awkward, scurries over and motions for the boys to follow him. They walk quickly across the grounds. A few boys look back and give a slight wave to the girls. Chasing Rabbit waves and catches a glare from Mrs. Trimble. She quickly puts her hand down.

"Now... in a few weeks' time, English will be the primary language, the only language permitted at this school. Does anyone here speak English?"

Timidly, Morning Star raises her hand.

"Wonderful. You can help me translate for the others, so please explain to the girls what I just said."

Chasing Rabbit and Little Moon stare at Morning Star, surprised by her willingness to help.

"Well, I hope you're as excited as I am for beginning your new life at this blessed school."

No one speaks. The rules laid out by Mrs. Trimble have numbed the children. Clapping her hands, she says, "Now, let me introduce you to the ladies who will assist me—Mrs. Burns and Miss Snodberry."

The two women stare openly at the children, whose eyes widen with curiosity. Mrs. Trimble notices, and admonishes them. "Close your mouths, ladies."

Miss Snodberry and Mrs. Burns quickly shut their mouths, but continue to stare.

Mrs. Burns is a plump, middle-aged woman with brown graying hair and Miss Snodberry looks like a beanpole with short curly brown waves covering her head.

"We shall do our best to insure you become decent children," says Mrs. Trimble, matter-of-factly. "If you have any questions or concerns, come to me directly."

Mrs. Trimble is in her late fifties and came to the school at the request of her pastor in Virginia. Pastor Williams had heard they were looking for a strict disciplinarian to run a boarding school for the Indians. She would have to speak the Sioux language, and also be fluent in the Bible and a devout Christian. Frances Trimble was perfect for the position. She never married after her beau ran off with another woman a month before her wedding date. Following her heartbreak, Frances moved out west with her father to an army post, where she served as a translator for the military. She settled in quite nicely taking care of him, but one day, a couple years later, he was killed by a suspected band of renegade Indians. Suppressing her grief and rage, she moved back to Virginia, where she devoted her life to God and the church. She would never give her heart to anyone again, but Him. Knowing He would never cause her heartache of the kind she had endured in the past—that was enough for her. She didn't care much for men or Indians, but would do her duty.

Chasing Rabbit stares at the three women, deciding the bossy crow lady was no one to mess with. She sees this place as a hostile fortress—nothing like her mother had described. There isn't anything pleasant about this place. Not the buildings, not the people.

Mrs. Trimble motions to the ladies to come close. Lowering her voice she says, "The children must remain separated at all times. We want no funny business going on. Who knows what they have been used to... gallivanting around like hooligans. We must remember the children are uncivilized. We must thwart any temptation of..." Catching herself, she touches her forehead in dismay. "God only knows what they are used to. So be vigilant... day and night. We are to dedicate ourselves to their salvation and save their wretched souls."

Miss Snodberry starts to say that she doesn't think they look uncivilized or vulgar, but is abruptly cut off when Mrs. Trimble admonishes her. "You cannot have a weak heart and coddle the Indians. I feel you might not be as strict as I would like, and yet, I cannot watch over you as well as the girls. They are wild, you know. Regardless of your sentiments, I expect you to set a good example, Miss Snodberry, at all times." Turning to Mrs. Burns she feels relief knowing the woman will be competent and firm. "At least the courtyard is large, and the fence in the center will keep them separated."

Chasing Rabbit is tempted to roam the grounds and explore

the area. It's so huge, there is no way to even throw a rock to the other end. Curious as she is about the dilapidated buildings, with flecks of gray chipping off, and what's inside them, she would rather explore the woods and go for a walk. After taking about twenty steps she feels a hand with an iron grip squeeze her wrist. Mrs. Trimble speaks through clenched lips. "Did you not hear me when I said disobedience will not be tolerated?" She snaps her fingers to draw Chasing Rabbit's attention, and gets a blank stare in return. So she whacks the girl's legs with her worn brown belt and speaks sternly. "Let's not begin our stay by causing trouble."

Morning Star quickly pulls Chasing Rabbit next to her, motioning her to behave. "Mrs. Trimble. This is hard for us, being away from our families and…"

Mrs. Trimble interrupts, "Now, that will be enough of that. You people are uncivilized and you don't know what is good for you, being brought up—well, bluntly put, in savagery. Just thank the good Lord we are here to help you overcome all that. So no more complaining about what is hard. Hard is what we ladies are doing for you. I have given up my life to come and help you people achieve a better life."

Morning Star is taken aback by Mrs. Trimble's cold and indifferent behavior. *How would that woman know how we've been brought up?* she thinks, her cheeks turning red. "We were raised with kindness," she says under her breath.

Startled by Mrs. Trimble's rebuke, Little Moon looks at Morning Star, and whispers. "I don't like it here. That lady scares me."

Morning Star holds her hand tightly. "I don't like it here, either, but for now we have to follow the rules and hope it gets better."

Chasing Rabbit furrows her brows, looking willful. "Why do we have to follow their rules? I didn't want to come here. I hate this place. I won't be ordered about by a mean ole scarecrow." Then she feels a rap on her head.

"Quiet, everyone," Mrs. Trimble says in a commanding tone. The children simply stare, wondering what will be next. "I will explain more as we go. Now, follow me and do as I do. Lift your legs high, one at a time, and march—like this."

Mrs. Trimble proceeds to demonstrate what she means, and awkwardly lifts one skinny leg high in the air, while stomping the ground with the other. Her bulky black shoes send dust flying as she barks her orders. "One, two... one, two... one, two..."

Mrs. Burns follows Mrs. Trimble's lead as well as she can, and pumps her stout legs up and down in unison, sweating from the exertion.

Miss Snodberry marches in the rear, looking like a billowy stick. Her loose-fitting dress blows about her twig-like legs as she shuffles and grinds to Mrs. Trimble's orders.

Chasing Rabbit and Little Moon hold hands, amused by the comic spectacle, while Morning Star takes hold of a bewildered Otter.

Mrs. Trimble marches the girls across the grounds. The only two structures not identical to the others is an outhouse set behind a row of oak trees, and, off to the side, a lovely brick house surrounded by sycamore trees with a stone path leading to its entrance. They continue walking until they come upon a barn. Mrs. Trimble slides the barn door open, and waves the girls inside. The cows moo as they walk past. Several pigs in a pen, grunting, seem to smile at them as they roll in the dirt. Outside the barn in a fenced area, a goat nibbles on grass, looking with curiosity as the girls pass by. The billy goat stretches its neck, showing his large teeth, and reaches for Otter's sleeve to nibble on as she tries to pet him. Loads of chickens are darting in and out, squawking as they run about the yard, pecking away at the dirt.

Then they move toward an oddly shaped building with rectangular corners and a slanted roof. One side almost touches the ground. The paint looks withered, and most of it is chipped off.

Chasing Rabbit stops as she stares at the peculiar looking structure, not wanting to go inside. A queer sensation rises in the pit of her stomach. She feels that bad spirits live inside. Her hesitation is short lived, as she is hurried along by the sharp-eyed, Mrs. Trimble.

The girls walk down a long dark hallway where the sound of Mrs. Trimble's shoes clunk and reverberate off the walls. Chasing Rabbit interprets the sound as an eerie warning. She looks up and swears someone is staring through a small window. The queer sensation mounts again.

"We will need eyes in the back of our heads at this place," Chasing Rabbit says quietly, looking back and squeezing her friend's hand. They are ushered into a large room with weather-beaten floors and crusty walls with an adjoining courtyard that has a large fire burning in a pit. Chasing Rabbit is famished and thinks for a fleeting moment that they might be roasting a pig or goat for their supper. But she smells no signs of cooking.

Mrs. Burns and Miss Snodberry observe the girls more closely now as they huddle together in the corner. Knowing they are not supposed to stare at the Indians, Miss Snodberry and Mrs. Burns can't help themselves. They are such an unusual group. "What a dour bunch," Mrs. Burns utters in dismay. But, Miss Snodberry is intrigued by their shyness. She had expected their skin to be red, like the name she had often heard them called— "Redskin"—but it isn't red at all. It's actually a pretty shade of light brown, tinted with a glow of golden raspberries, as they ripen in the fall. Nor does she think they look wild or dangerous, as she had been forewarned.

Mrs. Burns elbows Miss Snodberry in the side, and whispers. "Look at the getup they're wearing—animal skins and feathers." She wrinkles her nose in disgust. "Probably where lice comes from."

"I think the clothes are handsome," Miss Snodberry says, with a tinge of regret. Looking at Morning Star's beautiful dress, she says, "The beadwork on that girl's dress must have taken a long time to sew on. The design looks very complicated. I never was good in the sewing department—more for the outdoors and such." Then her glance moves to a little girl, *too young to be here*, she thinks, and wants to go over and comfort her.

"Close your mouth, Miss Snodberry," Mrs. Burns says, in annoyance. "If Mrs. Trimble hears you carrying on about the Indians, I wouldn't be surprised if she reprimands you. And stop gawking!"

Miss Snodberry doesn't respond as she watches the girls, feeling sorry for them. She wonders if her coming here was a good idea, after all.

Mrs. Trimble enters from the hallway and walks up briskly to the women and says, "Mrs. Burns and Miss Snodberry. You ladies will be in charge of removing the heathens' clothing. Please make sure every stitch is burned along with anything else they might have brought with them. I want any and all traces of their past gone. That is the first order of business. Second is hair-cutting. You don't have to worry about doing it correctly—just chop it off and burn it. Lice is common among the savages I hear, so be careful. Hurry to the fire, and just throw it in. Afterwards, you will proceed to the next room where new garments will be handed out." Mrs. Trimble claps her hands together to get the girls' attention. "Girls, I want everyone to stand in line behind Mrs. Burns and Miss Snodberry," she says, pointing with her strap. "You will undress and hand your clothes over. No need for shyness around here. Just be quick and do as you are told. We will dispose of your garments and put you in civilized clothes. But first, your hair will be cut, and then you will wash, thoroughly. Buckets are lined against the wall outside. So let's not waste any more time. We have a busy schedule to adhere to."

Morning Star translates the message, her voice trembling as she speaks. The girls stand motionless. A buzz of fear filters across the room. The girls look at each other, dazed.

Morning Star can't believe the woman's demands, and holds her breath. Tears are threatening to break loose. She wonders how they will survive this cruelty thrust upon them. She squeezes Otter's hand so hard the little girl cries out.

The first in line is Spotted Horse, who cowers as Mrs. Burns approaches and asks the girl to remove her clothes. The girl freezes. An exasperated Mrs. Burns rips off her dress in one swift tug. As she sees her clothing thrown into the fire, Spotted Horse screams and falls to the floor. Mrs. Burns looks on with determination, licking her lips. "You need to help, Miss Snodberry, and not just stand there staring. Now get moving!" Annoyed by the woman's tentative behavior, Mrs. Burns elbows her aside and says, "Watch how it's done." She is quick, considering her bulk, and sprints to another young girl standing against the wall, too frightened to move. In a blink, she yanks off her dress. Raven starts to cry as she stands naked, watching as her dress heads for the fire. Holding it at arm's length, Mrs. Burns hands it to a wide-eyed Miss Snodberry. "Now, hurry up, and take these rags to the fire before bugs start hopping."

Suddenly, all the girls take off in a run, circling the room, trying to find a place to hide.

Mrs. Burns looks exasperated, deciding this is a more difficult task than she expected. Miss Snodberry isn't much help, either. "I can't believe I let Mrs. Trimble talk me into this mess," she grumbles. She never had much use for children. They seem like so much trouble, red skin or white—doesn't matter the color. Hands on hips, she is not going to tolerate any of this nonsense and she tells Miss Snodberry. "Well, whatever your sentiments, we are up against a bunch of unruly hellions. You need to be of help here, instead of staring off in space." Vexed by Miss Snodberry's behavior, she gives her a push. "The sooner we get started, the sooner we finish with this wretched job." Nodding her head for emphasis, she sprints over to another young girl.

A hesitant Miss Snodberry picks up the torn dress and carries it to the burning pit, where the fire devours it in an instant. Unable to move, she stares at the flames as they lick upward, snapping. The smell is nauseating. Looking back at the frightened young girl, she is tempted to go over and console her, but that would only get her into trouble with Mrs. Burns. *I had better get used to this, or I'll go mad,* she thinks. *Maybe the children need discipline, but this is going too far.* This place reminds her of her adopted family. She suppresses a shudder, just thinking of them.

Her name was Rebecca Brown and she was seven years old at the time she was adopted by the Snodberrys. Thus her name was changed, as well. The Snodberrys had several children in succession after her adoption, and her job was to help raise them. Lucky Rebecca! She worked around the house day and night— cleaning top to bottom, cooking meals, holding crying babies, and washing the endless wave of soiled diapers, which she would then hang outside, no matter the weather. She was very quiet and was allowed no friends. Too busy for that nonsense, they told her. The only time she was allowed out was to attend school, but by the sixth grade, she was too busy with household chores and had to quit. Church was allowed.

Rebecca was tall and gangly, with long unruly hair, like a bristle—always full of knots. One day, something came over her and she felt a tinge of rebellion, so she went outside and wacked off her hair so close to her head that parts of her scalp showed. She then proceeded to slick it back with lard from the family tub and put on a pair of overalls. Her adopted family was outraged, and the pastor was even more so.

"Such outrageous conduct, considering the fine family that took you in. Makes me wonder about your motives..." Pastor Williams eyed her suspiciously. "Is it your intention to look like a boy? Do you know that homosexuality is a sin against God? The Bible clearly states..." He fumed, face burning red. "You are a disgrace to your church and your family!"

Rebecca's spirit died a little that day, but she dutifully grew her hair back and resumed her miserable life with the Snodberrys. *So much for being rebellious,* she thought. Then one day at church she met Mrs. Trimble, who invited her to join her at the boarding school. "Think of it as being one of God's servants," she said. "You will be a great help, being so familiar with children."

Anxious to leave the Snodberrys, and without hesitation, she enthusiastically accepted Mrs. Trimble's invitation. She had been raised to be obedient, or else. Now she would be daring and she would make her own decisions. She would cut her hair, as well. The Snodberrys were livid when they found out, but Mrs. Trimble prevailed. She had made her case with Pastor Williams. "It is God's calling to help the savages." So the pastor informed the Snodberrys that Rebecca would be on a higher mission. He was secretly glad to be rid of her, and prayed for forgiveness for his unkind thoughts.

Mrs. Trimble reminds Rebecca of the Snodberrys, and questions her hasty decision to come. "What in the dickens are you doing? You act like you're in a fog, for Pete's sake. Get over here and help me."

Miss Snodberry pulls herself together and hastens back

to a winded Mrs. Burns. "I think I'm getting the hang of this nasty business."

Morning Star is not going to have her beautiful dress ripped from her body and quickly lets it slip to her feet.

No wonder my brother is in love with her, Chasing Rabbit thinks as she looks at Morning Star. *She is beautiful. Maybe she is related to the White Buffalo Calf Woman.* That thought makes her smile.

Morning Star hands her dress to Miss Snodberry, who hesitantly walks to the belching fire. *How can I throw this piece of art into the fire and let it burn,* wonders Miss Snodberry. She glances back at Morning Star and sees her eyes fill with tears, and stops.

Mrs. Burns throws her hands in the air, so exasperated at the dawdling woman that she runs over and yanks it out of her hands. The flames roar as the exquisite dress explodes into a ball of fire. "That's how it's done, Miss Snodberry. Get a backbone."

Rebecca's hands shake. She stares at the fire for a lingering moment, watching as the flames rise. The nauseating smell fills the room. "Oh, dear God," she whispers under her breath. "Why am I here?"

Little Moon and Chasing Rabbit are next. "Let's hurry and get undressed before the big lady comes by."

Dresses in hand, they walk past a surprised Mrs. Burns and Miss Snodberry. They have decided to say goodbye to their clothes and pretend it's a ceremony for the dead—giving up their pretty dresses and moccasins. That's what it feels like for them. Death. Nearing the flames, they hold their breath, clutch their hands together, and throw their dresses into the pit. As sparks fly and tears fall, the girls shut their eyes, unable to watch. They feel like they are in mourning. Even Mrs. Burns is momentarily touched.

Otter is last. The little girl sobs and clings to her dress as Mrs. Burns tries to snatch it from her grasp. "For Pete's sake, let go." She gives a good yank and the dress and necklace go flying out of her hand. The necklace lands on the floor next to Mrs. Burns's feet. She bends down and picks up the hidden contraband. Holding it in the air she inspects the shiny object. "What do we have here, miss?"

Otter cries out, "No!" and begins to wail.

Mrs. Burns, resolved to follow Mrs. Trimble's orders, reprimands the girl. "Lesson to be learned, young lady—obedience. You were told to burn all your possessions. They are forbidden." Ignoring Otter, she turns to Miss Snodberry. "Take this trinket and throw it into the fire—at once."

Miss Snodberry dutifully takes the necklace, and gazes over at the hysterical girl. Then she walks over to the fire, and slowly opens her hand.

Little Moon smothers a sob, "Everyone is so mean here. I hope Hidden Spirit comes to help. He wouldn't let them treat us like this."

Morning Star has no answers. All she can do is console Otter the best she can. She hugs the girl tightly, and says, "We'll find something special for you. Don't cry, Otter."

Everyone is frightened and stunned, unable to understand this white man's school.

Grateful that task is over, Miss Snodberry looks around the room. Everyone is so quiet you could hear a mouse scoot past.

Annoyed by the absence of Mrs. Trimble, Mrs. Burns grimaces at the prospect of the next chore. "Look at their hair, Miss Snodberry. If you ask me, they look more like a horse's mane. Gonna take a month of Sundays to whack it all off. Can't believe Mrs. Trimble left us to do all this ourselves." Beads of sweat form on her forehead as Mrs. Burns holds a pair of scissors in the air. "We're going to be chopping hair next, girls." Clacking the scissors together she says, "No more long, unruly hair—or bugs. Easier to manage that way. Everyone stand in line, now, and come up front, one at a time. And don't any of you start a ruckus. Miss Snodberry, send the first one up."

Mrs. Burns slashes away as Miss Snodberry holds the strands. "Look at this mop," she moans. "I need a hacksaw to cut through this."

Miss Snodberry had been quiet throughout the process until now. She asks, "Do you think the girls will be more civilized after their hair is cut and they're properly dressed? Mrs. Trimble thinks so."

Mrs. Burns lets out a snort. "I'd say Hell would freeze over first." Choking back a laugh, she says, "They'll still be homely, no matter what we do. How many more are there, Miss Snodberry?"

"Just a couple," she says, and brings over a sobbing Otter.

"Oh, stop bawling," says Mrs. Burns. "Just cutting your hair for pity sakes."

Then comes Morning Star. "I hope this is the last one. My arm is about to fall off." Eyeing the girl, she says, "You've got a big wad of hair, so you best hold still or I'll chop off more than that." Without waiting for a reply she turns to Miss Snodberry. "Hand me that big pair of scissors over there. This girl's hair is thick as a sheep's coat." With a faint smile on her face and large scissors in hand, she starts whacking. "No different than sheering a sheep," she mutters.

Morning Star's lustrous hair falls to the ground in glossy waves. She is almost finished, except for three silky feathers attached to her long bangs. Mrs. Burns is ready to snap them off, but her scissors get entangled with the feathers. "Why on earth are you wearing those nasty things?" Fuming, she snips furiously at the feathers, which tremble each time the scissors come near.

"Damn," she says. Suddenly the silky feathers float up in the air, one by one, as if they have wings. "Blast it," she says, gawking at the feathers—scissors snipping frantically at the air. The long, silky feathers manage to stay just out of her reach as she runs around the room, determined to cut them into pieces. Then they float in formation out the door, like a flock of geese flies, as the girls shout excitedly at the mysterious sight. Mrs. Trimble hears the commotion and hustles inside the room. Hands on hips, she looks from one teacher to the other. "What on earth is going on?"

Mrs. Burns, red-faced and flustered, fumbles over her words, trying to explain.

Miss Snodberry is transfixed by the sight, and simply stares at the door, mouth wide open.

"Well, Mrs. Burns... Miss Snodberry... since no one will answer my question, are you finished?"

They both look at Mrs. Trimble, in a state of confusion. A perplexed Mrs. Burns attempts to answer. "Well... I... uh... I'm not certain."

"I say... how many more children need their hair cut, Mrs. Burns? You're not daft, are you?"

Miss Snodberry speaks up, amazement lingering in her voice. "Just two more, Mrs. Trimble."

Looking annoyed, Mrs. Trimble says, "Please hurry. You will make us late for supper. I trust you can finish." And she storms out of the room.

Mrs. Burns scratches her head. She wonders if this task is more than she bargained for. She isn't so sure she likes these Indians, or Mrs. Trimble, for that matter.

"Well, let me take a look around," Miss Snodberry says, interrupting Mrs. Burns's thoughts. She walks among the girls and concludes everyone is clipped. Then she spots Chasing Rabbit hiding in a corner, and hurries over to her. In a kind voice, she says, "Come with me, little girl." Taking hold of Chasing Rabbit's arm, she pulls the reluctant girl over to Mrs. Burns with her oversized scissors.

"I have no patience left, girl. So, you'd better not give me any sass. My nerves are frayed to the edges." Mrs. Burns grabs one of Chasing Rabbit's pretty long braids, ready to snip it off. But as the scissors come near, Chasing Rabbit's eyes widen, she suddenly comes unglued—and she snaps. All of her pent-up emotions surface and she bites Mrs. Burns's arm as hard as she can, producing a large red welt and vivid teeth marks.

Appalled at the girl's insolence, Mrs. Burns yells. "That little brat bit me!" Drawing her hand back, she swings at Chasing Rabbit, who ducks and kicks the woman in the shin. Then she starts running. Her hatred of this place is immense.

A shrieking Mrs. Trimble comes running into the room, banging the door open. "What the devil is going on?" Her eyes are smoldering.

Mrs. Burns yelps her response. "That girl about bit the skin right off my arm!" She displays her bleeding arm as proof.

Mrs. Trimble's body goes rigid and she rushes after the culprit. Mrs. Burns and Miss Snodberry follow suit, hurrying after the girl who is running away. The teachers finally corner Chasing Rabbit, and pounce on her, wrangling her to the floor.

Mrs. Trimble glares at the girl, seething. "Try that again and I'll wallop you so hard you won't be able to sit for a month." She squeezes Chasing Rabbit by the nape of her neck. "Hand me the scissors, Mrs. Burns. I'll show her whose running this place."

Mrs. Trimble proceeds to chop Chasing Rabbit's hair without regard, sending blood trickling down the back of her neck along with a nice size gash. "There, that should do it," Mrs. Trimble says, looking over her handiwork. A smile of self-satisfaction creases her face as she stands, wiping a damp strand of hair that fell over her eyes. Brushing it aside, she calls out, "Now, let's go outside where buckets of water and lye soap are waiting for you girls." She motions for the children to go.

The sight of the mysterious feathers is forgotten, as the girls obey the woman and silently walk outside. Mrs. Trimble hands each a bar of soap and tells them to wash and scrub thoroughly. "Get your ears real good. Bugs have been known to nest inside. I will be back to inspect."

Morning Star washes Otter's back gently as tears are flowing down the girl's cheeks. Otter sniffles. "That woman took my necklace."

"I know how sad you are," Morning Star says softly as she starts cleaning the girl's ears. "But when you go back home, your mother will make you a pretty new one."

Chasing Rabbit is washing her face when she gets the lye soap in her mouth and spits out the burning taste. "Yuck! This soap tastes awful!" She cries, and rinses her mouth with water—and then she spits again. The girls giggle as Chasing Rabbit makes a face.

Mrs. Trimble walks around the room like a military sergeant, barking orders. She watches as the girls wash, reminding them to scrub harder, flicking the leather strap against her leg. She's keeping a close eye on Chasing Rabbit, convinced that this girl spells trouble.

As Chasing Rabbit washes Little Moon's back she says, "This soap must be for cleaning floors. It stinks and tastes terrible." They both giggle as Chasing Rabbit puts some in Little Moon's mouth, which Little Moon quickly spits out. Just then a cold bucket of water splashes the girls. As they wipe the water out of their eyes they see, Mrs. Trimble standing nearby, bucket in hand. She says, "Maybe this will help speed you girls up. This is not playtime." Mrs. Trimble gives the girls a warning look as she walks away.

"Brrr!" Little Moon says, shivering as she stands naked, dripping wet. She turns to Chasing Rabbit and says, "I'm freezing, aren't you?"

Chasing Rabbit nods her head, wondering how they will survive in this place.

After Mrs. Trimble makes her inspections of ears and hair, she says, "Follow me, girls. We'll get you into some decent clothes and shoes, then take you to your rooms."

Heading down the hallway, the girls try to cover their bodies as best they can as they walk behind the woman, smoothing her taffeta dress as she marches smartly along. "Lift your legs, girls, and march."

They follow suit and a short distance later they enter a stuffy room that smells of mold and dust. Chasing Rabbit notices a small hole in the wall and hopes no one will be peeking inside. The cramped room is lined with stacks of clothes, all the same color, thin blankets, and faded yellow undergarments. There are two rows of long wooden benches with shoes and socks crammed underneath. A pretty young girl with sparkly blue eyes and hair the color of sunshine smiles at the girls as they walk in. But the smile freezes on her face as she looks in alarm at their shivering bodies and nakedness.

Mrs. Trimble says briskly, "Everyone take a seat." She points to the benches and waits for everyone to comply. "You will wait your turn to be summoned. Then you will go in an orderly fashion for your clothes." She taps the bench, "Girls, this is Ellie," waving her over with her strap. "She will determine your size and give you your clothes—starting with the smaller girls." Looking back at Ellie, she sniffs. "Are you listening to me or are you staring?" Mrs. Trimble pulls Raven off the bench. "We'll start with this one. She's a little chubby, so the smaller dresses most likely won't fit. Give her some of the older girls' dresses. They'll be a little long, so just cut off the bottom, and save the material for rags. She pokes the girl with her strap. "We'll be taking this extra flesh off soon enough with some good hard work. Next!"

Ellie can't speak. She is astounded by the callous treatment of the girls—some that are even too young to be here.

"Ellie! Stop staring and get moving. You act like the cat's got your tongue," says Mrs. Trimble, irritably, then turns to Miss Snodberry. "Please get the shoes ready to be distributed. Just get as close as you can to their size. If they are a little too big, give them an extra pair of socks to make them fit properly. Where the devil is Mrs. Burns?" At that moment the harried-looking woman hurries into the room, with beads of sweat dotting her forehead.

"Mrs. Burns, please get the blankets ready."

After the girls receive their clothes, Chasing Rabbit sits down and unfolds her pile. She holds up a coarse gray dress for inspection, wrinkles her nose and lowers her voice, saying to Little Moon, "This is ugly and scratchy, not soft and pretty like the clothes we wear. I bet it feels even worse on." Chasing Rabbit struggles with the voluminous dress, getting it stuck as she pulls it over her head and screeches in distress. Little Moon tugs and pulls and finally manages to undo the buttons. Then she helps Chasing Rabbit pull on the bulky dress, which falls past her ankles. Looking over at Mrs. Burns, she whispers, "We look just like them, only shorter." The girls burst into a fit of giggles.

Little Moon looks at the itchy wool socks as she slides her toes inside, then pulls on a pair of massive, heavy-soled black shoes. Trying her best to untangle the laces, she thinks, *this will take forever to figure out.*

Miss Snodberry sees the girl's dilemma and hurries over to

help Little Moon undo the shoelaces. Thankful for the woman's kind smile, she accepts her help.

Finally dressed, Chasing Rabbit stands up and clunks her feet on the floor. "I feel like my feet are weighted down with rocks. With these things on, I won't be able to run and play outside or catch fireflies."

Morning Star says, "I have a feeling we won't do much playing at this place, Chasing Rabbit."

Otter comes running, holding up the hem of her bulky dress, which is so long it falls to the floor in a heap and she trips over it as she tries to walk. Morning Star pulls her up and shakes the humungous dress as Otter cries out, "I want my mama. Can you take me home?"

"I know this place isn't home, Otter, or even close, but I'm afraid I cannot. Turn around, and let me fix your dress." Morning Star does her best, managing to tie it so Otter can walk without stumbling. "There," she says, "that's not so bad now. You look very pretty." Otter frowns, not believing Morning Star's words.

"Looks like everyone is finished here, so gather your belongings and follow me," says, Mrs. Trimble, striding throughout the room, scrutinizing the girls. "Let's march!"

Little Moon walks clumsily in her uncomfortable shoes, her feet sliding forward as she clunks along, trying her best to keep up with Mrs. Trimble. It sounds like a barrage of military men walking into battle as the girls' shoes pound in succession on the wooden floors, all doing their best to march.

The sun is almost down and it is a relief to be outside in the fresh air—away from the drab room. Mrs. Trimble marches smartly across the courtyard with the girls in tow. Chasing Rabbit notices a couple daisies poking up from the ground. It's the nicest thing she has seen at this place so far. Then Chasing Rabbit sees a small brick building set apart from the rest. She wonders who stays there, but has not long to wonder as they head into another dreary building. The difference in here is the wonderful smells wafting down the hallway. The girls' stomachs begin to rumble in hopeful anticipation. Nearing the kitchen, Mrs. Trimble calls out. "Mrs. Barlapp. Could you give a moment of your time, please?"

A snowy-haired lady smoothing her apron bustles out of the kitchen and smiles at Mrs. Trimble. "Girls, this is Mrs. Barlapp, our cook. I am so delighted she came on such short notice. She will be our blessing at the beginning and end of every day. Please be sure to thank her for her precious time, cooking for all of us."

The girls shyly smile at the woman, who nods in response.

The delicious aroma in the kitchen is overwhelming and the girls shuffle their feet and eagerly sniff the air, faint with hunger.

"Thank you Mrs. Barlapp. We will be along shortly. A most tiring day it's been."

Mrs. Trimble marches down the hall past the teachers rooms, and then comes upon two long rooms filled with rusted metal cots. Pointing to the first room she says, "The younger girls will stay here and the older girls will be housed in the next room. Come along girls, and make your beds."

Otter cries when her hand is yanked away from Morning Star's grasp.

Mrs. Trimble pulls Otter with her and says, "Hush, now. You are no longer a baby and we'll have none of that. Mrs. Burns, take the older girls to their room, and I'll handle this." Pointing inside, Mrs. Trimble continues. "This is to be your room, and I expect order and cleanliness at all times."

The girls stand quietly, afraid to speak.

Chasing Rabbit and Little Moon take Otter's hand as they walk hesitantly into the stark, drab room with its weather-beaten floors and flimsy cots. At the foot of each bed sits a pillow, a thin blanket, and a worn sheet.

"You may each pick a bed. Mrs. Burns will be in shortly to show you how to make it." She turns to leave.

The three girls walk to the furthest end of the room. Little Moon wrinkles her nose as she sits on the bulging mattress. "This feels hard, like my shoes. Maybe the floor would be better, Chasing Rabbit."

"Well, the floor doesn't look much better and we might get into trouble..."

Otter comes running over, holding her nose. "My bed smells like a skunk slept in it." Her lips start to quiver. "They don't like us, do they? Sobbing again, she says, "I want to go home."

Chasing Rabbit and Little Moon squeeze Otter's hands, and try to comfort her. "Let's turn the mattress over. Then it might smell better," Chasing Rabbit says encouragingly. As the girls lift the mattress, it smells even worse, so they throw it on the floor. "Whew," Little Moon says, covering her nose. "Let's try this one," she says, pointing to an empty bed. "Hurry before Mrs. Trimble comes back."

The girls hurry over and bounce on the bed. "This one is just as lumpy," Chasing Rabbit says with concern, "But at least it doesn't stink as bad." The girls struggle to move the bulging mattress, managing to toss it onto Otter's bed, as sweat drips down their backs.

"These clothes are hot," Chasing Rabbit says, rubbing her neck, trying to fan some cool air beneath the dress.

"I know," Little Moon agrees.

Otter says her foot hurts and kicks off her shoes, showing the girls her wound.

"Oh my, your heel is raw," says Little Moon, hugging the girl.

"Your heel looks painful," Chasing Rabbit echoes, and bends down inspecting the girl's gaping wound. "I wish I was home, where I could find a magic herb to make it better. I would have it fixed in no time." Otter looks so sad she thinks she might cry again, so Chasing Rabbit tries to brighten her up with her new idea. "Little Moon and I will shove our beds next to yours, so you won't be alone at night. None of us will be alone," she says, happily.

"Yes, let's do," Little Moon says, and smacks Otter's cheek with a kiss.

"Maybe we can get your bed softer by jumping on the lumps." The girls giggle as they climb on top of the bed, holding hands, and jump as hard as they can, up and down. "This should take the lumps out," Chasing Rabbit shouts at the top of her lungs.

"This is fun," Little Moon says with a grin.

Otter can't help herself, and laughs along with the girls as they jump harder. Suddenly, the mattress gives way and crashes to the floor, sending the girls tumbling over, hysterical with laughter.

Mrs. Trimble's shoes clank furiously along the hallway floor, as she storms into the room, shrieking. "What is the meaning of this?" She pulls Otter up by her arm, scolding her for her unruly behavior. Then she takes her strap and spanks Chasing Rabbit across her backside, soundly. Little Moon runs into the corner, fearful of the angry woman. Mrs. Trimble simply glares at the cowering Little Moon.

"Get up this instant and fix your beds," she says indignantly. "You children are like wild hooligans. And you…" Shaking Chasing Rabbit until her head bobs, "I can tell will be trouble." Mrs. Trimble throws the blankets on the beds. "Get busy, girls," she says in a huff, and strides off.

Mrs. Trimble bustles around the room, checking on the other girls who are doing their best to make their beds. She stops suddenly when she hears someone whistling down the hallway. Peering out the door, she gasps. "It's Preacher Crumm," she says, and covers her mouth in dismay. The sounds of boots echo on the wooden floor. He's strolling toward their room. "Hurry girls and stand in front of your beds." Momentarily disconcerted, she runs through the room, pulling the girls to attention. "Prepare for inspection," she cries out. Mrs. Trimble is flustered by his surprise visit, but secretly pleased that he finds the time from his busy schedule to come by, even if it's unannounced.

Preacher Jim waits at the doorway, scouring the room, as Mrs. Trimble assembles the children. "Girls. I would like to introduce your headmaster at the school, Preacher Jim Crumm." She put her hands together clapping, nodding for the other girls to follow her example.

Preacher Jim says magnanimously, "Thank you, Mrs. Trimble, for the fine introduction." He walks into the girls' room, shoulders straight back. Then he bows. "Welcome little heathens. This will be your sanctuary while you are here." He opens his arms wide, and says, "Seems quite adequate for sleeping quarters. Wouldn't you agree, Mrs. Trimble?"

Mrs. Trimble preens at the man, while bobbing her head in agreement.

Preacher Jim takes his time as he leisurely strolls around the room and comments. "I am most pleased you have consented to be the overseer of the girls, Mrs. Trimble. It's quite apparent that you are more than adept at taking charge around here. Must say, the Indians seem well behaved, standing at attention, properly dressed for their first day. We shall turn them around in no time at all… into good little Christians."

He walks down the aisle, nodding at the girls. Bushy gray eyebrows bob as he inspects each one, then stops by every bed and raises his hand and booms out, "How!" Then he clicks his heels together, as if he's addressing a troupe of soldiers and moves on to the next bed. That man gives Chasing Rabbit a funny feeling, although she doesn't quite know why. It could be because his smile doesn't reach his eyes, or maybe because of his rigid stance. But she knows that something is not quite right, as he stands before her, doing his stupid white man's interpretation of, "hello."

After he finishes strolling through the room, Preacher Jim beams proudly, pleased by what he sees.

"Well done, Mrs. Trimble," he says smiling at her. "Good job. We will have a lot of hard work ahead of us taming the heathens, so I will put you in my evening prayers and ask that God may give you strength. So forge on. That's what we used to say in the military. And now I bid you, good evening."

Mrs. Trimble claps her hands enthusiastically after Preacher Jim has left the room. "We will now have our dinner. Please follow me, and mind your manners in the dining hall."

Everyone is baffled by Preacher Jim's visit, but hunger fills their minds as they hurry after the teacher.

Entering the dining room with the rest of the girls, Morning Star finds it a little brighter than the other rooms.

Mrs. Trimble leads them past a large round table with a blue vase overflowing with white daisies perched on an embroidered tablecloth. Mrs. Barlapp buzzes about importantly, bringing platters of skillet fried chicken, mashed potatoes and gravy, along with green beans and piping hot biscuits. "Fresh out of the oven," she says, smiling at the teachers.

Stomachs rumble and mouths water as the girls eye the delicious food that smells like heaven. They walk past the teachers to their table, ecstatic, counting the minutes until they can eat. Chasing Rabbit swears she will devour every last bite.

Mrs. Burns ignores the hungry girls, busy perusing the table full of delectable dishes. Miss Snodberry shifts uncomfortably, watching the girls stare at the food as they pass by. She feels a twinge of guilt.

Leaning over to Miss Snodberry, Mrs. Burns says wickedly,

after the girls pass by. "Not sure the haircuts helped much." She proceeds to shove a buttered biscuit in her mouth and continues. "No matter what you do, they'd still be as homely as a hedge-post."

The girls march across the room to a long wooden table with a thick plank board, ready for seating. They cram together on the benches, anxiously awaiting their supper. Otter clings to Morning Star's hand. "I'm so hungry," she says, smacking her lips together. "My stomach hurts." Her eyes light up, anticipating dinner.

"My stomach hurts too," says Red Deer and Little Fox at the same time. The girls talk in hushed voices as Mrs. Barlapp bustles about the room, fussing over the teachers.

This will be a bright light after a horrid week, Morning Star thinks with optimism.

Little Moon notices the cuts on Chasing Rabbit's neck, and asks, "Does your neck hurt?"

Chasing Rabbit wipes away the dried blood that has caked into her cuts, and shrugs off Little Moon's concerns with a smile. "Everything hurts, from my feet to my head. But all I can think of is food. I don't think I've ever been so hungry."

Worried, Little Moon squeezes Chasing Rabbit's hand. "Mrs. Trimble cut your neck on purpose. I think she will do worse if you get into more trouble."

Chasing Rabbit is about to answer, but stops as Mrs. Trimble stands up and clanks a glass with her fork to get everyone's attention. "Order please, girls."

Everyone turns silent as they wait for her to speak.

"We will bow our heads in prayer and thank the Lord for our good tidings." She indicates for all to close their eyes, and begins.

"I thank you, Lord, for the generous ways in which you bestow upon us your bounty. I'm certain the Indian girls would like to thank you, as well. We give our blessings for the food we are about to receive that will nourish our bodies and we thank you for the wonderful man you sent to help the children. We are truly blessed to have Preacher Jim in our folds. Amen."

Mrs. Trimble gestures to sit down.

Mrs. Burns murmurs, "Amen," and reaches for the chicken, taking two large breasts, a generous helping of mashed potatoes, and a dollop of gravy for the center. Then she adds crisp green beans and two more biscuits to her crowded dish. Licking her lips, she dives in, takes a bite of the moist chicken and chews vigorously. "I certainly worked up an appetite today. The heathens are a load of work... more than I thought." She shoves a forkful of potatoes into her mouth, and then another.

Miss Snodberry eats her food in silence while Mrs. Burns continues to talk non-stop, devouring her food with gusto, her tongue darting lizard-like in and out of her mouth.

Mrs. Barlapp finally makes her way to the girls' table, placing two loaves of bread and butter in the center, and then hurries back with a jug of milk and a kettle of soup. Everyone waits in anticipation for the chicken and biscuits until it slowly dawns on them that their main course is the soup. Disappointment registers on every girl's face as bowls of soup are passed around the table.

Morning Star looks at the loaves of bread and the soup, which is mostly broth with hints of vegetables. "Well, this isn't much, but at least it's something," she says half-heartedly.

Chasing Rabbit points to the teacher's table. "Why can't we have some of their food, Morning Star? They have loads, and it smells so good."

Morning Star said, "I don't know. Maybe tomorrow will be better. Maybe tomorrow we'll eat what the teachers have."

Chasing Rabbit licks her lips, dreaming of a piece of that succulent chicken.

SUNSHINE GIRL

ELLIE IS ON her way home after helping Mrs. Trimble at the school. She feels sickened by what she has seen there and thinks she should tell someone—but, who? There is no one she can tell. Her parents are of the mind that hard work and discipline cover a multitude of sins, especially toward the Indians. That is their way. They believe in the rod and the Bible. She decides she will do whatever she can to help.

The little girl with the smiling, defiant eyes has caught her attention. She noticed the cuts on her neck and wonders how she had gotten them. They all seem so innocent, and yet her mother considers them "dangerous renegades." On Sundays, her father preaches, "We are all children of God," and wonders if that includes the Indian girls. *They look so sad and miserable at that place.*

Ellie lives about a mile from the school, in the outskirts of Hickoryville—a small town of a few hundred people. She and her parents just moved here a couple of months ago from Kentucky, so she is unfamiliar with how the townspeople view the Indian children. She never cared much for Kentucky, and she doesn't care much for her family. They disagree on about everything, so it really doesn't matter where they live. At seventeen, Ellie has big plans for herself—to run away from home someday and move to

New York City. As an adventurous, free-spirited, girl, she does not blend well with the small-minded people in these towns. She is also smart enough to know that a young girl traveling on her own is a risk... one that she is willing to take, and if her parents ever discover her plans, they will make her life even more difficult than they already have. She grimaces at the thought.

In the meanwhile, she dreams of the day she will be free of rules and restrictions. She is tired of her mother's dire warnings for not following the Lord's teachings. Opal would thrust the Bible in her hand demanding her to study the Book, and learn. Ellie isn't sure about the stories she has read from the Old Testament and shudders at all the murder and mayhem, preferring the New Testament. She feels the Bible must have been written by men who despise women, but like war. Who else would have written such words? She doesn't think they came from God, but rather from men who claim to have heard His voice, directing them. When she expressed her opinions to her mother, the woman was mortified by her accusations and slapped her face, leaving vivid marks on her daughter's fair skin. Opal concludes the girl's sins are even greater than those of Jezebel.

Ellie kicks a stone in her frustration as she walks home, thinking about this morning when her mother was angry over the dress she was wearing. In an agitated tone, Opal said, "Hold on there, Missy. Where do you think you are going dressed like that? Your ankles are on display and you look like a tramp. Just what the Devil wants. Not to mention those bright stripes, simply begging for attention. You will most certainly attract the wrong sort, and then tongues will wag all over town. You will not leave this house until you change. And where on earth did you get that lewd material?" Opal wrinkled her nose in disgust. "I bet it was from that awful Beatrice Hicks back home. I knew she was no good the minute I laid eyes on her. But what can you expect from a non-believer? I must say, Ellie, sometimes I'm ashamed to call you my daughter. Now, remove that rag immediately or I will tell your father about your indecent clothing!"

"I am not indecent," Ellie said, lowering her tone.

"What did you say?" Opal glowered.

Ellie lowered her eyes. "Nothing." She wasn't yet brave enough to openly sass her mother.

Opal continued her tirade as she grabbed for a modest dress in Ellie's closet. "You know how your father feels about women dressing to lure attention. The Lord wants none of that kind of behavior and neither do I, so take it off and put on this nice brocade dress."

Ellie frowned as she took the unattractive dress from her mother.

Opal saw the look Ellie gave in response, and pursed her lips primly. "It's proper attire for a good Christian girl, so as not to encourage glances from the opposite sex. They might interpret… well… get the wrong impression, and… oh, just forget it." Then she glared at her daughter, who delighted in seeing her mother fumble for words. "Just do as I say. I know what's best to keep you from sliding into sin," she said, slamming the door on her way out.

Finally arriving home, Ellie walks through the kitchen door, and sees her father and brother seated at the dining room table, hands folded, waiting. Opal scowls as she stirs the gravy on the stove. "Where on earth have you been?"

"Mrs. Trimble kept me longer than I expected," Ellie replies in consternation, as Opal shoves a pitcher of milk into her hands. "The girls seem so sweet and yet so sad. I feel sorry for them."

"Oh nonsense," Opal says, snorting. "They're wild savages, used to who knows what and… oh, never mind. We'll help them adjust soon enough, so don't go worrying, and don't stick your nose in where it doesn't belong. Dinner is almost ready. Take this gravy while it's hot, and go sit down." Opal bustles about for a few minutes before entering the dining room and sets a large platter of fried calf's liver with onions and boiled potatoes next to her father.

"I should have skipped dinner," Ellie says, barely audible, as she eyes the unappealing food.

Her brother, Ezekiel, gives her a nasty smile as she sits down. The boy resembles their mother with his light brown hair, brown eyes, and pointy nose. Ellie is aware he is the favorite. Spoiled and demanding. At fifteen, he wants to become a blacksmith. He even has a mentor in town, Ben Hadley, willing to teach him the necessary skills. It is unlikely Ezekiel will be allowed to follow his dreams, however, since he can't disappoint his father. "Follow in my footsteps, son, and you will make me proud," says Preacher Jim to his son on a regular basis. But Ellie hopes her brother will not become a preacher. One in the family is more than enough.

Ellie's thoughts drift off to the children at the school and how miserable they must be. She wonders what they will be eating tonight and hopes it wouldn't be liver. Her thoughts jolt back to the present as her father bumps her arm as he dishes out supper. She eyes the liver sitting on her plate. *Even though it's smothered in onions, it still looks disgusting*, she thinks, trying her best to hide her revulsion. *Preacher Jim's favorite meal!* Ellie thinks irritably. The aroma drifts up her nostrils. She tries not to gag at the smell, and covers her nose with her napkin. Her eyes widen at the sight of blood oozing from the meat, covering the onions with a reddish-brown color. Ellie thinks she might get sick and fights back to urge to vomit.

"Let's bow our heads in prayer," Preacher Jim commands after everyone is served. "Dear Lord, I would like to give thanks for this special day. The heathens have arrived in our midst. With your blessings, the school will be a great success. Thank you for letting me be your vessel of knowledge to guide the Indians while they're amongst us. Give me the strength I need to tame the wickedness from them. Amen."

"Amen," Opal echoes, as Preacher Jim serves dinner.

Ellie stares blankly at her plate. She cuts a small piece of liver, and chews. It is tough and rubbery. No matter how hard she tries, she can't swallow it. Her stomach starts to churn, and she gulps down the bile that rises. Finally, she spits out the liver into her napkin, feigning politeness, and forcing herself to take another bite. Then she quickly spits again. "May I be excused from the table? I'm not feeling well. I think it's the liver, it has upset my stomach."

Preacher Jim annoyed with his daughter's behavior, stressed curtly. "Your mother spends her day cooking and cleaning for you, and this is your thanks? If I didn't have so much on my mind… well, stay put until we're finished with supper. He looks over at Ezekiel and continues, "And take some lessons from your brother, then after you help your mother in the kitchen you will study the words of Leviticus tonight. Might learn how to be pious."

Ezekiel sticks his tongue out at Ellie, along with a chunk of half-chewed liver.

Ellie thinks her brother is as disgusting as the liver.

"You should be grateful you have something to eat," Preacher Jim drones on, while chomping on the tough meat. "The Lord gives us a bounty of food, and a wondrous cook," he adds with a grunt and takes another large bite, seeming to relish his meal.

Preacher Jim clears his throat and pushes his plate aside. "Opal, my dear. I know your days are going to be full now that you are teaching Bible class at the school. I thought I might hire Ezekiel's friend, Homer, to do odd jobs around the house, and to help you out. I do so admire your devotion to helping the underprivileged. Simply inspiring." Then he speaks about Sunday's sermon. "I believe I will talk about Adam and Eve and the temptation women bring into our midst. I see the women's new-fangled fashions that show off their ankles and such. Where this will lead…" Wiping his brows, he is silent for a moment, staring off in the distance. Then he comments about one of the parishioners. "Miss Stevens came to church last Sunday wearing immoral attire. We must not allow such behavior from our brethren. This will surely provide a straight path to the Devil." He glances at his daughter, then back to Opal with a slight nod.

Opal looks at Ellie and sniffs, then looks back at her husband. "That should be a most useful topic, dear. Maybe the message will keep the sinners at bay."

Ellie is sick of listening to this, and her thoughts wander off again to the girls. She is bored and wonders when dinner will end. Doing the dishes will be a relief.

LESSONS TO BE LEARNED, DEAR CHILDREN

THE NEXT MORNING is still dark when a firm hand shakes Chasing Rabbit awake. She squints in the darkness to see who it is.

Mrs. Burns cries out, "Time to get up," and moves down the row of beds, waking each of the girls along the way. "No heathens lounging in bed today or any other day," she says briskly, clapping her hands together. "So up, up." Chasing Rabbit notices the moon is still shining brightly and wonders why they have to get up so early. Still sleepy, she rubs her eyes, gives a loud yawn, and looks over at the tiny girl next to her, snuggled in a ball, sound asleep.

"Time to wake up, Otter," Chasing Rabbit says, brushing her face lightly. She climbs out of bed, stretching her limbs.

Little Moon yawns and stretches, looking around in the dim light. "It's so early," she says, confused by Mrs. Burns's demands. "I'm still tired."

Chasing Rabbit agrees, yawning, while pulling on her big baggy dress. As she slips it over her head, it falls to the floor in a heap. Struggling, she calls upon her friend. "I need help, Little Moon. It's so dark in here I can't figure how to get this big thing on." Little Moon rushes over to help and the girls giggle as they tug and pull on the dress, finally turning it around to the right side. "I will never get used to wearing this ugly thing," Chasing Rabbit declares.

"Me either," Little Moon agrees.

Chasing Rabbit sees Otter is still sleeping, and shakes her. When that doesn't work she tickles her feet, trying to wake Otter up. Then she pulls the sleepy girl out of bed while Little Moon helps her dress in her over-sized clothes. Once the girls finish tucking in the material around Otter's waist, they follow Mrs. Burns into the hallway. With their ill-fitting outfits dragging along the floor, they shuffle in their clunky shoes as they walk.

Morning Star can't believe this is really happening as she climbs out of bed. Their lives have been shattered in a matter of days. Her insides quake as she tries to get ahold of her fears, which have become her constant companion, especially when she closes her eyes at night. Now, in the darkness, she stumbles over the hem of her dress, her heart heavy in anticipation of what is to come and goes out the door to find the girls.

Chasing Rabbit, Little Moon, and Otter see Morning Star coming down the hallway and go running over. They hug one another, so happy to see each other. "What a horrid night," Morning Star says, and swoops Otter up twirling her in the air. Did you sleep well, little one?" Otter giggles, and then buries her face in Morning Star's neck. "I cried at first for my mama. But Chasing Rabbit and Little Moon held my hand until my eyes closed."

Morning Star gives her a tight hug and kisses her cheek. "I wanted to cry, too."

The girls all hold on to each other, as they follow Mrs. Burns in the early morning hour, wondering where they are going.

Chasing Rabbit yawns, as she stumbles along. "My mattress almost hit the floor, and it creaks when I move, but I was so tired it didn't matter."

Little Moon squeezes Morning Star's hand. "I had a bad dream, but I tried to be brave. All I could think of was Mama and Papa."

"Hidden Spirit was so near in my dream last night, I could almost touch him," Morning Star says softly. "I saw his eyes staring at me. He said something, but I can't remember…"

"He knows we hate it here," Chasing Rabbit says miserably. "If Hidden Spirit comes, let's run away with him and live in the hills."

Morning Star smiles at the willful girl, wishing it were true that Hidden Spirit would come.

The girls are quickly ushered along into a building outside—a stuffy room where they see a petite woman standing by the door, arms folded, watching the girls enter.

Chasing Rabbit whispers to Little Moon. "She looks grumpy. Maybe it's too early for her, too. I wonder where the girl with the sunshine hair is. She seemed nice."

Otter jumps, reacting to a loud rap on the table. It seems all the teachers like to scare the girls with a loud noise. The girls wonder what kind of teacher she might be.

Mrs. Trimble enters the room. "I will be the translator for your new teacher, Opal Crumm. I would like you to repeat after me, "Oh-pp-aal krrr-ummm.""

The girls repeat it several times before Mrs. Trimble says, "Good. Mrs. Crumm is here to teach you every morning about your new God—the one true God." Everyone looks at her strangely. "You will soon forget your Spirit God, for he is sheer nonsense. Your new Spirit God, who is goodness and light… you will call Lord, Our God. Repeat after me. L-oor-dd Ow-er G-aud. This is the only God you will worship from here on out. Only Him. Also, as I have told you, you will learn our language—which is English. After a few weeks of practice, that will be the only language you will be allowed to speak. If you are caught speaking your native tongue, you will be punished and your mouth will be washed out with soap. Is that clear?" she says, holding up a bar of lye soap for inspection.

Everyone nods their heads.

"We will teach you our ways, the white way, even though your skin is red. Our mission is to help you girls become assimilated into the world... You're lives will be forever changed... for the better."

The silence in the room is deafening, except for the beating of hearts. All the girls try to comprehend the meaning of the new rules. Morning Star feels a chill, listening to Mrs. Trimble. She wants to get up and run as far away as possible from this awful place, but she knows she can't leave the girls.

"Also, for as long as you are here, the barbaric dances of yours that I have heard about will not be tolerated. It is never to be discussed or practiced."

Morning Star's head begins to swim. *What else can they take from us?* she wonders, as a gnawing fear starts to rise in her chest. We can't forget about their culture or their families. But she is afraid that is their plan—*to make us forget who we are.*

Opal stands and starts to speak, as Mrs. Trimble interprets. "This will be our place of worship each morning and evening. I will be instructing you in the ways of our Lord, God Almighty. We celebrate our God by obeying His commandments and delight in His words. Through your new Savior, you will be born again and you will rejoice! Now, it's time for the morning prayer, so please stand." The girls obey and stand, numb, trying to comprehend Mrs. Trimble's words, in the early morning hours.

When the long and boring prayer is over, Mrs. Trimble taps the board and signals the girls to sit. Opal points to a picture of an odd-looking man with pointed ears and a long pointed tail. He holds a big fork and has fire coming out of his mouth.

He must be a powerful chief, Chasing Rabbit, thinks.

Mrs. Crumm frowns at the picture and repeats. "Devil… Devil… Devil. Bad Devil… Bad. Evil… Evil… Evil." Chasing Rabbit thinks maybe he isn't their great chief, after all. Just someone Mrs. Crumm doesn't like. Well, she doesn't like Mrs. Crumm—with her stern face and silly switch, or Mrs. Trimble either.

Then Opal points to a picture of a white man with a beard, asleep on some boards, "Jesus," announces Mrs. Crumm with a smile. "This is Jesus. Repeat, Jeee-suss… Jeee-suss. He is Good… Good."

"I guess she likes this guy," Chasing Rabbit whispers to Little Moon. "I liked the other one better."

Chasing Rabbit catches Morning Star's attention as they both roll their eyes, wondering how long this will go on.

After an hour, Mrs. Trimble claps her hands and says, "Class is over. "We will adjourn to the dining hall where we will partake of the Lord's bounty. Follow me."

"What does 'bounty' mean, Morning Star? I hope it's a lot of food. I'm still hungry."

Following Mrs. Trimble, Chasing Rabbit and Little Moon hold hands while Morning Star carries a half-asleep Otter. "I can't believe they make us get up so early just to listen to that," says Chasing Rabbit in a grumble. "We learned about good and bad a long time ago."

"They sound silly," Little Moon, says with a big yawn.

"They think the sleeping man is more powerful than our Great Spirit," reasoned Chasing Rabbit. "I wish the Great Spirit would come and tell them we want to go home."

Otter sniffs the air, as they pass the teachers' table, loaded with food.

"Tell them we're hungry," Little Moon adds.

"All that food makes my stomach growl," says Chasing Rabbit, longing for the pancakes, bacon, fried eggs, and steaming cups of coffee.

"I hope we get some bacon today," says Little Moon, wistfully. "Maybe some eggs, too."

Morning Star takes her sister's hand, hurrying the girls past the table. She has a sinking feeling they won't get much more than they had last night, but tries to sound hopeful. "Let's hope so."

Otter's eyes light up and she licks her lips. "I like eggs, too."

Mrs. Barlapp hustles over to their cramped table with a pot of hot cereal. "Good morning, girls," she says, while dishing the cereal into the girl's bowls. Little Moon gets her bowl filled first and hungrily takes a spoonful. Mrs. Barlapp stops serving and with raised brows, slaps the spoon out of her hand, and scoffs. "Young girl, you must wait until everyone has been served. You need to learn some manners. We never eat until we say our prayers." Mrs. Barlapp gives her a stern look and continues serving the girls.

"How would she know that?" grumbles Morning Star, and hugs her little sister, who is close to tears. "Don't pay her any mind, Little Moon. These women are all grumpy. I don't understand why they sent us here." Morning Star bites down hard on her lip, and says, "I'm sure things will get better here, girls."

Chasing Rabbit is not so optimistic, and looks at Morning Star, doubting her words.

"We must pray to the Great Spirit," Morning Star, says, noticing Chasing Rabbit's defiant look. "We must stay strong and not let these people frighten us. At least we have each other and when times are bad…" Morning Star stops mid-sentence, staring at the teachers, then continues softly, "… which I think will be often. We must remember to pray."

Morning Star is worried for the stubborn and rebellious Chasing Rabbit—so like her brother. *But here, in this place, it won't bode well for her,* she thinks glumly. Morning Star speaks in a whisper. "I think these people could be cruel if you disobey their rules, Chasing Rabbit. I saw the look Mrs. Trimble gave you this morning."

Hiding a smile, Little Moon says. "Maybe it's because you bit the fat lady's arm." Morning Star holds back a laugh.

The girls hungrily slurp down their cereal in a couple of minutes, then stare at their empty bowls, hoping for more to come. Mrs. Barlapp brings a loaf of bread and plops it on the table. Morning Star hops up and cuts the bread for the girls, hoping that will fill their empty stomachs. Then they wait for the teachers to finish their breakfast.

When the teachers finish their savory breakfast and Mrs. Burns scoops up the last morsel on her plate, Miss Snodberry stands up and comes to the table and says, "Good morning, girls. I will escort you to Mrs. Trimble's class. Please follow me down the hallway to your classroom."

In the narrow room, there is a long crack in the window, and the wall is stained with brown spots, where water seeped in. The furniture consists of ten desks with a small bench in front for two girls to sit together.

As the girls file in, Mrs. Trimble is standing up front writing a long list on a chalkboard—their practice for the day.

Mrs. Trimble raps her desk. "Everyone, please take a seat. Miss Star, please come up front. I understand you can speak our English language fairly well. I must say I am impressed by your knowledge and willingness to learn, so you will be my class helper. Now put that girl down, and come up here."

Morning Star takes Otter and squeezes her in between Little Moon and Chasing Rabbit.

Looking around at the class, Mrs. Trimble says, "Everyone must pull their own weight while at this school. There will be no shirking of duties." Looking at Morning Star, she says, "Now, please distribute these boards to the children. They will have to share. Then come up here and help me interpret. I would like you to go over a list of words I made for the girls to practice. I will say the word, then you will repeat it. We have a lot of work ahead of us. I expect each one of you to pay close attention in class. No disruptions will be tolerated. Two weeks should be sufficient to learn English well enough for everyone to communicate with one other. Do I make myself clear? Good. Let's get started."

"Miss Star. Ready."

Morning Star goes over Mrs. Trimble's list, speaking slowly:

Stand
Sit
Sing
Pray
Bedtime
Morning
Undress
Outhouse
Yes
No
Preacher Jim

This seems to go on for hours, during which time Mrs. Trimble walks up and down the aisle, clacking her strap, letting the girls know that if they do not follow along or if they dare to doze off, a sharp smack on the hand will follow.

At long last, class is over. The girls' minds are numb from the endless repetition. With stiff bodies and sore behinds from the hard seats, they trudge silently behind Mrs. Trimble to the dining hall.

Morning Star walks beside the girls, and whispers, "Mrs. Trimble forgot to put boring on the board. Boh-ree-ng!" The girls cover their mouths in laughter.

After their lunch of soup and bread, Mrs. Trimble hurries over to Morning Star. "I made a work schedule for the week and I want you to come and help me with the duties I have laid out. I need to know each child's name and their capabilities." Looking at Mrs. Burns, she says, "Their names are so odd, I fear it will take an eternity to learn them." Mrs. Burns agrees. "Now, I want to make certain we have the right girl for the right job. Mrs. Burns and Miss Snodberry will accompany me to the classroom as we go over the details." She hands Morning Star the list and tells her to come along directly.

Later that day, Morning Star finds Chasing Rabbit and Little Moon and holds up the sheet of paper. "I have the list of chores." They huddle together while Morning Star reads to them.

SCHEDULE OF DAILY ROUTINE:

Out of bed: 5:00 a.m.
Prayer service with Opal: 5:30 a.m.
Breakfast: 7:00 – 7:25 a.m.
English Class with Mrs. Trimble: 7:30 a.m. – 12:00 Noon
Lunch directly following class

CHORE DESCRIPTION:

Pick up dishes after every meal
Wash laundry, hang to dry, iron
Mend (sewing, hemming, etc.)

Sweep floors, mop floors, scrub floors
Clean staff rooms, make beds, change sheets
Wash windows, clear cobwebs, kill rodents
Additional duties, as needed

KITCHEN CHORES:

Peel, chop, slice, dice
Rinse dishes, wash dishes, dry dishes, put away dishes
Bake, core, can
Fetch buckets of water, collect eggs, collect firewood, etc.
Anything else Mrs. Barlapp requires for meals

SUNDAY: CHURCH:

Chores to follow services

"This list is endless," Morning Star, says in dismay. "With this schedule, we will drop into bed every night, exhausted. Otter is too young to be on her own. I will ask Mrs. Trimble to let her help me with my chores in the kitchen. She is having such a hard time here." Worry creases her brow. "She seems so sad now. It's hard to make her smile, or see there may be hope of someday going home."

"We're kept here like prisoners," says Chasing Rabbit angrily. "We'll have no time to play or explore. I think we should run away, and soon…"

"No, Chasing Rabbit," admonishes Morning Star. "It will be too dangerous. Let's pray every night to the Great Spirit that Hidden Spirit will come." Her voice trembles at the mention of his name. Then, she feels a faint glimmer of hope rise from somewhere inside. Surprised by the feeling, she says, "Let's do the best we can while we're here. Besides, we have each other. Not to mention all these chores," she adds with a touch of irony. "Anyway, we have no choice." Morning Star hugs a silent Otter, who seems to be in a daze. She clings to Morning Star, and wraps her arms around her neck.

Chasing Rabbit, Little Moon, and Morning Star stare off in the distance, lost in their own miserable thoughts, staring at nothing in particular. A little bit of life and joy slips out of girls on this bleak day.

OFF TO CHURCH WE GO

I T'S SUNDAY MORNING when the girls are allowed to sleep in until six o'clock. An excited Mrs. Trimble runs into the room clapping her hands. "Everyone, up! This is a very important day for you. I want all of you girls to look your best, so spend a little extra time washing, and brush the dust and wrinkles out of your clothes. We will be going into town to hear Preacher Jim's sermon. I want the townsfolk to see how well behaved you girls are, so they don't fret about 'wild Indians' and such being close by. Let's make a good impression. We leave here promptly at eight o'clock. No dilly-dallying on the Sabbath."

The girls are excited, but Chasing Rabbit is not sure this will be any fun, and she grumbles to Little Moon. "It will be good to leave this place, but why can't we have the sermon outside, so we can look at the trees and sky?"

"I don't think the white people do it that way," Morning Star says quietly, as the girls wait in the hallway.

"Come along, girls." Mrs. Trimble says with a flourish and hustles outside where she instructs everyone to gather in a straight line. She looks around to see if everyone is present, and is annoyed by a tardy Mrs. Burns. "Where on earth is that woman?" she asks irritably. A moment later the harried-looking woman huffs out the door, pinning her boxy hat to her head.

Mrs. Trimble starts walking, lifting her legs as she goes. "One-two, one-two." She turns to the girls, and orders, "Follow me, and march!"

Little Moon and Chasing Rabbit moan in exasperation.

After a mile or so down the road, their legs feel like jelly and the girls tire of marching, so Chasing Rabbit and Little Moon decide to skip instead. Disobedience gets them a whack on their legs. "This is the Lord's day, Missy, so mind your manners," says Mrs. Trimble, indignantly. She turns and marches back to the front of the line.

Mrs. Burns looks completely frazzled as she pumps her legs up and down, wiping her brow.

Miss Snodberry follows behind the girls, not even bothering to march.

By the time the girls arrive in town, sores and blisters emerge on the girls' feet. Morning Star carries a quiet Otter, as Little Moon and Chasing Rabbit limp along beside her, moaning in unison. "This is silly."

In town they pass neat houses with curtains hanging in the windows and bordered with fenced-in yards.

Up ahead is a whitewashed building with a bell on top, ringing a pleasant sound.

When the children file in, the townspeople, already seated in the pews, abruptly stop talking. Some stare, while others whisper amongst themselves. A few of the parishioners openly point. The children look shyly down at their feet, but not Chasing Rabbit. She looks boldly at the crowd. She hears a woman say, "Imagine! Indians in our midst. What will happen to our town next? Not sure I'll be able to sleep a wink." Chasing Rabbit stares at the woman, and hisses. "I'd like to punch that lady right in the nose." Before Little Moon can respond, Mrs. Trimble quickly ushers the girls down the aisle to the front pew.

On the left side of the aisle, the wide-eyed boys watch as the girls walk past. A couple of them wave as their eyes fill with longing to see their friends. They look just as homesick as the girls.

Seated separately from one another, the boys and girls are not allowed to walk together to and from the church, nor are they allowed to exchange words once inside. They are instructed to stare straight ahead at all times, eyes on Preacher Jim. But exchanging smiles is difficult to ban.

Although the boys and girls rarely run into each other at school, occasionally Morning Star or Chasing Rabbit see one of the boys, and sneak in a hello.

Chasing Rabbit whispers to Morning Star, "Who do you think will be worse—Opal or Preacher Jim? I bet he's just as bad as she is." Morning Star can't help but burst out laughing. A stern reprimand follows. "Quiet!"

Preacher Jim walks to the pulpit, pleased at the large turnout. He gives the parishioners a nod, then subjects the room to a careful scan, nodding at a few of his favorites—those who are generous when the collection plate is passed around. His eyes swivel to the front row, and he gives a broad smile to the children, opening his arms wide as if encompassing them in his folds. Preacher Jim proceeds to embellish his tales to the eager parishioners, who are curious about the heathens in town. "Everyone. I would like to welcome the children from the boarding school. They have come from a long way off—from Satan's den, as you know. They will now have a chance to redeem themselves in the eyes of the Lord. A few months ago, I heard His call, asking me to save these reprobates that are sitting in our midst. Well, I responded with a resounding, 'yes!' I even shouted it out at the top of my lungs. 'I will save the heathens, my Lord, from a lustful and barbaric life. And I will bring them to you.' How could I refuse?" A polite round of applause filled the church. Looking pleased that he had their rapt attention, he opens his Bible and clears his throat—all set to start his sermon, which he begins in a combative voice. "Today's topic is about the perils and pitfalls of women and their charms…" His words come to a screeching halt when the church door swings opens with a bang. A few parishioners gasp at the interruption, and turn around to identify the latecomer. A low buzz filters throughout the room as the parishioners express their shock at Ellie's tardiness and improper behavior.

Ellie enters with cheeks flushed and defiant eyes, boldly making her way to the front of the church and sitting directly behind the girls. The dismayed congregants whisper among themselves. Momentarily taken aback, Preacher Jim gives Ellie a furious look, but manages to keep his composure and continues on. His voice rises sharply as he pounds the pulpit with his mallet, causing it to wobble precariously back and forth. "This is God's House. So all ye sinners beware! The Devil comes disguised in many forms, waiting to catch us off guard. Beware of a pretty face that will tempt you with her guile and lead you on the path toward temptation. Rise up and resist, if you can, and pray mightily. God is forgiving and He understands man's desires as women flaunt their bodies and petulant faces before us. I warn ye, take heed and pray, pray with all your might."

After a while, the words all blend together, and Chasing Rabbit figures everyone is doomed, especially the women. She can't understand why the preacher thinks women are bad. The room is stuffy, and she soon dozes off. Then a booming voice startles her awake. "Let's all stand and sing our praises to the Lord."

Opal hurries up front, opens her pages, and begins to play the piano with gusto. Never mind that it is off-key and out of tune. Opal isn't the least bit deterred as she clangs away and belts out her favorite song, "Glory Be to God." The parishioners do their best to follow along.

Uncertain of what to do, the children stand and hum along.

After service is over the parishioners file outside, waiting to greet the preacher and shake his hand. Some are not sure what to make of the Indians in town, but are relieved to hear their new preacher was once a military man and decorated with honors. This makes some of the townsfolk a little more comfortable about the Indians' presence. They just hope no coloreds will follow.

As the girls walk back to the school, they talk about the boys, wondering if their side fares any better.

"They look real sad," says Chasing Rabbit absently as she sits on the ground to slip off her heavy black shoes—revealing bright red sores. Little Moon sits down as well, removes her shoes—displaying raw heels. "I need more socks so my shoes will stop sliding," she says with a moan. Cradling her feet, she pops a bulging blister on her toe.

Morning Star looks at the wounds and says, "Why don't you walk the rest of the way barefoot. Mrs. Trimble is so far ahead she won't notice, and I don't think Miss Snodberry will tell."

The girls turn and look at the woman who is standing close by. She walks over and speaks nervously as though Mrs. Trimble might hear. "Just hold your shoes until you get to the school. I'll find you more socks so your shoes will fit better." Before the girls can thank her, she hurries down the road. The girls stand, and quickly follow behind.

After walking a short way, Morning Star comments, "Preacher Jim seems peculiar. His eyebrows jerk up and down as he talks. It's like he's looking at the boys and us at the same time. He is odd…"

"I know." Chasing Rabbit says, agreeing. "Yesterday he saw me outside and patted my head and told me that I'll soon be one of God's little angels. What does he know? He always says odd stuff."

Then Little Moon speaks up. "Did you see Long Hair? He

looks as lonely as we do. He snuck a wave, and got hit on the head, two times."

"I guess if you're a Christian, it means you don't have to be nice," Chasing Rabbit says. "And probably means you're not to sass the guy on the cross."

During their first week at school the children are kept busy learning their regular routine and work schedule. The pace is grueling, and each child is expected to keep up—no exceptions.

Chasing Rabbit's chore is to do laundry. After lunch, she drags an old whiskey barrel down to the stream that still reeks of the aged spirits and she fills it to the brim with water. Mrs. Burns follows the girl to the water's edge. She is supposed to show her how to wash, but instead she simply tosses a bar of lye soap into the bucket and says, "Stick the dresses in the water, get them wet, and scrub hard. A little elbow grease does wonders." Then she shoves a washboard in her hand. "Don't forget to rinse the clothes real good before hanging them up." Before Chasing Rabbit can ask her any questions Mrs. Burns hustles back up the hill as fast as her stout legs can take her.

Picking up a large gingham dress, Chasing Rabbit submerges it into the water, getting it sopping wet, just as she was told. Then she rubs the soap onto the fabric, and scrubs it on the washboard. The dress slips from her grasp, and she scrapes her skin on the sharp board. The lye soap stings like a bee and Chasing Rabbit hops around the bucket, wincing in pain. After looking at the huge pile clothes and then at her red, cracked hands, she decides to use just a small amount of lye soap. "I'll forget the scrubbing part, too. I don't care what they say. I'm not even halfway finished with my chores, and my hands are raw." She blows on her wounds in dismay, while looking at the amount of clothes lying before her. Plunging another humungous dress in the water she swishes it up and down, wrings it out, lugs it over to the clothesline, and heaves it over the top. Chasing Rabbit wonders if her arms might fall off. She's not sure that she can lift another soggy dress, but plows ahead. By the end of the day, she is so tired that she can barely drag the buckets or herself up the hill, so she plops down on the ground to catch her breath. Chest heaving, she's grateful to be finished with her chores for the day. Of course, *tomorrow will bring more of the same drudgery,* she thinks, but the one bright spot is, *I get to be outside.* Yawning, she rubs her eyes trying to stay awake. But they begin to sting, then burn furiously, turning a deep scarlet. Her eyes swell and tears begin to drip. They hurt so bad, she rubs them even more, and she starts to scream and hop wildly around in circles. Mrs. Trimble happens to be walking outside, and hears the girl. She hurries over, livid. "What on earth are you doing out here—one of your savage, wicked dances? And why are you crying?"

"I got soap in my eyes and it burns like mad. I can hardly see," Chasing Rabbit says frantically.

"Oh fiddlesticks and baloney. Go to the kitchen and get a bucket of water and rinse your eyes out. Here, follow me inside."

*

Little Moon is assigned to milk Bessie, the big brown-eyed cow in the barn. The girl has never milked a cow before, but is excited to try. Mrs. Trimble announces to Mrs. Burns, "I have my hands full at the school and your help is sorely needed. I think you are more than adept at showing the girls a few of their chores—like how to milk a cow!"

"Well," Mrs. Burns says with a sputter, "I've never milked a cow in my life."

"It certainly can't be that difficult, so give it a try. The worst that can happen is you get a couple squirts. The girls can mix it with water, if that's the case," Mrs. Trimble sniffs.

Mrs. Burns walks inside the barn and grunts as she plumps her wide bottom on the stool next to Little Moon, "Watch how it's done. It can't be that hard." She scowls as she grabs ahold of the cow's teats, and yanks. Nothing happens. She tries again, this time with a little more force. Nothing comes out. Little Moon giggles, as Bessie kicks her hind legs, almost knocking the bucket over. Mrs. Burns screeches in alarm as the cow kicks its legs again. As she leans back to get out of the way of the dangerous hooves, she falls off the stool with a *thump*. Mrs. Burns has had it with this stubborn cow and says, struggling to get off the ground, "Figure it out for yourself!" She heaves herself up, huffing her way out of the barn.

Little Moon is glad the lady is gone and sits tentatively on the stool, talking to the cow. "I think the lady doesn't like you Bessie, but I do. I hope we'll become good friends. I could use a friendly face around here." She looks at Bessie's tail switching back and forth. "Now don't kick me like you did Mrs. Burns. I've never milked a cow before, so be patient with me. I won't hurt you." Little Moon gingerly takes ahold of the teat and pulls, with no luck. After a few tries Little Moon manages to get a small amount of milk in the bucket. It takes a week before Little Moon can get the hang of milking the cow. When she finally does, she is able to squirt the milk into a bowl without losing a drop.

Little Moon and Bessie become good friends and she tells the cow everyday, "I love you, Bessie." Then she scratches her ear. "The best part of my day is coming out here to be with you." At the same time each day, Bessie waits for Little Moon to start milking her, and softly moos as the milk starts to flow. When Little Moon finishes her chore, she gives Bessie a hug, a kiss on the nose, and scratches her ears, assuring her she will be back later. Then she runs over to the stream to help Chasing Rabbit with the laundry. She loves being near her friend in the outdoors, even though it's hard work. She doesn't know how Chasing Rabbit does all this by herself, and is grateful to be with her friend.

*

Morning Star convinces Mrs. Trimble to let Otter work with her in the kitchen. She wants to send the little girl out to pick vegetables in the garden and pull a few weeds.

It's Morning Star's chore to help Mrs. Barlapp prepare the food—breakfast, lunch, and dinner. The children's menu never varies. Breakfast is always cereal, and usually served with lumps because Morning Star is always racing back and forth with her many chores. Mrs. Barlapp is most demanding and hovers over her, scolding. "Don't burn the bacon... and hurry and get the teachers' food on the table before it gets cold. I swear you're slower than molasses in the month of January. Do you have lead in your feet?" Not wanting to upset the woman, Morning Star swallows her fear and hurries even faster. The one thing that Mrs. Barlapp isn't that concerned with is the girls' food, and she pays little attention to how it's prepared. Morning Star does her best to make it for them. "I have enough on my plate without having to worry about the girls' supper as well. Milk, bread and butter, and soup with a few vegetables, is more than sufficient. You may toss in some leftover meat on occasion. I'm sure it's better than what they eat back home. If the meat is a bit sour, don't worry. It's suitable enough for the children," Mrs. Barlapp assures Morning Star, who looks at the off-colored meat, dubiously. "Won't taste it in the soup, anyhow. Just add a little more water. No wasting of food in my kitchen."

Sometimes Morning Star can smell the spoiled meat as she stirs, and the rancid odor drifts up her nostrils, causing her to worry that the children might get sick. She thinks adding extra salt will help cover the taste, but it doesn't. With no choice,

Morning Star brings the pot of soup to the table. Chasing Rabbit sniffs the soup as Morning Star sets it down, and starts serving the girls. "It smells like something died in here. Give this smelly stuff to the teachers," she says, pushing the bowl away.

Morning Star has no words for the feisty girl, and hurries back to the kitchen to sneak some extra bread and butter, hoping that will fill their stomachs. At least, it won't make them sick.

The teachers' meals are a different story. Sumptuous dishes are painstakingly prepared, and Morning Star's mouth waters from the wonderful aroma filling the kitchen each day. Mrs. Barlapp takes great pride in making delicious, hearty meals for the staff.

Morning Star serves the teachers first, then the girls. When Mrs. Barlapp isn't looking, she grabs some food off the large platters and sneaks it over to the girls to share. One time she snuck a large hunk of roast beef to the table. The girls devoured it in a flash. It wasn't much, but it makes the girls happy to taste something other than their daily ration of soup.

One morning, Morning Star gets up the nerve and asks Mrs. Barlapp, "Why don't we eat the same food as the teachers?"

Indignant at the inquiry, Mrs. Barlapp throws her shoulders back, and bristles. "These women are doing you a great service. They're trying their darndest to educate you girls, so that when you go home, you will have skills and you won't be ignorant. The only reward they get is my good food. You girls have plenty to eat, so stop complaining. You're lucky to get what you do. Now, get back to work."

Morning Star can't believe the insensitivity of the people at this place, and the gall of Mrs. Barlapp. She throws down her towel and blurts out before she can stop herself. "The teachers think we want to be here—to become like you people. Well, we don't. Mrs. Trimble knows nothing about our culture, and neither do you. No one cares to learn, either. No one bothers to ask if we are happy here and they never comfort the girls who cry at night for their mamas. Everyone is unhappy, and all we want is to go home." Surprised by her outburst, Morning Star's face burns with fury and she holds her hands to keep them from shaking.

Mrs. Barlapp's eyes bulge at the girl's candid words. Waving her pot in the air, she explodes. "I should knock some sense into you... you ungrateful little savage. You should be ashamed of yourself. But I don't think you have any shame in you. You're lucky I don't tell Mrs. Trimble about this. If I had my way I'd tell the whole lot of you to skedaddle back to where you came from. You're more trouble than you're worth. I say she is not strict enough. If I had my way, I'd give you a walloping you'd never forget. Now, I tell you once more. You get back to work before I change my mind and tell her what a despicable heathen you are." Then she storms back to the stove, and turns over the ham, grease splattering in every direction.

Morning Star recoils at the callous words. She dislikes Mrs. Barlapp more every day and her hatred of this place grows deeper. She wishes Hidden Spirit would come and take her away. She would never come back to this horrid place, no matter what they threaten. She would hide out in the hills with Hidden Spirit. Her parents would understand, once they knew what was going on at the school. These people are heartless.

As the days pass, turning into weeks, then months, Little Moon laughs less often. There isn't anything fun about being at the school. At night, Otter hardly says a word or smiles when Chasing Rabbit tells her stories. Most of the time her eyes glaze over. She is as tiny as a willow stick and will hardly eat. Chasing Rabbit notices, and is getting nervous about her little friend.

One day when Little Moon is helping Chasing Rabbit dump the dirty water, Little Moon is unable to keep her lips from trembling. She asks Chasing Rabbit about Hidden Spirit. "Do you think your brother will come and take us home? I miss Mama and Papa and I don't want to stay here. I don't think they will let us go home. The only thing nice about this place is Bessie and you and Morning Star. You have to come to the barn to meet her, Chasing Rabbit. Bessie is what keeps me from going mad. I talk to her all the time. I think she understands what I'm saying, and she feels my sadness. I think I would die without you and Bessie."

Chasing Rabbit has a gnawing feeling inside that haunts her about this place—a bad feeling that won't go away. She tries to hide her feelings from Little Moon and pretends all will be okay. "I love cows, too. Maybe I'll sneak over when I don't have piles of wash," Chasing Rabbit says, brushing a mound of soap off her friend's nose. "Maybe I'll think of a way we can escape." Chasing Rabbit isn't at all sure how to accomplish that, but she needs to say something to lift her friend's spirits. "Maybe I'll pray extra hard tonight to the Great Spirit, and He will help me think of a way."

"I will pray extra hard, too," says Little Moon.

Chasing Rabbit sits for a few minutes before voicing her thoughts. Then she says, "Preacher Jim is really strange."

Little Moon looks up in response.

Without waiting for a reply, Chasing Rabbit continues on, as she sloshes the clothes around in the bucket. "The other day I was going to the outhouse and I saw him coming down the path, holding his Bible in the air, talking to himself. When he spotted me, he hurried over and said he wanted to pray for my soul. He asked me to bend on my knees while he talked to the Lord. It took forever and I had to go really bad and couldn't wait for him to finish. Soon as he did, I jumped up and hurried to the outhouse as fast as I could, and I locked the door. I stayed inside an extra long time, hoping he would be gone, but when I opened the door, he was still there, waiting. My stomach thumped at the sight of him and I heard him say, 'God help the wayward ones.' I didn't answer and took off in a run—and didn't stop until I was at the school."

Both girls sit in silence and contemplate the strange man while continuing to work. Then they look up as they hear someone in the bushes. It's the yellow-haired girl, staring at them. *Why is she hiding here? Is she spying on us?* Chasing Rabbit wonders, a bit fearful.

Ellie has been watching the girls, curiously. She wants to approach them, but hesitates. She knows that Mrs. Trimble would be furious and she isn't certain the girls would want to talk to her—not that she would blame them. She can clearly see that the girls are unhappy, and wishes that she could reassure them, but she doesn't want to mislead them, either. Then, when the girls look her way and they wave timidly, she finally gets up the nerve. "Hello, girls," she calls out.

Little Moon and Chasing Rabbit stare at the girl, too surprised to reply.

"What is your name?" Ellie asks, curiosity getting the better of her.

Chasing Rabbit speaks first. "This is Little Moon. I'm Chasing Rabbit."

"Those are pretty names. What do they mean? I've never heard any like it before. So unusual."

"Well," Chasing Rabbit says, straightening her shoulders proudly. "When I was born, all the rabbits in the area came to visit. Hundreds of rabbits danced around me and chased one other, round and round in a circle. They were so excited about my birth they couldn't stop running and hopping. That's what my father says, so he named me Chasing Rabbit, after the rabbit family."

Delighted by the story, Ellie says, "That's wonderful. I wish someone would have danced around me when I was born."

Little Moon says, shyly. "I was born when the small moon glowed in the sky. That's when Mama knew my name."

"You girls are so lucky to have such interesting names. Mine sounds boring compared to yours." Ellie looks around the school grounds. "You must be unhappy here… away from your families."

Little Moon and Chasing Rabbit nod vigorously at the same time.

"My father is… well…" she says, fidgeting, "he believes he is helping. He doesn't understand other peoples' customs or their beliefs. Only his. If you don't believe in what he preaches, then off to Hell you will go. The Devil will be waiting around the corner to snatch you up."

"Is that where the pitchfork man lives?" Chasing Rabbit asks.

"Well, it's complicated to explain," Ellie says, smiling, "but, yes."

"We believe in the Great Spirit, and sometimes I can see Him in the sky. He doesn't care what you believe in, as long as you don't hurt Mother Earth and all her animals."

"We take care of each other, too," Little Moon chimes in, importantly.

Chasing Rabbit and Little Moon are delighted to have the pretty blonde girl sitting next to them, talking about their families. They are proud of their culture and of being Sioux.

Reaching out to touch Ellie's hair, Chasing Rabbit says, "It's so pretty. I wondered if it felt like the sun." Ellie smiles at the inquisitive girl, "I'll bet your hair was just as pretty before they cut it."

The girls frown. "We have never cut our hair before," Chasing Rabbit says. "That is not our custom. We cut our hair when someone close to us dies and they go to the other world." She looks at Ellie. "It feels like death at this place. I don't like it here."

"I don't, either," Little Moon says.

"Mrs. Trimble tells us we're not supposed to talk in our

language anymore," Chasing Rabbit says sadly, "or wear our own clothes. They took our dresses and burned them—like they were bad—and we can't even wear our moccasins that were soft and never gave us blisters. I hate it here. And… Mrs. Trimble and the others call us 'savages'."

Ellie gasps, and gives the girls a hug. "Oh, girls," Ellie says. "I am really sorry what they are doing to you. It makes me really mad they say such awful things. If I could I would smack everyone of…" Trying to keep her anger in check, Ellie thinks she should change the subject and sweetly asks Little Moon and Chasing Rabbit. "Tell me more about your families. I find your stories fascinating."

Chasing Rabbit beams. It feels good to have someone to talk to. The sunshine girl likes them and they like her. The girls bask in her attention.

Ellie is enthralled by their stories and pelts them with more questions. She is so engrossed with their lives that she forgets that the girls have work to do. Then her eyes stray to the pile of untouched laundry, and she says, "Oh, my goodness girls. I've been so selfish, pestering you about your lives back home. I fear you won't get your work finished, and there's so much to do. I don't want you to get into trouble, so please let me help."

Chasing Rabbit gratefully agrees, since there is an extra pile today, with the addition of sheets and blankets.

The girls scurry about, gathering the clothes.

Ellie picks up a heavy dress and shakes it out. "This big thing must belong to Mrs. Burns. It weighs a ton," she says, as she starts to dip the clothes in the water and begin scrubbing.

The girls giggle and smother a laugh at Ellie, who is up to her elbows, soaked with water and lye soap, like she knew what she was doing. Chasing Rabbit warns her. "Don't get that stuff in your eyes, Ellie, it burns really bad."

Ellie grins and says, "I know. My mother, that is Opal, likes to use it on the floors and has washed my mouth more than once for sassing her." She makes a funny face that makes the girls smile. Ellie pulls the heavy dress from the tub, and hangs it on the line that almost dips to the ground from the weight. Wiping her hands she stands for a moment, then questions the girls some more about Mrs. Trimble and her rules. "I bet she's just like my father," Ellie says somberly. "She treats him like he's something important and worships his every word. Makes me sick."

"I think she is unhappy," Chasing Rabbit says, "because she frowns a lot... and she always carries her strap. I felt the strap across my legs. She hits real hard."

After hanging the last sheet on the line, Ellie spots her father walking the grounds. "My father is coming. I'd better leave before he catches me here." She quickly ducks in between the sheets. "I'll come back as often as I can," she says, sprinting toward the barn.

Preacher Jim strolls over to Little Moon and Chasing Rabbit, scrutinizing their work.

Chasing Rabbit becomes nervous and drops a dress on the ground.

Preacher Jim frowns. "You must be more diligent in your duties, young girl. Don't want you doing sloppy work. Now, wash that dress again, and hang it carefully. Remember, the eyes of the Lord are always upon you." His eyebrows shoot up in a nervous twitch. Then he's off again, strolling the grounds, Bible in hand, quoting The Lord's Prayer.

VISION QUEST - AGAIN

HIDDEN SPIRIT SITS up in the early morning light, contemplating the unusual stick. He thinks it might be good for firewood on a cool evening until he sees it move, ever so slightly. Then he looks closer, but sees no further movement. The darned thing would appear out of nowhere, and then simply disappear. Restless with worry, he has been thinking about the girls—particularly Morning Star. He decides it's time to visit Plenty Feathers and talk to him about a vision quest.

At Grandfather's camp, Hidden Spirit paces back and forth by the fire. Troubling thoughts crease his brow. Finally, at Plenty Feathers' request, he sits down near the fire. "I see your heart is troubled, *Mi-thakoza,*" says Plenty Feathers. "I think it's time for you to commune with the Great Spirit—to seek His wisdom and solace. In the darkness, voices will come and strange things will happen and you may hear things that trouble your heart. Let all your thoughts go. This time, in the pit of darkness, things will be different."

Hidden Spirit ponders Grandfather's words. "I want to go to the Black Hills where Broken Feather has gone. I will feel his spirit there in the hills."

"Could be dangerous, leaving the reservation," Grandfather says, full of worry. He sits quietly, and ponders Hidden Spirit's request. "You are right, though. The Great Spirit will hear you more clearly in the Hills of the Gods. It will be worth the trip— and the punishment, if we are caught."

Plenty Feathers knew the Black Hills well as he had traveled there many times in his youth. He would find the same spot he once used for his own vision quest long ago. "Let's purify your body before you go to the hills, and make a sweat lodge to clear your thoughts."

The two men set about gathering wood and lava rocks. The heat will hold well with the rocks. Once all is set, Hidden Spirit immerses himself in the searing heat, staying there for hours.

The next morning at daybreak, Hidden Spirit and his grandfather leave camp, bringing along the star blanket that Leaves Dancing had made. Hidden Spirit wears only a breach cloth, his body cleansed and his mind now readied. For seven days, he will consume no food or water.

In the cool morning light they walk with purpose, passing deep ravines and hidden gorges filled with birch trees and open meadows. Nearing the rancher's land, they walk silently through the grasses, past the cattle, and into the thick forests filled with Black Hills' spruce and quaking aspens. Hidden Spirit breathes in the scented pines as they pass by clear running streams. His heart is full of sadness and anger as he walks through the land that had once been theirs to roam.

In 1868, his tribe had signed a treaty with the Great White Father. The white man told his people, "As long as the grass shall grow and the rivers flow, and your dead lie buried, the Black Hills will forever be yours." It was the Sioux's sacred place where the people came to pray and to bury their dead. But when Custer discovered the golden rocks in 1875, the treaty was no more and their land was taken back. Giant scars are now visible in the sacred valley, where miners left gaping holes.

Hidden Spirit is filled with anger, surveying the destruction. "Grandfather, the white eyes are worse than locusts, destroying everything in their path—our sacred hills tarnished by their footprints. I hate them and what they have done."

Plenty Feathers looks around with longing. "Yes, my grandson, it is a travesty, but we must try our best to let go of anger and hold to our knowledge from the ancient ones. It will not serve us well if we don't." Hidden Spirit forces his thoughts away from anger and concentrates on what lay ahead.

As they climb the steep hills, Grandfather now walks with a spring in his step, like he had as a young man. Being here among his ancestors makes his energy soar. At the top of the hill, he stops and looks around at the beautiful vista surrounding them on every side—his arms outstretched to the heavens. "Where east meets the west, and the sun and moon kiss," he says serenely. "This is the most sacred place of all in the *Paha Sapa*. They walk a little further and come upon a group of cottonwoods—the talking trees, as the Sioux call them—their sacred trees.

Grandfather looks wistfully at the hills. "I well remember this place, which will soon be my home. The memories of my ancestors make me proud, Grandson. I feel alive in the home of my brothers, even though they have gone with the buffalo. I feel their presence and find my weary bones comforted by them."

Hidden Spirit can feel the energy as he nears the sacred place. He remembers his last vision quest, and tries to quell a shudder. He reminds himself he was not ready back then and wonders what will await him this time, in the hole of darkness. He can already hear the whisperings in the wind, and feels a shiver run through him. He knows they are close.

Within a short time, Plenty Feathers finds the opening he was looking for, and removes a worn buffalo hide that is concealed with branches and accumulated brush. Beneath is a small hole in the ground, just enough room for Hidden Spirit to sit. Grandfather says a prayer as he opens his medicine pouch and sprinkles some pungent sage and pine inside. Plenty Feathers hands the star blanket to his grandson. "It's time, Mi-thakoza."

Hidden Spirit lowers himself in, and Grandfather smiles. "*Wakan tanka kici un*," he says, covering the opening with the buffalo robe. "I will be back when I hear the call."

Inside the cool pit, Hidden Spirit sits on the pine needles and sage, and breathes deeply. The walls are moist and damp, and the pungent smell of the earth, mixed with pine and sage beneath him, is calming.

As he sits alone in the darkness, he listens, prays, waits, and wonders. He can hear the beat of his heart—the only sound in the hole. He worries about Morning Star and his sister and Little Moon, and he prays to see them in his vision. Now he is ready to go to the spirit world and unravel its mysteries. "Take me beyond the realms of darkness," he asks. "I seek for answers that trouble my heart." He feels the wind begin circling his body, as he lies bare on Mother Earth. Time begins to fade until he cannot tell day from night or how long he has been inside the damp pit. He sinks back into the calm and concentrates—his hunger long forgotten. A rumble comes from above. *It must be thunder,* he thinks, as the ground jolts violently, knocking him over. Then, a scream whistles by. His body goes limp with fear as he hears giant wings swoop down and he feels long piercing talons grab him by the neck. Another thunderous *boom* echoes, carrying him high over a mountain—soaring beneath a whoosh of flapping wings. Suddenly, the sharp talons let go of him and he lands atop a massive hemlock tree. Frightened, he looks carefully around. Lightning flares shoot jagged streaks across the sky, illuminating the outer world. Then in another flash, all is calm. A moment later, the wind picks up and rises to a high-pitched crescendo. He sways on the creaking branch and clings tightly—wondering if he is in the afterlife. And then he slips.

Spiraling down into the unknown depths, he passes through spewing lava that singes his lungs as the red-hot core pulsates in the darkness and reverberates around him. Hidden Spirit hears the cry of death echoing loudly, and he can breathe no more. He feels his life drift past and he reaches out to pull his body back, but it seems impossible. "No! No! Don't go!" he cries. "I don't want to die in here." The more frightened he becomes the further his body drifts away. It is only when he steels himself to relax that he slides back into his body.

A large owl flies by and beckons to him. He jumps onto its back and clings desperately to the bird's neck as they rise higher and higher. Feeling a cool burst of air, he inhales deeply, relieved to be out of the fiery depths and into the light. The bird carries the boy through the forests, rich with spruce and willows. Hidden Spirit can hear his ancestors whisper, "*Toksha ake wac inyuankti*," as the owl drops him onto another large hemlock tree, where he lands on the highest branch. The boy can hear the trees whisper in the breeze, "Thank you, our friend, for coming. We are your brothers, Oh, Great One. We are in trouble. Our leaves and limbs are givers of life. Please help. Do not let the unenlightened ones destroy us—for if they do, all of life shall wither and die." Then the hemlock starts to weep.

Hidden Spirit feels droplets of water falling, slowly... like a heavy mist. Then a warm wave of salty tears splashes down, mingling with the rain, and drenching him with sadness so deep it reaches his inner being. The tears now fall so hard it's like hail, as Hidden Spirit clings to the slender branch. He feels the love of the trees and their sorrow, emanate from their inner depth, giving him insight into the vastness of their roots. Feeling as if he is dying, he starts to weep with the swaying trees. The hemlocks gather him into their velvety limbs. He can hear the call of the willows and the oaks and the pines and quaking aspens all crying out—" Help us, spirit being. We beg you, help!" Their cries reach out across the sky, and into the ethers and beyond. For a fleeting moment, he can see into their future. It is fading. He screams. The trees are all gone. He clings desperately to the weeping branch, wanting to give them comfort. Then, he prays to the Great Spirit, and senses a burst of life flow through him and the trees.

Losing his balance, he starts to slip and grasps at the quivering branch, but to no avail. He tumbles through the air, whirling at a dizzying pace as piercing screams follow. Hidden Spirit no longer can tell if the screams are coming from him or the trees. A bolt of lightning snaps, then Hidden Spirit finds himself whirling round and round, on the back of an eagle. They soar out into the brightness, flying across the grounds of a fortress.

Hidden Spirit blinks, dismayed by the images before him. He sees Chasing Rabbit washing a large pile of clothes. Little Moon is beside her. The eagle and the boy swoop down over the girls' heads, and he shouts out to them. "Chasing Rabbit... look up. I'm here. Little Moon, hello..." Then he is abruptly whisked into a large kitchen, and alights beside Morning Star. He gasps at the sight of her—saddened by the loss of her long hair and the sorrow etched in her beautiful face, which appears older. He whispers, "Morning Star, Can you see me? I'm right next to you. I see you standing in your sadness. It makes my heart grieve so. Look for me in your dreams, my love. I will be back." He reaches out to touch her face, when, suddenly, he is swept along by the eagle's wings. He fights to stay with her, but is locked in an iron grip. He and the eagle are now gliding across the universe. It feels as if he is the wind, impelling himself forward. Then he soars into a glacial blue world, full of misty ice and wonder. A chilling echo startles him and he shivers at the words. "If you are brave, my boy, dare to look deeper. There you will find the edge of the unknown… where death duly beckons."

Hidden Spirit looks down and sees a young girl sitting by a stream, splashing her feet. Thoughts flash through his mind. "Who is this?" he questions aloud. The light is searing in its brightness, and he squints, shielding his eyes. The girl looks like Otter, and he wonders what she is doing in this place. He looks further downstream and sees another girl, walking, but he can't quite make out the face. As he strains harder to see, he almost falls off the eagle's back. The girl looks like Chasing Rabbit. But that can't be. He had just seen her a moment ago. As soon as he starts to panic, the vision fades. Fear grips his heart.

Before he can ponder his vision any further, the boy and the eagle land next to a riveting young Indian—strong, powerful, and handsome.

"Welcome to the other world, Mi-thakoza. I see you have grown to be a fertile young man. You do our people proud."

The handsome warrior comes in closer from the glaring light. He is suddenly older now, great lines creasing his still striking face. He wears a large war bonnet ringed with black feathers, and carries a stick.

"I see you have many questions and heavy burdens on your mind. You, Hidden Spirit, are one of the great ones left to save our people. Our traditions are slowly disappearing, and soon will be gone—like the buffalo. You must light the way for our people and give them hope, even though death is all around."

Hidden Spirit stares. It's his grandfather, Broken Feather, who left this world near the time of his birth. He trembles at the sight of him.

Broken Feather speaks gently. "I will show you sacred rituals that only you shall perform. When you achieve these, I will give you more. But first, you must learn restraint."

Broken Feather reaches out, and lightly brushes his fingers across Hidden Spirit's face. It feels like the cool, misty air he just came from. The noble-looking Indian encircles Hidden Spirit with mesmerizing eyes, and then vaporizes into a cloud of smoke.

A large spotted owl, the size of a horse, lunges down and takes Hidden Spirit on his wings, then dives into an indigo stream. The frigid waters rush over his body and he struggles to breathe. He can feel his skin crack. His blood pours into the water as vivid scenes unfold. Then he is hurled through the air. Hidden Spirit is now looking at a dead Indian, whose eyes stare blankly. As he approaches, the Indian comes alive and sits up—handing him a sacred pipe.

"This will speed your prayers to the Great Spirit, my grandson," says the withered voice. When Hidden Spirit awakes, he notices that he is back in the damp pit. Scared, shivering, and afraid to move, he wonders if he is alive or dead. He can't distinguish between the two.

Hidden Spirit is crouched down covering his eyes and lying on a bed of black-tipped feathers when a bright light glares inside the pit. Then he hears his name. "Grandson, your time is up. Come."

He blinks his eyes and squints into the blinding light as he slowly begins to stand. He is weak, dazed, and naked. Unable to speak, he takes the hand of his grandfather, who helps hoist him out of the hole.

Plenty Feathers speaks to him gently. "I see your visions were powerful, Mi-thazoka." He holds the star blanket in his hands, and wraps it around Hidden Spirit's shoulders, helping him down the hill. A stick floats out of the pit, following behind.

DEVIL AND THE REDSKIN

IT SEEMS TO Chasing Rabbit that they have been here forever. She has lost track of time and nearly all hope of leaving this place. The weather is starting to change—the nights are cooler and the days are growing shorter. But everything else follows the same dull routine: work, prayer, study, more work, and little sleep.

Chasing Rabbit sits by the stream scrubbing clothes as Miss Snodberry hurries over, holding a dress.

"My dear, Mrs. Trimble said to tell you that you're getting careless in your duties. Her dress wasn't cleaned properly, so she wants you to wash it again—thoroughly, this time. It's her Sunday best."

Chasing Rabbit looks at Miss Snodberry, nods her head, and continues to scrub. Then she asks without looking up, "Does Mrs. Trimble tell you when we get to go home?"

"Well, my dear, I don't think it will be for quite some time. We are teaching you new skills so that when you go home you will be able to pursue your dreams."

Chasing Rabbit looks puzzled. "What dream is that? So I can be grumpy like Mrs. Trimble and pray to that white guy on the cross? We loved our life before they made us come here. When I was little, my father used to hunt buffalo and elk and deer.

Then the white eyes came and killed them all. We like praying to our Great Spirit, not your guy on the boards. Opal gets mad at us because we don't believe in that guy. Then she tells us we are like the Devil and will go to Hell. Our dream is to leave this place, and never come back! Maybe Opal will go to Hell, she talks about it so much."

Miss Snodberry looks stunned by the girl's outburst, then her face softens and is full of anguish, and reaches out to smooth Chasing Rabbit's hair.

The girl pushes her hand away.

"I really believe Mrs. Trimble has your best interest at heart, even though she seems grumpy. I think Opal does as well. I wish there was something I could do to help, but if I did, Mrs. Trimble would have my hide and send me packing. I'm sorry." She then hurries back up the hill.

Chasing Rabbit watches Miss Snodberry leave and thinks, *it would be nice if she tried to help us, even if it meant her hide.*

Chasing Rabbit has done her best to follow the rules, but they are so strict, and she's sick of it here *and*, sick of all this work. She hoped they would get tired of her by now, and send her back home. Then she would get help for everyone.

The next day in Mrs. Trimble's class, Chasing Rabbit whispers to Little Moon and gets her knuckles rapped. Then earlier that same day in Opal's class, she scoffs at her lecture and asks, "How is it that your God can be so kind to the white man and so cruel to us?"

Mrs. Crumm stops mid-sentence, and turns around to face Chasing Rabbit. "As I've already told you, your people's beliefs are akin to Devil worship, plain and simple. Before you can reap the Good Lord's benefits, you must tell Him that you were wrong—that you weren't brought up any better. It would help if you prayed nightly, tell Him you believe in His words, and that you will let go of all that heathen nonsense. Then, the Lord will make your life better. Since you have disrupted my class once again with your poppycock, you can now stand in the corner for the remainder of class."

As Chasing Rabbit passes by, Opal whispers under her breath. "The Lord surely won't want a trouble-maker like you."

Chasing Rabbit sticks out her tongue in response, making the girls giggle.

Furious at Chasing Rabbit's behavior, Opal reports her to Mrs. Trimble. "That Rabbit girl is nothing but trouble. She's wild and incorrigible and has a nasty tongue. Just wanted you to know."

At breakfast, a frustrated Mrs. Trimble tells Mrs. Burns what Opal has said.

Between mouthfuls, Mrs. Burns offers her advice. "I know you hate to bother the preacher with his hands full and all—plus his Sunday sermons—but I think you should send the girl to him."

"If she doesn't straighten up, I think I will, regardless."

A few days later Chasing Rabbit is hauling the buckets of water, ready to start her chores, and stares at the massive pile of clothes. Deciding it's far too nice outside for work, she is tempted to roam the vast grounds. She has never been to the other side and wants to see "the forbidden territory." She wants to find out if the boys hate it here as much as she does. Passing under the fence, she spots Long Tail, who is busy chopping wood. Excited and nervous at the same time, she simply bursts out without thinking, "Long Tail, it's me—Chasing Rabbit! How are you?" Her cheeks flush.

Long Tail looks up and smiles, rushing to meet her. "Chasing Rabbit, it's good to see you. I'm glad you're okay." He lowers his eyes. "It's really awful here. Mr. Darrell is cruel, and he beats us. Three of the boys have died. Limping Bear, Stands Tall, and Big Nose."

Chasing Rabbit feels her heart sink at the news, and tears well up in her eyes. "How did that happen?" She reaches for Long Tail's hand, and puts it to her cheek. Abruptly, he jerks his hand away, and runs back to his work.

Turning around to see what frightened him, she spies Mrs. Burns flying across the grounds. By the time she nears Chasing Rabbit, her face is purple with fury, and huffs breathlessly.

"What in God's name do you think you're doing amongst the boys? You know this place is off limits." Grabbing Chasing Rabbit's arm, Mrs. Burns says, "Come with me, you little troublemaker. We'll see what Mrs. Trimble has to say about this." Glaring at Long Tail, she orders him to stop staring and get back to work. Mrs. Burns hustles off to find Mrs. Trimble while pulling a frightened Chasing Rabbit, who stumbles along.

In the kitchen, Mrs. Burns finds Mrs. Trimble with Mrs. Barlapp, discussing the dinner menu. She waits impatiently, tapping her foot, staring at the girl.

"I think a nice lamb stew will do—with those tasty potatoes you fix with that odd spice you like. It's not often we get a fresh lamb for supper. Wonderful neighbors we have in town."

"How about a nice apple pie to go with that?" Mrs. Barlapp adds, firmly.

"Marvelous," Mrs. Trimble says with delight, and looks over at Mrs. Burns, whose face, by this time, is twitching with anger.

"Sorry to disturb you, Mrs. Trimble, but I caught this girl sneaking over to the boys' side," she says, lifting her brows. "I caught her just in time, before any kind of…"

"Yes, yes," Mrs. Trimble says, sternly. "I thank you for your sharp eyes though, Mrs. Burns. Must be vigilant at all times at this school. I do declare, you need eyes in the back of your head with these wild ones." She shoots an icy glare at Chasing Rabbit. "How dare you disobey my rules that were clearly stated when you arrived? Now you will suffer the consequences of your brazen actions." She motions for the girl to follow her to the next building over, through its enormous hallway, which apparently hasn't been cleaned in a long time.

"You will scrub this entire floor until it shines and I can see my face in it. I suggest you get a bucket and brush and start scrubbing. That is, if you want any sleep tonight."

Chasing Rabbit's shoulders slump as she sees the amount of work ahead of her and sighs.

"You will not be having dinner, either," she continues irately and stomps off down the hallway and sees Mrs. Burns walking toward her. The ladies look back at Chasing Rabbit, talking to each other.

She overhears Mrs. Trimble saying to Mrs. Burns. "I'm going to see if Preacher Jim has any recommendations for this incorrigible girl. I am at my wits end."

"Yes, I'm quite certain he will have some tricks up his sleeves." says Mrs. Burns. "He is very diligent about the children's behavior and…" The words drift off down the hallway as the two women walk out of earshot.

Chasing Rabbit finds a bucket, brush, rags, and lye soap. *They use that soap for everything*, she thinks, grimacing. She hates the smell of that stuff—her hands are still raw from scrubbing the clothes, and, it burns. "This job will take forever," she grumbles, looking at the dirt caked about an inch thick on the dilapidated floor. She doubts that Mrs. Trimble will be able to see her grumpy face on these old boards—no matter how hard she scrubs. Sloshing water onto the floor she takes the heavy bristle brush and shoves it back and forth. "Hidden Spirit, are you ever going to come? I wish you would hurry," she says, feeling trapped—her brush leaving muddy streaks as she inches her way down the hallway. She sloshes more water on the floor and continues scrubbing. Soon all is quiet in the building except for the bristles scraping against the boards. *It must be dinnertime*, she thinks, her stomach rumbling, *but not for me*. She works as fast as she can, determined to finish, but she is getting tired—bone tired. Her arms are so stiff she can hardly move them. A big bruise forms on her knees. She sits on the floor and rests for a moment, rubbing her sore knees, then looks down the big, long hallway, not believing the amount of work left to do. *The pictures of those guys hanging in Opal's classroom reminds her of this place—nothing but punishment and suffering.*

Delighted she had hidden her bear claw from the teachers, Chasing Rabbit pulls her blue stone out of her pouch—and kisses each of her precious items before returning them to their hiding place. As she starts back to work, she begins to sing the owl song and thinks of her mama, and how much she misses her. "Oh, sweet owl, I hear your hoot in the night. Oh, smart owl, can you guide me into the light? Your big round eyes, are so beautiful and bright..." Then suddenly she hears her name being called. "Chasing Rabbit." She thinks for a moment it's her mama calling her. Then she hears it again.

"Chasing Rabbit. Over here!"

The girl looks bewildered as she stands up and sees Little Moon hiding in the doorway.

"I brought you some food," says Little Moon breathlessly. "It's not much, but it looks good. Morning Star snuck some leftovers off the teachers' plates, when Mrs. Barlapp wasn't looking. You must be starving."

Chasing Rabbit runs over and hugs her friend. "Oh Little Moon, thank you. My stomach is rumbling really loud." She looks at her friend with concern. "But I don't want you to get caught sneaking me food." Pointing to the long hallway, she says, "Mrs. Trimble will have you doing this next."

"Morning Star told me to be careful," she beams, handing her a carefully wrapped napkin, "and I was."

Smiling at her brave friend, Chasing Rabbit sniffs the food hungrily, and devours the roast pork and bread. "Um-m-m-m, this tastes good. So much better than what they feed us. Would you like a bite?"

Her friend shakes her head, no. "That's for you."

Licking her fingers she smiles at her friend. "Thank you for bringing the food, Little Moon. But you must hurry back—and don't get caught." She kisses her cheek. "I'll be there soon, I think. I hope."

By the time Chasing Rabbit finishes scrubbing the floor, it is well past ten o'clock. Mrs. Trimble is tired and cranky as she comes to check on her progress. Hands on her hips she says, "It's not a very good job. I'd say it's not much better before you started. I suppose you have been lollygagging your time away, daydreaming and such like usual. I think I'll have you... Oh, just go to bed. My head hurts thinking about all the trouble you cause me."

Chasing Rabbit leaves, exhausted. It takes all her energy to make it to her room. As she changes into her nightdress she hears Otter crying. Weary, she crawls into bed beside her, and holds her hand.

Otter says softly, "I don't feel well, Chasing Rabbit. Can you tell me a story?"

Stifling a yawn, Chasing Rabbit hugs Otter, and tells her the story about a buffalo hunt.

"Everyone celebrated the feast," she says. "There was a big dance and women were cooking over the fires as the buffalo roasted. The smell was so wondrous it drifted into the other world, where the Great Spirit looked down and smiled at our happiness. Can you smell the buffalo cooking over the open fires, Otter? Let's pretend we are home celebrating and eating, with juice dribbling down our chins. We can eat until our stomachs bulge. Yummmmm."

Otter stops crying, clinging tightly to Chasing Rabbit's hand. "I love that story, but it makes me sad," she says, starting to cry again.

Chasing Rabbit holds her friend and starts to sing the owl song. When she sees that Otter has finally drifted off to sleep, she kisses her cheek and then passes out from exhaustion.

The next morning, Chasing Rabbit is jostled awake by a deafening sound. Mrs. Burns is banging two pans together as she walks through the room.

"Everyone up! It's getting late," she says, banging the pots together. "No oversleeping today. The morning is waiting, so get out of bed and thank the Lord for the new day."

Chasing Rabbit feels as though she had just gone to sleep. She can't believe it is already time to get up. Stretching out her sore arms, she stumbles out of bed. Her eyes seem stuck together as she rubs away the sleep. After pulling on her oversized dress, she walks to her morning class.

Opal awaits the girls at the door with a brisk, "Good morning girls. Get to your seats! I have a busy schedule today." Everyone files in, yawning.

As they enter the classroom, Chasing Rabbit and Little Moon are caught up in conversation, talking about last night and how tired they are of waking up at the crack of dawn every day and have forgotten about the sleepy Otter.

Little Moon says, "I bet Opal talks about the big black place again. It's her favorite subject."

Chasing Rabbit bristles. "She always tries to scare us about that place—telling us that's where we'll go when we die. I'd rather be with the guy that breathes fire than be with the people at this place. They'd probably make us work even harder than we do now."

Little Moon covers her mouth to laugh, but then turns serious, and says, "The other day Raven told me she hates the color of her skin. I saw her scrubbing her arms really hard, and I asked what she was doing. She told me she was washing the red color off her skin."

"I heard some other girls talk about wanting to be white. It makes me mad the teachers say bad things about us."

"Shush, girls! Class is started."

Opal starts the morning routine of taking roll call. When she gets to Otter, she hears no reply.

"Does anyone know where Otter is?"

No one answers.

Chasing Rabbit whispers to Little Moon. "I told her a story last night, and she said she didn't feel good. But she fell asleep before I finished."

Little Moon says she is probably with Morning Star.

Opal continues, annoyed. "No one has permission to miss my class unless I am told beforehand, and it had better be for a good reason."

Chasing Rabbit raises her hand, and Opal gives her permission to speak. "I think she is ill, Mrs. Crumm. She didn't look well last night. She said her belly ached. This morning, her head was really hot, so she stayed in bed."

"Oh, fiddlesticks!" she says. "Most likely that's just an excuse not to work. I will inform Mrs. Trimble about her absence."

Opal raps the desk. "Let's get started. Time is wasting." She opens the Bible and reads from the book of Psalms. The girls yawn. When she finishes, she starts her lecture about sinners.

"This will be the life of torment you will suffer, if you don't entrust your life to Jesus, the Son of God. This is important. When you girls go home you will…" Opal's words get drowned out as a loud cheer erupts at the sound of the word, 'home.'

"We're going home!" Everyone is standing now, cheering at the news.

Opal tries to regain control of the class, and demands. "Everyone quiet down. This is outrageous," she says, seething with fury. "I don't know why I bother to help you girls… to have an understanding of what awaits you on the other side. I told Preacher Jim beforehand that all this work would be a waste. It's no wonder that… oh, what's the use."

Silence filters throughout the classroom, as the girls stare at the agitated woman. "Class is over," she says, fuming, and huffs out of the room.

The bewildered girls walk toward the door, filled with disappointment. Thoughts of going home are now dashed.

Morning Star is there to greet Chasing Rabbit and Little Moon and gives each of kiss on the cheek. "Good morning girls," she says. "I thought I would get Otter. Is she with you?"

Chasing Rabbit and Little Moon shake their heads.

"We thought she was with you," says Chasing Rabbit. "She didn't want to come to Opal's class. Her head was hot, and I was so sleepy I forgot to ask if she was going to the kitchen. She wasn't feeling well yesterday."

Morning Star looks up and down the hallway. "I'm worried about her. I'll go outside and see if she's in the garden or the barn. She loves it out there. You girls check the room. Hurry."

Concerned for the whereabouts of their little friend, the two girls run down the hallway, hoping to find her in bed. Chasing Rabbit feels guilty for leaving her. Inside the room, she peeks under the bed covers, and calls her name. "Otter. Are you in here?" No answer. "She must be outside," Chasing Rabbit says, worriedly. Little Moon agrees, and they run as fast as they can down the hallway again. Mrs. Burns and Mrs. Trimble see the girls, and Mrs. Trimble calls out. "What are you two doing wandering the halls? There is no running in here, as you very well know. Into the dining room, now."

The two girls scurry past Mrs. Burns and Mrs. Trimble, and head into the dining hall to wait for Morning Star.

Mrs. Trimble wonders what that Chasing Rabbit is up to. Her patience is wearing thin with the child. "That girl is a slacker," she comments to Mrs. Burns. "The floor is worse than when she started cleaning. I let it slip though. I was too tired to administer more punishment. Probably getting too soft," Mrs. Trimble laments. "For the life of me, I can't get used to their silly names," she blurts out. "Maybe, I'll change them to something like… Henrietta or Margaret. Good Christian names. I should have done that upon their arrival, but I wanted to make the girls feel at home, and now look at the mess I've made. Nothing but trouble and my body is weary."

"Pray to the Lord and ask for strength." Mrs. Burns replies. "I say, give them an inch and they'll take a mile. Must say, we had our hands full when those heathens first arrived," the memories still fresh in her mind.

Mrs. Trimble feels rebellion runs deep in that Chasing Rabbit. She considers discussing the problem with Preacher Jim.

*

Morning Star is trying to squelch her fear as she runs into the kitchen, telling Mrs. Barlapp, "I'll be right back." Mrs. Barlapp opens her mouth to respond, but the girl is gone before she can get a word out. Morning Star flies out the door and runs to the barn, calling, "Otter, are you in there?" She stops and listens for the sound of Otter's voice, but all she can hear is Bessie mooing and the squawking of the chickens. Walking inside the barn, she inspects all the stalls, and again calls out to Otter. This time she hears a moan. "Otter, where are you?" Looking around in the dim light, she finally finds the young girl lying in a stack of hay, trying to sit up. "Oh, my sweet Otter. What are you doing out here?"

"I don't feel good."

Morning Star gathers her up in her arms. "Why didn't you tell me you were sick?"

"I always feel better out here," says Otter weakly, as Morning Star picks her up, takes her hand, and walks her to the kitchen.

Mrs. Barlapp is at the stove, tossing hunks of ham into the skillet as it spits and sputters from the hot grease. Waves of tempting odors float across the room.

"What on earth are you doing with that child?" Mrs. Barlapp demands, pointing her fork at Otter. "That girl will be spoiled rotten, if you ask me, with all that coddling you do." She hurries over to make a pot of coffee on the potbelly stove.

Morning Star sits the ailing Otter in the corner, wrapping a towel around the shivering girl, as Mrs. Barlapp gives her a nasty glare.

"She's ill, Mrs. Barlapp. I think she needs to go to bed."

"Nonsense. Probably has gas, is all. Nothing like a good dose of castor oil to cure her ails. Now, we don't have time for that nonsense. I'm running behind," Mrs. Barlapp snaps, bustling about the kitchen. "The potatoes haven't been peeled yet and there's eggs to be cooked." She nods toward the bowl. "Start peeling. See about the girl later."

Morning Star's muscles are tense from worry as she peels haphazardly. Glancing over at Otter crouching in the corner, she can see her face is as pale as a ghost. Half of the potato goes into the bucket and what is left goes into the sizzling skillet. Morning Star doesn't care. She can't wait for breakfast to be over as Mrs. Barlapp bosses her about, sending her on numerous errands. Finally breakfast is ready. Laden with platters of ham, potatoes, and eggs, she carefully sets the dishes down at the teachers' table. Mrs. Barlapp follows behind with the coffee.

Morning Star takes a pitcher of milk and bread to the girls' table. Little Moon and Chasing Rabbit are anxious for news about Otter. "Did you find her?"

Morning Star nods her head. "In the barn. I'm taking her to bed when I'm finished. I don't care what Mrs. Trimble or Barlapp say."

"We want to come with you," Chasing Rabbit says with pleading eyes. "I don't care what Mrs. Trimble says, either."

"No, Chasing Rabbit. You're already in trouble. Come when class is over. I have to go now." She kisses each girl on top of their head before dashing back to the kitchen.

At the sight of Morning Star, Mrs. Barlapp throws her hands into the air, furious.

"That girl threw up on my floor, and it smells to high heaven in here. Get it cleaned up before my food is ruined."

Morning Star looks at the mess, and then runs over to Otter, who is shivering uncontrollably.

"Otter," she cries, touching her forehead. "You're burning up," she says in alarm. "I'm taking you to bed."

Morning Star picks up the frail little girl and rushes her out of the kitchen as a livid Mrs. Barlapp expresses her outrage, shouting. "You get back here and clean this mess up. This very instant!"

Morning Star ignores the woman and pushes past her. She hurries with Otter down the hallway and into her room, where she lays the girl gently on her bed. Morning Star can hardly believe this is the same little girl who came here months before. "You're so frail," she whispers, and quickly pulls off Otter's stained clothing, then wraps a thin blanket around her shaking body.

Otter's eyes flutter open as she looks at Morning Star, and says weakly, "I tried hard not to get sick, but I... I..." Her teeth chatter as she speaks.

"Shhh," says Morning Star as she rubs her burning forehead, her body soaked with perspiration.

"I won't get to see Mama, will I?" Otter says, in a muffled tone.

Morning Star nods her head, and smiles. "Of course you will... very soon." She is frantic with worry as she tries to comfort Otter and holds the little girl in her arms, wiping her brow with a sheet. Otter's eyes are sunken with fever and fatigue. "Don't talk now, little one," says Morning Star, kissing her cheek. "You need to save your strength so you can get well." She murmurs under her breath, "Please get well," and rocks Otter back and forth. By now, Otter's breath is so slight that Morning Star has to put her ear to the girl's chest to make sure she is breathing. Otter is quiet now, eyes closed, her head on Morning Star's shoulder. Then, suddenly, Otter's eyes open wide, and she stares at the wall.

"Someone called my name, Morning Star," she whispers. "I saw a warrior wearing a big war bonnet. He said his name is Broken Feather." Her face lights up. "He seems happy to see me. He told me that I will have a new home soon, where I will float on the clouds and sing with the birds." Otter's face beams as she struggles to breathe. "He is waiting for me." Otter touches Morning Star's face, her voice so faint, Morning Star can barely hear. "Can you see him?"

Morning Star shakes her head, afraid to speak, afraid to look up.

"He's right here, beside me," says Otter as a smile crosses her face. "I can almost touch him. Morning Star... look!"

Keeper of the Souls – Book 1

A soft glow flickers above, seeming to dance around the little girl. Otter smiles as she stares at the image that only she could see. She looks so peaceful that Morning Star cannot argue with her. As she struggles to sit up, Otter's tiny hands reach toward the invisible being. Her body tingles with excitement. She takes one last valiant breath, then her body falls limp and slumps down into Morning Star's arms.

The light hovers above Morning Star and the lifeless Otter for a brief moment, twinkling ever so slightly, then whizzes off, leaving the tearful Morning Star in wonder. "What will I tell your mama?"

Otter's eyes stare off into the distance, her serene face contoured in peace. A slight smile forms on her lips. *She looks beautiful.*

Morning Star runs her fingers across Otter's forehead. For the first time in months, the child looks happy. "I'll tell your mama that you're home," she says between tears, "with people who love you."

Morning Star rocks Otter back and forth, singing the death song, then she whispers, "Goodbye, my little friend."

Chasing Rabbit and Little Moon fly into the room, eyes aghast. They look at Otter's limp body and then at the distraught Morning Star. Her face says it all.

"No, Otter," screams Chasing Rabbit. She runs over, takes Otter's hand, and kisses it. "I'm sorry I didn't help you this morning. Please don't go!" Falling to her knees, sobbing uncontrollably, she begs her friend to stay. "Come back, come back."

Little Moon's heart is filled with grief and she stares blankly, unable to speak. Tears stream freely down her face as she bends over and kisses Otter's pale cheeks, dripping pools of tears.

The three girls cling to one another, cradling Otter, trying to ease their pain. It seems like a bad dream. It's hard to believe their little friend is gone from this world so soon. Morning Star thinks of Otter's mother and the pain she will feel upon receiving the sad news.

Then something inexplicable happens. Morning Star sees a glimmering orange glow, and nudges Chasing Rabbit and Little Moon. "Look! Over by the window. Do you see a faint light? It's glowing."

Chasing Rabbit and Little Moon scrunch their tear-stained eyes and notice an orange light flicker in the corner, throwing rainbows of colors against the wall. Then the soft glow whizzed overhead. The face of Otter reflects in the light. She's smiling. The girls cry out and wave as the soft glow whirls and dances happily around the room. "Otter, we see you... we do!" Beside themselves with happiness, the girls blow kisses. "Goodbye, Otter. We love you." In unison, they say, "*Kadishday dayden.*"

As the light disappears, a lone black feather drifts in from the window and falls to the floor. The girls rush over and pick up the feather, a parting gift from Otter.

TROUBLE COMES RIDING INTO TOWN

I T'S A WARM autumn evening as Will Wigley sits on the porch rocking back in his chair, smoking a wilted cigar. He is waiting for his friend Jeb Snodgrass, while calculating some plans. Will is twenty-one years old and about to retire. He came from nowhere and grew up on the road with his Pa. They would never stay in one place for long—always on the move. His pa wasn't much of a fighter, but he was a real good thief and gambler. Occasionally he got caught cheating at cards, but he could usually talk himself out of trouble. He even robbed a train once and took nine-year-old Will along with him to bag the loot. Will liked that. With Pa holding the gun on the passengers, he thought himself real slick when he said to them, "I'll take whatever po-ssessions ya got, an don't be cheating me, neither." His Pa spent most of his money on drink and women of ill-repute and he taught young Will everything he knew about his trade, which included keeping a straight face and being darn lucky. When Will was sixteen, his Pa got shot robbing a bank. The sheriff caught Will and told him, "Two possibilities, young man. You could either go to jail or join the army." So, Will joined up and found himself in the stockade a few times for misbehaving. He had just been doing small stuff, like stealing whiskey and cheating the soldiers out of their pay while playing cards.

He even stole a load of food from the kitchen to sell back to the soldiers. But the time he got into real trouble was when he stole the sergeant's horse. The captain had had it with Will by then and threatened to lock him up for good. "You've got a break, boy. This is your lucky day. There's a post on the Indian reservation, and no one's volunteered for the job. So, if you don't want the stockade, that's where you're headed."

Will put up a fuss at first—no way he wanted a post with no women or booze, gambling to occupy his time. But realizing he had no choice, he quickly agreed. Once he settled in on the reservation, he got to snooping around and thought to himself, *this could be a money-making little business.* Fortunately for him, the captain never mentioned a thing about his misdeeds to the good Otis Peale, who was trusting and at times, gullible. So Will decided to impress the man with some stories he'd made up. "I shot my way outta a situation with a band of renegades. They had me surrounded, so I killed the nasty savages. Then there was the time I saved a drowning woman from a raging river... swam way out in the middle to save her. Drug her back ta shore and gave her some mouth ta mouth... 'susatated her back ta life." Bragging about his military prowess, he chortled, "I'm dedicated to servin' my country an' would be real honored ta serve you, too."

Peale about fell over at those words. "Well, I am most grateful to you and the captain. You never know when I might need somebody such as yourself." Patting Will on the back, Peale said, "The storage house will be your job, and you can run it any way you see fit. Order what you need. I've got a load of work to do here. Plus, the missionaries got a passel of souls to save."

Will about wet himself at the news and went on his way, passing the two missionaries.

Snickering at the sight of those old sourpusses, Will hollered out. "Howdy, ladies. Mighty fine day ain't it?" And gave a bow.

The missionaries scooted to the other side of the road, giving him a suspicious look.

Homely bunch, for sure, Will thought. *They stick their snouts in the air like they is somethin' real important. They can kiss my sweet ole ass.*

Peale would have to be mighty desperate if he had eyes for either of those old bags. *I'd say he ain't gotta dog's chance in Hell of gettin' 'em in the hay, neither.* Will bursts out laughing at his thoughts. Still, those two snippety ole bags were relentless in their quest for saving souls. Once they came by and tried to convert him.

"You need to set a good example on the reservation, young man, and that requires your attending church." His eyes bulged out at those words. He wasn't having any of that malarkey, so he said, "Get on outta here," and he shoved those two righteous do-gooders right out the door, lickety-split. The missionaries bristled as they hurried away, looking back in dismay at the rude young man. He gave them the finger for good measure and hollered, "Go tote your Bible business elsewhere," and slammed the door shut. He snickered to himself. *I got my own idea of convertin'.* "I'm gonna convert me some fine young ladies that's ripe as summer rain. They're gonna work fer me in my whorehouse when I'm finished here with my business."

Will can hardly wait to get out of this place, but in the meantime he has a lot of figuring to do. At the rate he's going, he calculates he should be able to skedaddle out of here in another couple months at the most. Ever since he arrived, he has been selling off supplies—a little more each month. He even requested that the government send out another shipment—and they complied. Will wiggles in his seat thinking about his profits. *Like stealin' candy from toddlers,* he thinks. *It's that easy.*

He grins to himself, thinking, *I got my supply house 'bout full to the brim. When those Indians complain, I tell 'em that's all I got—maybe more next month. Some of 'em even come beggin', sayin they're starvin', asking why the government ain't sendin' their food. I tell 'em some made-up story, like they got held up or some such baloney. After all, I gotta business to run. Peale doesn't do anything when the Injun's whine to him. He says that's not his job, and for them to come and see me. I do thank my daddy for teaching me how to use my noggin'. He said I could steal people blind if I wanted— that all I had ta do was be smart 'bout it. I'm gonna be smarter'n my pa, though, and not get shot dead.*

Will is feeling pretty confident, wondering when Jeb would show up. He wants to finalize his plans with him.

Jeb is a 19-year old who likes to think of himself as a sharpshooter, like Billy the Kid. He brags and blusters, "I'm gonna be just like him." Although Will doesn't expect that to happen, he keeps his opinions to himself. Jeb is from a dirt poor family in Virginia, the oldest of eleven siblings. When he was fifteen, he ran away from home, taking odd jobs of any sort. He made it through the fourth grade and Will made it to the fifth, barely. They met in a Nebraska saloon, where Will was playing cards and Jeb was sweeping the floor. Once Jeb saw Will cheat, but he didn't say a word till afterward. "That was mighty slick," he said. They sat at the bar talking late into the night. Will told him he was on his way to the reservation. Jeb laughed at him for going. He couldn't believe it.

Well, he ain't gonna laugh now when he sees what I've been up to, Will thinks to himself with a grin. *Jeb can't count real good, so I could cheat him outta his cut and he wouldn't even know it. I could tell him it's a fifty-fifty split right down the middle and he'd be happier than a hog in shit.* The only thing Will can't stand about Jeb is his nose-picking. It's a nervous habit, which Will finds disgusting. But other than that, Jeb is a perfect partner.

Just before suppertime, Jeb finally arrives. Hooves come flying down the road, and he hollers out, "Is this the right hell-hole, or did I miss it?" Howling with laughter, he hops off his horse, rubbing his behind. "Oooh, I'm a bit stiff. That's quite a ride from Tucker," he says, smacking his lips. "Ya got anythin' ta loosen me up a bit?"

Will walks over, and shakes his hand. "Ya made good time, Jeb. Mighty glad to see ya."

"What ya got up yer sleeve? Bet it's somethin' real big," says Jeb, looking around, curiously. "No wonder they gave this place to the Injuns." He chuckles. "Just a bunch of weeds and dirt. How do you stand it here? A man could get mighty lonely with nothin' for company but some ugly squaws." Jeb hesitates a moment, eyes Will, then says cautiously, "Or maybe you like 'em."

Will glares at his friend. "I got more 'portant things on my mind right now, Jeb, like makin' money. Lots of it. Then I'm gonna have me all the whiskey and women I want. Yer lucky I'm countin' you in on the deal. Let's go inside and have us a drink."

As they walk inside, Jeb takes a look around the room, and lets out a whistle. "Nice little set-up ya got here."

There is a table with two worn chairs next to a window with torn yellow curtains, and a rusty brass bed with a saggy mattress in the corner and a drape for a partition hanging over the front. In the middle of the room sits a pot-bellied stove, with a tin pot of coffee brewing on top. A small leak is coming out the stovepipe, but that doesn't bother Will. He has all the comforts of home.

Jeb says, sniffing, "Ya got anythin' stronger than what's brewing on the stove?"

Will bends down, reaches under his bed, and pulls out a heavy case full of some strong brew. He yanks out a shiny bottle and pours Jeb a glass of whiskey. Before Will has a chance to fill his own glass, Jeb drinks it down in one gulp.

"How 'bout another one of those, partner? Heck of a long ride," says Jeb.

Will pours him another and Jeb drinks that one down just as fast. Jeb begins to slur. "Fill 'er up, partner, I'm just gittin' started." Will is getting annoyed as he hands him the bottle and watches as Jeb downs a good portion of the whiskey in one long swallow. After letting out a satisfying belch, Jeb sits the bottle on the table. "That took care of the dust in my pipes," he says, wiping his lips. "Might need another snort for my sore ass."

"Look here, we got business to attend to, an' I don't want ya gettin' all liquored up. So this one's it. Then I want ya to listen up."

"Just was thirsty, is all," Jeb says, wiping some grime off his chin.

"I gotta big job for ya, if ya think yer up for it," says Will. Need a man that can handle his pistol with a steady hand an' can shoot faster than a bolt of lightnin'."

"Think ya called the right man, Will. What's this all about, anyways? Get caught cheatin' at cards and got someone ya want me to settle with?"

Will pulls up a chair and says, "Remember Elmer Fink, who drove the stagecoach for a bit and now works in a livery stable in Tucker?"

Jeb nods. "Yeah, he's a grouchy ole coot, always chewin' and spittin' out his tobacco."

"Yup, that's him. I got a note I want ya to take to him. It explains where he's gonna pick up a wagon full of whiskey and where we're gonna meet him. Everything's in there. He can wire me if there's a hitch. Then we're gonna head over to the post at Henderson an' sell it to some thirsty soldiers. That'll give us some booty. An' wait'll ya see my big stash of food. Come an get a gander of this." He walks to the door in the back room and swings it open, with a big proud grin.

Jeb's eyes widen as he looks inside. There is enough food to feed an army. Sacks of beans, flour, salt pork, coffee, sugar, and more. "That's why I like bein' yer partner," says Jeb, slapping Will on the back. "You don't do nuthin' halfway."

"Now, once you finish with Elmer, there's somethin' else I want you to do," Will says, collecting his thoughts. "I know you're good with yer gun, and yer a good tracker, besides. So I want ya to go into the hills and find this Injun kid who calls himself Hidden Spirit—or somethin' like that. He lives up somewhere in those hills. I got me some unfinished business with him. Caught him off the reservation a while back huntin' on some rancher's property. But, dang, he got away. Sneaky kid. Ain't seen hide nor hair of him since. What you're gonna do once ya find him, is shoot him in the head—dead."

Jeb looks at Will suspiciously. "Why don't *you* go on up there?"

Annoyed, Will says again. "I told ya. I got lots to tend to right here. Peale likes me to stay close by in case any problems get loose with them Injuns. So if we're gonna split fifty-fifty down the middle, then you gotta earn yer share of the profits. I've done everythin' else. Remember, I'm the brains around here an' yer the gunslinger."

"Well, yeah," Jeb says, puffing his chest. "I been known to be as slick as a whistle with my pistol, an' faster'n a jackrabbit chased by a pack of coyotes."

Hiding a grin, Will says, "Here's an idea. Why don't you take a bottle along for company? Might keep ya from gettin' dry along the way. And ta make it more interestin'... ya catch that Injun kid, and there's five Lincolns waitin' fer ya."

Jeb's eyes light up at the thought of whiskey, but wonders about the Lincolns—not sure what or who that is. *Might be more whiskey*, he thinks, so he blurts out, "Deal."

Will thinks he'd just leave out about how strange these Indians can be... dark magic around them, and stuff. *He'll find that out soon enough.*

A couple of weeks have passed since Jeb left the reservation. Will is working in the storage room one afternoon, counting the sacks of flour and coffee and beans and everything else he has stashed away. Concentrating on his work he doesn't hear Jeb ride up. Will is startled when his partner runs inside his living quarters, hollering up a storm. "I need me a drink. A big tall one... and don't bother with no glass, neither. Hurry it up!"

Will drops a bag of flour and comes running out of the storage room, looking at Jeb like he is crazy... eyes all bugged out. "What the dickens is wrong with ya? You come running in here like a wild man, hollering an all. Some fine partner yer gonna be." Will looks at Jeb quizzically, and says hiding a grin, "You act like ya seen a ghost."

Panting, Jeb says in a high-pitched voice, "Well, I'm tellin' ya... there's somethin' fishy going on in those hills, an' don't be laughin' ta me 'bout ghosts. I seen 'em with my own two eyes."

Will hands Jeb a bottle of whiskey to calm him down. He wants to get to the bottom of what he is talking about. "Whaddaya mean, ya saw a ghost up there?"

Slugging the whiskey, Jeb says, "After I finished my business with Elmer, I rode in the hills like you said. Stopped at a few other camps 'long the way... and then I come upon a camp with some Injun sittin' by his tepee an' smokin' a big ole pipe. I thought I'd ruffle his feathers a bit, so I hollered out, 'Hey ole man, I'm lookin' for some Indian kid they call Hidden Spits...

somethin' like that. Ya seen him 'round these hills?" Will takes a real big drink, and continues.

"Now I was real polite-like 'til I saw he was ignorin' me and just kept on smokin' his big ole pipe. That made me real mad, so I says, 'Whaddaya doing sittin' out here like you's some kinda stachew.' The ole man still didn't answer, so I hollered, 'Are ya deaf or just plain stupid?' I figured he's a little of both an' I was gettin' sick of these Injuns, anyways. Besides, if they see me comin', they just turn their backs on me like I wasn't there, an give a smirk. I woulda liked to shoot the whole dang bunch of 'em, but I didn't want to waste my bullets. This was the final stick in my craw, so I decided I was gonna have a little fun… see if'n he answers me this time. I pulled out my pistol and hollered real loud, just in case he was deaf. That Injun looked old enough to be six-feet under, all withered an' wrinkly-like. So I says, 'Hey, Chief, why don't ya let me have a look inside o' that wikiwup of yers. You got any hides in there? I could use me a nice warm beaver skin. Or how 'bout some liquor? You Injuns get caught drinkin' the juice, an' they'll send ya to the clinker—the crazy way it makes ya act, an' all.' The old man still didn't say a word, so I pulled out my gun and gave it a twirl, thinking ole Chief might react. He didn't, so I took aim an' shot a feather hangin' from his pipe clean off. The ole coot just sat there an' didn't blink er even budge. I was really gettin' mad and I wasn't gonna let him get the better of me, so I says, 'How 'bout I blow yer head off? Maybe that'll get yer 'tention.'" Jeb takes another slug of whisky. "Next thing I knew, I felt somethin' ruffle my hair, and my hat started to lift right off'n the top of my head. I grabbed ahold of it an' shoved it down, real tight. I glared real hard at that Injun, an' he just stared straight ahead, like nothin' happened. Thought it was the wind, but I was a little more cautious this time as I swung my leg 'round my horse, an' looked around real good to see if anyone else was there. Coast was clear, so I hopped to the ground. But soon as I did I felt this stinging jolt shoot right up my leg, like I stepped on a big-ass rattler or something. It gave me a twitch I couldn't stop. Then, outta the blue, the twitchin' stopped… quick as it started. I fell to the ground, hard…'bout knocked my front tooth loose. That Injun starts a-laughin', tryin' to make a fool outta me. 'Lookie here,' I told him. 'I ain't nothing to mess with.' That's when I pulled out my gun and told him to stick 'em up—real high, too. 'I'm gonna take a look inside that tepee,'" I said. "Then, out of the blue, something real big flew over and walloped me on the side of my head. I gotta big ole lump right here, too. Well, when I looked at the ole coot, I 'bout jumped outta my britches. Something was drifting on over. I had ta blink a few times. Then I saw two big ole eyes starin' right at me. No face or nothin'. Just eyes starin' outta a big feathered hat, floatin' on over. Real spooky-like. Now I was done, so I hopped on my horse and rode like the devil outta that place. You ain't never sendin' me back there again, no matter how much liquor you give me. Don't care 'bout those Lincolns, neither—whoever they are."

"Now, Jeb, sounds to me like you was seeing things, is all. Some people get all scaredy-like being around them Injuns. Some say they can do that to ya, but they ain't done that to me, and I been here a good long while. Here, have another drink and settle down."

DEATH AWAITS FOR THOSE WHO DALLY

TWO DAYS HAVE passed since Otter's death. Preacher Jim hurries inside the dining room to make an announcement during lunchtime. "I will hold services in Opal's classroom after supper for the Otter girl, who recently passed. Everyone may attend." A lilt of excitement fills his voice. "Also, my children, I have a special guest, who will be arriving momentarily. After services you will sing a song that Opal has selected to welcome him."

Then he strolls out of the room, his face beaming.

Otter's body lies in a gunnysack on Opal's table in the classroom, surrounded by a mound of colorful wild flowers that Miss Snodberry recently picked for the services. She wonders why he would use a flour sack to bury her in, thinking the little girl deserves better. When Miss Snodberry timidly mentions it to him, Preacher Jim shrugs off her concern. "We don't have the money for a coffin. This will do fine. Just pick a few more flowers to cover the bag and scatter them over the top. She won't know the difference... and the good Lord won't mind, either. He will smile upon her, regardless."

That same evening, Preacher Jim stands up front nodding at the girls as they file into the room and circle the table to view Otter's body.

Chasing Rabbit holds Little Moon's hand as they near their sweet friend and she bursts into tears—Otter's memory still raw in her mind. A wave of sadness fills her. She tries to focus on her last vision of Otter—swaying in the light. But all she can see now is Otter stuffed inside a sack, like her life held no meaning… especially for these people. The sadness takes her breath away, as Chasing Rabbit touches the lifeless body in the flour sack, and whispers in her grief, "*thechihila.*"

Preacher Jim clears his throat, signaling everyone to take a seat. "My children, this is indeed a solemn occasion. One of our little ones has departed this world, and is on her way to heaven to be with Jesus, who will be waiting at the pearly gates to welcome her. I know everyone's heart is heavy with sadness, but life must go on."

The girls are silent as they listen to Preacher Jim speak. "As you have most likely heard, a few of the boys have died, as well. Mr. Darrell said they were unruly, and that strict measures had to be taken. I gave them a Christian burial. Of course, the Otter girl will be buried separately from the boys." Preacher Jim lowers his voice and speaks solemnly. "You must understand that it was the Lord's wish to bring this little heathen into His folds. You must be grateful she came here—in time to become one of God's children, rather than suffer the path to Hell. It is unfortunate that the boys still had the heathen blood in them and were too wild and unwilling to follow our rules. But fret no more about them. I have prayed for their salvation and asked the Lord to make an exception for them and to receive them into His fold. Please concern yourselves about where you will go when the Lord calls."

Preacher Jim straightens, smiles, and calls out. "Now, it is with great pleasure and honor to surprise you with our special guest, Mr. Otis Peale. He has traveled from your reservation out here to see your progress. I am sorry to say it is in time of sadness that he arrives, but we will sing praises to him. Make him proud of all your accomplishments."

The girls look with skepticism at Otis Peale, especially Chasing Rabbit, who openly glares at the man. "He's the reason we are here," she says to Little Moon, with bitterness.

Opal quickly rushes over and assembles the girls around the piano, instructing them. "We will sing, 'Jesus Loves Me.' We have sung this song enough times by now, so there is no excuse for not doing it correctly." She plunks a few chords on the piano and says, "Let's begin."

In hushed tones, the girls sing:
Jesus loves me, this I know,
For the Bible tells me so,
Little ones to Him belong,
They are weak, but He is strong...
Yes, Jesus loves me...

Otis leans over to Preacher Jim. "Well done, Jimmy. You have surprised me with how well behaved everyone is. I know you feel bad that one of your heathens has died, but that is to be expected. So, congratulations! I didn't think you would be able to turn them around."

Preacher Jim beams in his delight at his friend's words. As the children file out of the room, he bids them good-night. "Good job, girls. Now go finish your chores, and say your prayers before bedtime."

*

Chasing Rabbit is sick of it here—rules, work and the incessant preaching. And she is sick of hearing how sinful their parents are and that the Great Spirit is so evil. So on this bright sunny day she looks up at the blue sky, wishing she could float along on the big puffy cloud overhead. Her arms aching from scrubbing the piles of clothes, she decides she needs a little exploring. It doesn't matter to her the consequences—she is used to them by now, getting into more trouble with each passing week. A few days earlier, Mrs. Trimble found sand in her dress, which made the woman livid. There was also the day Chasing Rabbit left her chores unfinished and had her ears boxed as punishment. She was also caught speaking her Lakota language, for which she got her mouth washed out with lye soap and the strap. Mrs. Trimble was beside herself with this unruly girl and would like to tan her hide, but good. Instead she decides to leave that endeavor to Preacher Jim. *He will put Chasing Rabbit in her place, once and for all,* she thinks. *He has the hand of God. He will remove her insolence.*

*

Chasing Rabbit has heard rumors about the boys who died after they tried to run away and were caught. Preacher Jim had told the girls that they were unruly and savage, and needed to be punished for their crimes. 'The boys brought their demise upon themselves, so where they end up, is no longer my concern.' He designated a spot up the hill, behind the school, for their burial site. No services were provided. The girls were not even allowed to go there to say their goodbyes and Mrs. Trimble didn't have the decency to tell the girls what happened. She simply said when asked, "It would only cause some type of ruckus and disrupt your classes. I didn't want any of that. Besides, it wasn't necessary."

Today, on this sunny morning, Chasing Rabbit is determined to see where the boys are buried. So off she goes, leaving the last pile of laundry for later. Scurrying across the grounds, she waves to one of the boys, who looks back at her in surprise as she hurries up the hill through a row of oak trees and stops for a moment to look at the surroundings. She sees a family of squirrels scampering about, reminding her of a time when she would play—running and laughing with her friends. She sighs—wishing she were home with her family. Then, realizing she had better hurry, she sprints off once again. Nearing the top of the hill, she skids to a stop, and looks on in dread. "It's Preacher Jim!" She moans.

He is on his hands and knees, with head bowed, near a mound of dirt. *It looks like a gravesite*, she thinks. "It's probably where he buried the boys," Chasing Rabbit whispers, feeling an intense wave of sadness course through her. Chasing Rabbit slowly slides behind a nearby sycamore, and presses her trembling hands against the tree. Gathering her resolve, she slowly peers around the side to watch Preacher Jim—and listens, with mouth agape.

"Dear God… dear God… my life is in torment with all the lost souls at this school. I try and try, but the demands are great. One of the young heathens died, and I could not prevent it. Do not blame me for her death," he begs. "The boys on the other-hand are a different matter. I didn't take the time to work harder, dear Lord, to change them, to turn them into God-fearing Christians. I don't know what more I could have done. Please forgive my shortcomings. I have been hearing voices lately, commanding me, to bring them to you. I'm sorry I displease you." Then, Preacher Jim starts to bang his head on the mound of dirt, up and down, while bemoaning his fate—about the heathens, the school, the sacrifices he makes everyday. Blood drips from his forehead, after much repenting, then he abruptly stands, as if a bolt of lightning had struck him. He runs as fast as a jackrabbit while screaming out for forgiveness as he looks to the sky with hands raised.

Chasing Rabbit is rooted to the spot, eyes wide, and before she can move a muscle, Preacher Jim runs smack into her, knocking them both off balance. The preacher yelps in surprise, and sputters. "What in the devil are you doing up here?" he asks, his eyes flickering with anger. "Spying on me?" Chasing Rabbit's throat constricts, and she stammers. "I... I... uh... I wanted to see Otter," she gushes out, "and the boys. I wanted to say goodbye to them." She quickly looks down at her feet. "I wanted to pray that they would go to heaven," she says, trying to conceal her lie. "With that white guy on the cross."

"I think we have some serious work ahead of us," Preacher Jim says, pulling at his brows. "You know this place is off limits to you. I believe Mrs. Trimble stated that fact quite clearly. Now you have put me in a wicked, dreadful position. I will have to ask the Heavenly Father what to do." Preacher Jim pulls at his brows again. "I offer you my guidance and service, but you rebel and sneak around like a thief. My time is valuable, but I will sacrifice it to save you," he says, looking upward, "I have given my word."

*

Chasing Rabbit walks down the path, kicking stones on her way to Preacher Jim's office. She doesn't care if she is late. It's just another miserable day at this miserable place, and she is tired of going there. It seems like she's been going there forever. She can't understand why the Great Spirit sent her to this awful place and looks up to the sky for answers, kicking another stone as she moves forward. "I hate it here, Great Spirit. Please send us home." Hearing no reply, she trudges off down the path. *I hope He gives me an answer soon because I'm not sure how much longer I can stand being here among the white people forcing me to change.* A twinge of guilt fills her. She reprimands herself. *I shouldn't be thinking of myself, especially since Otter just died.* She looks up the sky once again, and whispers, "I hope you're happy, Otter. I'm not, but I'm trying to be good." Absently she pulls her bear claw out of her pouch and looks at the long curved nail. She closes her palms tight, squeezing as hard as she can until it bites into her hand, leaving imprints. Closing her eyes, she imagines being as strong and fierce as the bear. She feels the bear's power trickle up then surge throughout her body. *I know it will help me get through another boring lecture, with Preacher Jim,* she thinks. *It will help me be brave.* Looking toward the barn, she sees Little Moon running toward her, seemingly upset. As she approaches, she hugs her friend tightly around her neck.

Little Moon is breathless. "Do you think we'll all die here, Chasing Rabbit?"

Taking her hand, Chasing Rabbit asks, "Why do you say that, Little Moon? Has something happened?"

"I had bad pictures in my dream last night about darkness filling me up. And today in the barn I heard Mrs. Burns say to Miss Snodberry that at the rate we're going, we'll be lucky to see God's green fields. I think she was mad at Brown Dove for not doing a good job cleaning out the chicken coop. But the bad feeling hasn't gone away, and I'm afraid."

Chasing Rabbit touches her friend's cheek. "I have something that might make the bad feeling go away," she says as she holds up the bear claw and presses it into Little Moon's hand. "Hold this real tight, and wait for the power to come. Then you won't be afraid anymore."

Little Moon squeezes the bear claw, and closes her eyes.

"Can you feel its power yet?"

Little Moon waits a moment, still squeezing the claw tight. "My arm is tingling," she beams, opening her eyes. "You're right. It does have power. You're very lucky to have a bear claw. I wish I had one. Then, I could be brave like you."

"Well," Chasing Rabbit says, "why don't you keep it for a while? Hidden Spirit wouldn't mind. He'd be sad to see you afraid, and would want you to stay strong."

Little Moon can hardly believe it as she looks at the bear claw in awe. "Oh, Chasing Rabbit, are you sure? Your brother said it was special. It's your totem."

"I can share my totem with my best friend, can't I? You keep the bear claw with you. I'll be fine. Besides, look—I still have my special blue stone." Smiling, she holds the stone up to the light, watching the brilliant colors sparkle.

Little Moon feels better. "Maybe you could tell Preacher Jim about our Great Spirit, and how wonderful He is. He could pray to Him like we do, in secret. And he might even like the Great Spirit better than the guy on the boards. Maybe then he'd be nicer to us."

Chasing Rabbit isn't sure about that, but smiles at her friend. "I guess I'd better hurry. I'm already late." She takes Little Moon's hand, and kisses her cheek. "I'm glad you're my friend," she says sweetly, and then turns and walks down the path, kicking a big round stone, sending it skittering aside. Halfway down, she turns around to see Little Moon waving at her, shouting, "Thanks, *mi-kola*."

A few minutes later, she's at Preacher Jim's door, ready to knock, then stops and groans as she reads the new sign on his door, chiseled in crooked letters: ENTER THE KINGDOM. Butterflies flutter in her stomach. *The Kingdom surely isn't here*, she thinks, as the door abruptly swings open. Preacher Jim is standing there—his bushy eyebrows bobbing in annoyance. "Well, well, my little child of God is late," he says, waving her inside.

The preacher looks disheveled—his hair askew, shirt stained, and his face haggard. *He seems odd today*, she thinks, then dismisses the thought. *He's always odd.* But the feeling she has in her belly makes her uneasy. "Take a seat," he says gruffly, and gives her a strange look. "I'll be back momentarily."

Chasing Rabbit swings her legs back and forth to ease her

apprehension and boredom. She looks around at the spacious room and its heavy furnishings, which she has etched in her memory. A few ugly red brocade chairs frame the fireplace and a bulky wooden desk stands near the window with carvings of the cross on its battered legs. A large, pale blue rug with holes and frayed edges sits underneath. The top of the desk is strewn with papers and books, and in the middle sits a dimly lit kerosene lamp with black smoke curling up, drifting across the room and casting a hazy glow. She wrinkles her nose from the acrid smell.

Preacher Jim goes to his desk, and then walks over with his Bible in hand, and sits next to her, crossing his long legs, idly swinging his foot up and down. As if collecting his thoughts, he says, "I heard the words of the Lord last night, and guess what He said?"

Chasing Rabbit doesn't particularly care and stays quiet, not trusting her voice or her words.

Preacher Jim continues in a low voice. "He told me I should read to you from the Book of Psalms, so that you may believe His words. He tells me that you are defiant and must be reigned in." The preacher opens the Bible carefully, and starts to read in a monotonous tone. "Blessed is the one who does not walk in step with the wicked..."

Chasing Rabbit wishes he would just dole out her punishment, so she can leave. She doesn't care if she has to scrub floors for a week straight, or go without dinner; she just wants to get out of here. She thinks, *nothing can be worse than sitting in this smelly room with this wretched man.* Finally, after what seems like hours of tedious repetition, Preacher Jim, slams the Bible shut and says, "I must make you a faithful follower, my child. I can see that you are resistant."

Chasing Rabbit says nothing, but looks at him with a trace of defiance and malice.

"Now, stand up before God, and tell Him that you believe."

Chasing Rabbit crosses her arms, and says, "Why?"

"Because the Bible tells you so," Preacher Jim retorts angrily. "Now, I want you to recite this verse." He positions Chasing Rabbit precisely in front of him. "Repeat after me, and pay heed to what I am saying. 'The Lord is my shepherd, I shall not want. He maketh me to lie down in green pastures…'"

Chasing Rabbit shifts her feet, eyes defiant, and without thinking of the consequences, she hollers out, "The Lllooooorrrd is a big, fat shepherd."

"No, no, no!" says Preacher Jim, flying off the couch. Fury crosses his face in alarm. "How am I supposed to help you if you don't recite His words correctly? You are making a mockery of me and of Him." Shaking her crossly, he says, "Now, stand straight, and do this again." His voice was deep and angry. "Do not dishonor His words this time."

Chasing Rabbit decides that this is meaningless. Preacher Jim will never convince her to forget her Great Spirit. So she boldly states. "The Lord is a shepherd," she says with a grin, while brushing a strand of hair from her face. "He is a goose in green pastures, laying big fat eggs." Chasing Rabbit wonders if she has gone too far after seeing Preacher Jim's face bulge with fury and then turn a violent shade of red.

"Are you daft?" Preacher Jim says, as if in shock, then shakes his head. He bolts off the couch and whacks Chasing Rabbit over the head with his Bible. "Since you are not stupid, and you are not deaf, you must be tainted with evil."

He looks momentarily crazed as he flails about the room. He starts speaking in words that sound like gibberish. Chasing Rabbit's eyes widen and backs away as she hears him say something like, "*Ooomma, oomma.*" She watches in fear as Preacher Jim falls to his knees and weeps aloud, "Oh dear Lord, what am I to do with this unspeakable heathen? She, who defies me at every turn!"

Cringing at his behavior, Chasing Rabbit worries about Preacher Jim's actions and is not sure if she should run or call out for help.

Preacher Jim brusquely rises to his feet, and then he looks around the room, as if coming out of a stupor. His glance falls upon Chasing Rabbit and glares at the girl, announcing, "God is very displeased with you… with your conduct at this school. You have been warned several times." Then he folds his hands across his chest and closes his eyes and whispers. "But God is also… forgiving." Suddenly, raising his hands in the air, he cries out as if a light has gone off in his head. "He can see all." He says valiantly. "I might be able to save your soul from Hell, after all. The demons have filled you with their pernicious tentacles. They want you to resist." His brows twitch excitedly as he looks at Chasing Rabbit, who sits staring at him, ready to run. "I will remove your sins, my child," he states with authority, and pats her on the head. "I was sent here by the Lord to help you repent. Don't you see? The road of the wicked will be over."

He hurries to his desk and pulls out a long strap from the drawer, running his hands back and forth over the smooth leather. Looking back at Chasing Rabbit, he cracks the strap across his legs, then walks over, and sits beside the girl. "Bend over my knees, child, and let me begin. I will remove your demons."

"No," cries an astonished Chasing Rabbit.

Preacher Jim yanks Chasing Rabbit off the couch. The look in his eyes is wild. He pulls her over his knees and she resists, kicking and screaming. Furious, he shoves her down to the floor and puts the heel of his foot on the small of her back. He cries out, "Let this girl be saved in thy name, Oh, Lord!" He whacks her bottom with the strap and shouts again. "Praise be, Oh, Lord."

Chasing Rabbit is so furious that she wants to slug him between the eyes. She grits her teeth to hold back a cry, as he holds her firmly to the ground. Her tongue tastes the grime from the floor.

"Now, the path to salvation can be easy or it can be hard. It's entirely up to you." His heels push down even harder as Chasing Rabbit tries to wiggle free, when another *whack!* is heard. The sound reverberates across the room like a bullet. A trickle of sweat drips off the side of Preacher Jim's face. He absently brushes it away and raises his hand in the air, with tears streaming down his face. He cries out. "I beseech thee, Lord! Help me to remove this girl's demons." After each crack of the whip, he shouts, "Let the Demons be gone. Praise the Lord!"

When he is spent and regains control, he speaks in a hoarse voice. "Now, I will read, so you will understand how to be submissive to thy Lord." He picks up the Bible and starts reciting a verse, his voice barely a whisper. "I have hidden Your word in my heart that I might not sin against You…"

Chasing Rabbit is stunned. She wills herself to remain strong. She can't fall to pieces now and give up, or into this man. Her thoughts are of her brother, Hidden Spirit. She can see his face and his smile, and feels his strength. It seems to flow throughout her body. Their people are warriors of the Plains—unafraid to fight. She can't bear being next to this crazed man any longer. And so, without another thought, Chasing Rabbit twists out of Preacher Jim's grasp and runs over to his desk, panting, and spies a letter opener on top of a pile of papers. In a blink, Chasing Rabbit scrambles atop the desk, scattering the papers and books on the floor. She grabs the letter opener, as the sharp tip flickers in the light, reflecting weird shapes from the kerosene lantern. She stands on the desk, and bravely brandishes the weapon in the air, daring the man to come near.

The startled look on Preacher Jim's face widens in utter shock and his eyes glaze over in surprise. Uncertain if he's seeing things, he blinks a couple times to make certain he's not. The image of Chasing Rabbit wavers before him, and he gasps, clutching his chest in alarm, he inches his way closer. He sees the darkness of the Devil around her. *She has a pitchfork in her hands,* he thinks, and cries out. "The Devil's tool!" He blinks even harder, wiping his brows, faint with terror. Suddenly, his vision clears, and he sees she's just holding his letter opener. Relief floods through him, as visions of the Devil dancing around her disappear. He's so relieved he bowls over, and howls with laughter. Slapping his knee, he practically dances around the desk before he regains his composure. "It's the Devil making you do this," he says animatedly, and flings his arms wide. "You are possessed. Now, drop that thing this instant. The Lord will forgive you, as shall I."

Chasing Rabbit flinches, wondering what to do, but decides to stay the course. She keeps her feet firmly planted on the desk, standing tall, resolve filling her.

Preacher Jim's eyes darken and narrow as he slowly advances toward the girl—his eyes flickering ominously. Nearing the desk, he bangs his fists down with such force that it rattles the lantern. It sends waves of fear shooting through Chasing Rabbit. She tries to gauge her next move, her eyes darting toward the door, as her heart thumps painfully against her ribs.

Preacher Jim enraged, lunges for Chasing Rabbit, but she dodges his long boney fingers and whirls around and kicks at him, knocking over the lantern. A wave of smoke drifts up. Before he can react, she plunges the knife into him, grazing his shoulder.

Preacher Jim howls with pain, clutching his wound.

Chasing Rabbit quickly slides off the opposite side of the desk, scattering his papers in every direction and takes off in a run.

The preacher's face turns ashen. He drops his Bible on the floor, ranting, "You little beast," then scurries after her. She is quick, and her feet are flying, but is no match for Preacher Jim's long legs, as he quickly advances and catches the back of her dress, savagely pulling her back. Preacher Jim whirls her around so hard, she's unable to keep her balance as her shoes catch on the uneven floorboards—hurtling her onto the corner of his massive desk. An earsplitting thud echoes in her brain and reverberates throughout her entire body. She sees bluish stars swirling around her head, twinkling brightly, then, the starlight gradually dims. Trying to hold onto the desk, her fingers slip and she gasps for air. As if in slow motion, Chasing Rabbit slumps to the floor and sucks in her last, shallow breath. Pools of blood stain the desk and splatter down the side, leaving imprints of her hands as blood drips down onto her cheeks. Visions of her life float past. She sees her parents smiling happily in their youth. Now they are sitting at their small table, talking in hushed tones. Her mother is weeping. Her father is trying to console her, but is unable. He holds his head in his hands, his grief-stricken face filled with pain. She wants to comfort them. Then her vision wavers, and blurs—everything turns to darkness. The cold wraps around her as the room slowly fades away. There is nothing now but a low hum. Suddenly a burst of light shimmers, blinding her. She hears a buzzing sound—the force pulls her into an effervescent tunnel. Looking down, she sees her beautiful blue stone skid across the floor and land against the wall, flickering—sparkling.

Chasing Rabbit reaches down to touch it, but is quickly whisked away by the light, floating past her beloved treasure. Her last gaze is of Preacher Jim standing over her body.

DESPERATE LITTLE MOON

LITTLE MOON PUTS the bear claw in her pocket. She hopes it wasn't a bad omen for Chasing Rabbit, giving her totem away. It makes her nervous remembering her dream of last night—of a voice calling for help. She hurries to the barn where Bessie is waiting. She loves that cow and likes telling her stories about her life and where she came from and about her mama and her papa. Whenever she feels blue, she can count on Bessie to listen patiently as she chatters, while swishing her tail back and forth.

Opening the barn door, she stands for a moment and listens for Bessie's "moo." It makes Little Moon smile. "Hi, Bessie," she says, grabbing a bucket and pail. "I see you are still eating. You must be related to Mrs. Burns. She eats a lot, too, but you're much nicer." Setting the pail under the cow, she says, "I have a lot on my mind today, so try to be good and don't kick the bucket over. I always get into trouble when you do that."

Bessie turns her head, still munching, and looks at Little Moon with her soulful brown eyes. Little Moon pats her rump. "Let's get a big bucketful today. Then I'll lick the cream off the top before I take it to the kitchen. That's the best part of this job—being with you and licking the delicious cream. Ready, Bessie?" Little Moon grabs the cow's teats, pushing and pulling until rich and creamy milk splashes into the bucket. "My best friend gave me a special gift today, but I'm a little scared," she says, as she stops milking for a moment and holds the bear claw in the air for Bessie to inspect. "It's to make me brave," she says proudly. Bessie kicks her hind legs as if to say, keep milking. "Oops, you almost knocked the bucket over. I guess I'd better pay closer attention." Little Moon puts away her bear claw, smiles at Bessie, and continues milking. "I'm not at all happy here, Bessie, but you know that," she says, sadly. "I always feel better telling you my troubles. I wish you were my teacher, but what I wish for most is to go home. I would miss you a lot, but I miss my parents even more..." Her voice trails off, and she brushes away a tear. "Preacher Jim and the teachers talk bad about us because we're Sioux. I don't know why. I was happy back home with my people. They treated me special and they loved me." Little Moon is quiet for a moment, and then says softly. "Preacher Jim makes me nervous. He acts like he cares about us, but I don't think he really does. He's not nice like you are, Bessie. And you know... maybe I shouldn't have taken the bear claw. I'm worried that I did. It's Chasing Rabbit's totem. What if something bad happens?" When the bucket is filled to the brim, Little Moon scoops a big dollop of cream off the top, licks it off her fingers, and smacks her lips. "Thank you, Bessie. Your milk is real good." Little Moon moves the bucket to the side, and rests her head against the cow's rotund belly, rubbing it gently. "I love you, Bessie. You always make me feel better," she says, before going silent, deep in thought. Bessie's tail swishes back and forth in a soothing manner as she chews her cud.

Little Moon stands up reluctantly, and hugs the cow. "I guess it's time to clean your stall now, so please don't kick me." She finds the wooden rake by the barn door, and begins to clean away the soiled hay. "Whew! You have a lot of droppings today. I think you eat too much," she says with a grin. "But all that poop'll make the garden grow, real big." She throws a bucket of fresh water on the floor, and then fills another for the cow, patting her one more time. "Goodbye, Bessie. See you tomorrow."

Walking outside, Little Moon looks toward Preacher Jim's office, wondering if she should peek into the side window. She wants to see what is going on. That icky feeling she had is still with her.

On her way, she sees Mrs. Trimble running from Preacher Jim's office shrieking, almost hysterical. "Chasing Rabbit is dead, and Preacher Jim's been wounded!"

Little Moon cannot believe what she's hearing.

Miss Snodberry stands in the middle of the grounds, shaking from the news.

Little Moon begins to cry, thinking, *this is not real. The teachers are lying. It can't be true.*

Mrs. Burns hustles across the yard after Mrs. Trimble. "Good Lord! Whatever happened?"

"That little troublemaker almost killed our preacher. Now she's dead."

Little Moon feels her heart sink as she crumples to her knees. *It's true!* She tries not to give into the pain, but the blood is pounding in her temple. With the bear claw in her possession, she is supposed to be strong, but the news hits her like a rock. Her throat constricts, so she can't even scream. Wanting to drown out the pain, she hits her head on the ground, over and over. Her pain doesn't diminish. All she has is a lump the size of a goose egg on her forehead and an aching head. Mrs. Burns, ignoring her, rushes by carrying a blanket.

Little Moon pulls herself off the ground. She has to see for herself what is going on. Without thinking, she rushes to the window in Preacher Jim's office, where she wipes the tears from her cheeks and the grime from the cracked pane.

Peering inside, she feels her world collapse. There is Chasing Rabbit, lying on the floor, covered in blood. Little Moon's body goes numb. She can't move—she can only stare in disbelief. Recalling her dream, she realizes she should have listened to its warning. A hundred frantic images swirl in her head, and she covers her eyes to block them out. The sight of her friend lying there is too much to bear. "Chasing Rabbit. You can't be dead. I'm sorry I took your bear claw. Forgive me. Please don't be dead! Please don't be dead! Please don't be dead!" Repeating this over and over again.

When Miss Snodberry manages to gain control of her emotions, she goes inside Preacher Jim's office to see what she can do. After a moment, she notices Little Moon staring through the window, and runs out the door and kneels beside her. "Chasing Rabbit hit her head on Preacher Jim's desk. He was trying to stop her from leaving, but she put up a fight. She found a letter opener on his desk and stabbed him with it. He wasn't hurt too badly. Just a little cut." She touches Little Moon's face, and speaks calmly. "Let me walk you back to the school and put you in bed. You shouldn't have had to see any of this."

Little Moon just stares at Miss Snodberry, as the woman takes her in her arms and tries to console her. Little Moon shoves her away. "Why didn't you help her? Help us? You knew we were miserable, but you wouldn't do anything. You're just like them. I hate you!"

"I did my very best, Little Moon. I did. Please don't be angry with me."

The child stands up, glares at the woman, and walks away, leaving a stricken Miss Snodberry in tears. Little Moon doesn't know where she is going and doesn't care. She doesn't care what might happen to her. She just knows she is never coming back to this place again. She would rather die. Death is all around this place—creeping inside her soul. Her best friend is gone and it's too hard for Little Moon to imagine life without her. Chasing Rabbit was her last shred of hope. Little Moon's mind is a frantic mixture of fear and panic, and she starts to run as fast as she can, clutching the precious bear claw. Tears stream down her face, blinding her as she runs wildly into the woods, squeezing through thick scrubs and low-lying bushes. In her haste she stumbles over a log, and suffers a deep gash on her shin. She barely notices the blood flowing down her leg as she leaps back up and runs until she can go no further—finally collapsing on the damp ground. She wants to die—better out in the open than at that school. Her sides heaving, she lies down on the moss-covered earth, ready to go to the otherworld. Her life no longer has any meaning. Tears gush down her face and Little Moon whispers through a cloak of tears, "You didn't get to see Bessie, Chasing Rabbit. And now you're… gone." She stops, hearing someone calling her name—and then she feels someone pick her up.

"Little Moon, what are you doing here?" Ellie asks incredulously, searching the child's pale face for answers, and gently shakes her, but Little Moon doesn't respond. Frantic with worry, Ellie feels something is wrong—terribly wrong. She wonders what has happened, and clings to Little Moon, rocking her back and forth. Tenderly brushing away wisps of hair from the girl's eyes, she finally gets the girl to respond. "Little Moon, please tell me what happened."

Uttering a few undistinguishable words about the afterlife and Chasing Rabbit is all that Little Moon can manage. Ellie shakes her again, gently. "Please tell me what happened. Please. You can't stay out here. It'll be dark soon. If my father catches you, you'll get into trouble. I must take you back."

Feeling dazed, and unsure of what to say, Little Moon looks up at Ellie, trying to tell her what happened but, her spirit is gone and her heart is full of agony. She bites her lower lip to keep them from quivering. Grasping Ellie's hand, she manages a faint, "Chasing Rabbit left for the other world... where Otter is."

Ellie is stunned, hoping she didn't hear correctly and gasps. "You mean Chasing Rabbit is dead?" The little girl nods her head. She gathers Little Moon in her arms, holds her close, as tears tumble down her cheeks. "Oh no! This is impossible. Are you certain?" She rambles on. "Not Chasing Rabbit. I can't believe it. How did it happen?"

Sounds of boisterous laughter startle Ellie out of her reverie, making her jump as she looks in dismay, seeing her brother and his friends coming down the road. She shudders. "Oh no! It's Ezekiel." He spots Ellie and comes running over. Ellie holds tight to Little Moon and prepares for a likely altercation. She has just heard the worst news possible, and now this. She stiffens as he walks near.

Ezekiel looks at Ellie, at first in disbelief, then scowls, as he sees Little Moon crouched beside her. "What the Devil are you doing out here with a squaw? Pa will be livid if he finds out, and I'll make sure he knows what you're up to."

Ellie can see the corners of his mouth turn upward, and smirks. He looks over at his friends in exaggerated annoyance. He's with Abe Laskey and Homer Banks, who also seem surprised.

Ezekiel doesn't care much for Indians. In fact, he loathes them. His hero is General Custer, and he keeps favorable articles written about him on the wall of his room. He hates the fact that Custer was killed by a band of renegade Indians at the Battle of Little Bighorn. He doesn't care about the truth or the reason why they fought. Custer was a real man... and he idolizes him. Custer hated the Indians and so does he. That's all that matters.

Abe Laskey, on the other hand, could care one way or the other, about the Indians. He cares about his prestige in town, and that's pretty much it. Being the son of a local rancher, he's wealthy and popular, and has his own agenda. Abe's dazzling blue eyes light up upon seeing Ellie, and smiles.

Homer is a newcomer to Hickoryville. His parents run the local newspaper. Word around town is that the paper is too liberal for most folks in the area, but the Banks family pays no mind to the gossip. They like to write about subjects they find interesting to enlighten the community with their newsworthy topics. Homer sees Ellie sitting on the ground and his face burns bright red at the sight of her.

Ezekiel continues to badger his sister. "I asked, what are you doing with the squaw, Ellie?" He shoots her a critical glance. "No one can understand why you like hanging around them. They're butchers. It's one thing for Pa to run the school for those redskins, but for you to be friendly with them is downright embarrassing." Ezekiel struts around her, saying, "Pa should whip you. You know you're not to be interfering with his work at the school." Then he looks over at Little Moon, eyeing her up and down and then over to Abe and Homer, and snickers. "Looks like that squaw is good an ripe—an ready to bed. 'Bout the right age too, wouldn't you say, boys?"

Homer and Abe are stunned by Zeke's crude comments, but before they can answer, Ellie runs up to Ezekiel and shoves him back.

Shaking so hard, Ellie's not sure what to do, and feels her insides tense into a knot. She impulsively blurts out. "Shut up, Zeke! I'd call you a pig, but pigs are better than you!" Trying to control her fury, she states. "There has been an accident at the school." Rage, sadness and incredulity, consume all her all at once. "One of the little girls died today."

"Who cares, besides you?" says Zeke. "They're nothing but troublemakers. I don't know why Pa bothers with them, anyhow. Folks in town say the only good Indian is a dead one. I'd shoot 'em all for a nickel and give you five cents change."

"I think you're disgusting and..." not able to finish her words, she holds tight to Little Moon.

Ezekiel yanks Ellie off the ground as Little Moon whimpers, trying to hide. He leers into Ellie's face. "Aren't you supposed to be home, learning how to cook or scrub floors? You're not even good at that, from what Ma says."

A stinging sharp slap across Ezekiel's face startles him. Livid, he grabs her upper arm and spins her around, threatening her with a balled fist. "I ought to knock some sense into your..."

Abe hustles over and quickly intervenes, pulling Ellie out of his grasp. "Take it easy, there Zeke. You can't hit a girl... especially one as sweet as your sister." He gives Ellie a wink. "Best to simmer down and forget this."

Tall, handsome, and muscular, Abe had a slightly crooked nose and shaggy blond hair. He stands facing Zeke ready to fight, but Zeke backs down as he sees Abe's resolve, and says, "Guess I got a little carried away to see my sister with a squaw is all." Zeke reluctantly lets go of Ellie who looks at Abe gratefully as she runs over to soothe a frightened Little Moon.

Abe makes a lot of women in town swoon whenever he nears, and he enjoys flirting with them openly. But Ellie is not swayed. She finds him too arrogant. Abe's family's cattle ranch employs a number of local folks, who are beholden to them for their livelihood. At seventeen years old, the boy has a rugged self-assurance about him and a keen eye for pretty women—especially Ellie. That she shows no interest in him makes her even more appealing. He figures, with a little patience on his part, sooner or later she will come around. *She's well worth the wait.*

Ellie brushes her silky hair off her face and looks over at Homer, who shuffles his feet awkwardly. "Hello, Homer," she says, preparing to leave with Little Moon. "Thanks for fixing the step by the kitchen the other day. My foot almost went through the board."

Homer's face pales before turning a deep shade of crimson. Shyly, he looks at his feet. "I… I… uh… I pulled s-some weeds yes-s-s-t-terday and p-p-planted a… a m-maple in the yard." His face is boiling hot as Abe and Zeke about fall over themselves in laughter.

Ellie recovers from her fury, hides a smile and thanks Homer for his thoughtfulness. She has never given a thought to Homer or even spoken to him before today. She notices that he has big emerald green eyes that slant upwards and a mop of unruly red hair covered in cowlicks and a face full of freckles that dot his cheeks. He looks like a mottled apple, she thinks with a smile.

Ezekiel and Abe like to make fun of Homer—and they enjoy needling him whenever he is around. It's like a game for them. Homer can't shoot, ride, hunt, or partake of any other 'manly' pastime. They hang out with him solely for sport, something to do when they're bored, which is often. Homer knows he is not nearly as good-looking and self-assured as Abe, or a big talker like Ezekiel, but he wants friends and is willing to put up with their mockery and abuse of him. Better than being alone in this town.

Homer has a secret crush on Ellie, and Abe would be furious to find out. No sense getting worked up over her, though, as she wouldn't be interested in him. Still, it's a nice dream and he does have something in common with her. He admires the Indians and their culture, and loves reading stories about their lives. In his spare time, he even draws pictures of their famous chiefs—his favorite of whom was Sitting Bull. He knows about the boarding school and sits above the hill behind the school for hours, watching the children and drawing their solemn faces as they go about their chores. Homer keeps his feelings bottled up, a habit he learned early on back home, where he was bullied and beaten up. They called him a sissy for preferring reading and drawing to hunting. He gets his artistic nature from his mother, and that makes him proud. Ellie makes him tingle—just looking at her. He imagines telling her how he feels about her—that he admires her not only for her loveliness, but her spirit, as well—something he knew he lacked. Maybe someday, if he ever gets up the nerve and can talk without stuttering or making a fool of himself—maybe then he will show her his drawings. He sighs, wishing he were a little braver, or, at least, a bit dashing. *Maybe I should learn how to fight, or at least shoot a gun* he thinks. Then, just as quickly, he rejects that idea.

It is well past dinnertime and getting dark as the girls make their way back to the school. The children should be in their rooms, saying prayers and getting ready for bed. Ellie wants to get Little Moon some food before she goes to sleep, so she peers in the dining room window to find out if anyone is still around. Fortunately, Mrs. Barlapp has gone for the evening, so Ellie puts her finger to her mouth, signaling Little Moon to be quiet, and then tiptoes into the pantry where she finds some freshly baked loaves of bread. Opening the larder where they keep the meat, she slices off two large hunks of beef, still warm from supper, and pulls Little Moon into a corner, where they can sit and eat without being detected.

Little Moon shakes her head no when Ellie offers her the food. "I'm not hungry," she states tearfully. But Ellie insists she try a bite, so she reluctantly takes a piece of meat and chews slowly—discovering she is ravenous. Little Moon crams the bread and meat into her mouth, eating as fast as she can until it is all gone, then licks her fingers. Now the stress and horror of the day are taking their toll, and fatigue is setting in. The little girl's eyes grow so heavy she can barely hold them open. A big yawn follows.

Ellie pulls Little Moon off the floor, and brushes away the crumbs. "I think we had better get you to bed. I don't want you to get into trouble."

The girls start down the hallway, where they hear Mrs. Trimble with Mrs. Burns coming around the corner, saying, "Oh, what a positively dreadful day!"

"I think we should be a little more careful at night, maybe lock our doors," Mrs. Burns says warily as Mrs. Trimble stops mid-stride—her eyes practically popping from their sockets in disbelief.

"Mrs. Burns, look!" says Mrs. Trimble. "There is that friend of that murderous Rabbit girl with Ellie. What in the world is she doing here? Holding hands with the heathen, to boot." For a moment Mrs. Trimble is at a loss for words. As the girls draw nearer, she recovers and is furious. She glares at Little Moon, and barks, "where have you been?" And then fixes her stare at Ellie. "What on earth are you doing with this girl? She should be in bed by now, prayers said. Does your father know where you are, or with whom?"

Ellie glares back defiantly, shoving Little Moon behind her.

"We have been looking everywhere for that child. If I wasn't so tired, I would strap her behind, but good."

"It's not her fault for running away. She saw... she saw her friend through the window, covered in blood."

Mrs. Trimble speaks civilly, despite her anger. "Preacher Jim said the girl went stark raving mad. He was trying to remove her demons when she attacked him—stabbed him in the shoulder with a letter opener. Can you imagine? That man must be a saint not to blame her for her abominable behavior. He made an excuse for her—said her mind was taken."

"You are the head mistress and you should know that isn't true. She was a lovely girl. And she certainly wasn't possessed. My father might be though."

The color drains from Mrs. Trimble's face, leaving it a pallid white. She couldn't believe Ellie's outspokenness, and she blisters. "You speak of things about which you know nothing. You're lucky that wicked girl didn't kill your father or severely wound him. That red-devil Rabbit girl was trying to run away when your father tried to stop her and she tripped. She got what she deserved, as far as I'm concerned. Please leave now. It's getting late, and we have a busy day ahead of us." She flicks her strap, looking threateningly at Little Moon.

Ellie clenches her fists, furious at the woman. *I had better leave before I do something I might regret.* Tomorrow, she will figure out a way to help Little Moon. *My father has them all fooled,* Ellie thinks, bitterly. *And they're fools for believing him.*

Mrs. Trimble's voice carries down the hallway as she speaks to Mrs. Burns. "Why should a fine man such as Preacher Jim, who devotes his life to the children and the parishioners, have such a wicked child as that one?" She marches on, pulling Little Moon beside her. "He certainly has his hands full, and with his own flesh and blood, as well. It's simply disgraceful."

Mrs. Burns agrees. "Indeed, it is."

Leading Little Moon by the nape of her neck into her room, Mrs. Trimble says, "Say your prayers quickly and get into bed before I lose my temper and wallop you a good one."

WEASEL FITS

OPAL IS SITTING by the fire knitting, seething over the fact that her headstrong daughter has not been home for hours and has once again missed dinner. Her husband is still at the school, mulling over the disturbing events of that darned Chasing Rabbit. Oh, she could wring her neck. Well, now she wouldn't have to worry about that. The weight must be heavy on her husband's mind with the constant turmoil at the school and rigorous demands. Plus, there was also that incident of the Otter girl dropping dead this week. *Well, the load of the weary shall be lightened*, she thought. Opal has her own hands full, and she is sick of trying to convert those girls. She wouldn't mind sending them packing.

Worst of all, she can't believe her daughter likes being around them. They are a bad influence—brought up in an atmosphere of savagery. And she is appalled by the gossip going on.

It crosses Opal's mind that she might be too lenient with the wayward girl, but she knows she has the perfect solution for her. His name is Frae Beadle. Frae is a plain-looking thirty-five-year-old thriving butcher in town, and a devout Christian. He is short and stocky with somber pale gray eyes, bulging muscles, and bristly brown hair—a perfect match for her headstrong daughter. Opal has noticed he likes to flex his muscles whenever

Ellie is around and figures his strong body compensates for his plain appearance. *He would be no one to cross,* Opal thinks with satisfaction. *He would most assuredly keep Ellie firmly in line.* Furthermore, since her husband is adamant about keeping non-believers from joining his family, Frae would get his full approval.

Leaving the school, Ellie walks home, despondent over Chasing Rabbit and deep in thought. As she nears her house and rounds the corner, she stops—hearing a man's voice near the back porch. Creeping around the side to see who is there, she feels her breath catch at the sight of Frae Beadle, and she quickly hides behind a knobby oak tree.

Frae is standing by the door talking to Opal, who invites him in. Luckily for Ellie, he declines.

"I'm sorry Ellie's not here, Mr. Beadle. She should be home soon. She helps out at the school on occasion. Horrid business going on there."

"Yes, I heard. It's quite distressing, to put it mildly. I'd use stronger words, but I shall not use the Lord's name in vain."

Ellie sees Frae's face jut forward in a frown as he leans in closer to Opal, sharing her disapproval, and states irritably. "I'm concerned about her association with those Indians, Mrs. Crumm. People are starting to talk. Might not be good for my business or for me—having that kind of nonsense going on."

"Well now," says Opal. "She's a headstrong girl and, Lord knows, I've tried my best to rein in her willfulness. Someone like you, Mr. Beadle—could remedy her willful behavior."

"Well," Frae says, puffing his chest, "I might consider proposing to Ellie with the understanding she would never go near that school again." He leans toward Opal, and lowers his voice. "That is, after we're married."

Ellie's eyes pop when she hears Frae's reference to marriage, and gasps. *I have to get closer,* she thinks, and quickly slides around the tree to hear better—her mind whirling at the news. Without paying attention, she knocks her head on a low-lying branch, causing her hair to get tangled in the woody stem. "Damn," she curses, trying to get untangled from the limb. Suddenly she stops and slaps her hands over her mouth. To her horror, she realizes her mistake and panics. "Please don't let them come over," she moans, and crosses her fingers, hoping they didn't hear her. She is acutely aware her mother and Frae have stopped talking. Ellie pokes her head around the tree and slips out, "Oh no." She notices they are looking her way, and holds her breath, trying not to shake.

Frae jerks his head toward the tree and cranes his neck, looking to see what's out there. Flexing his muscles, he heads in Ellie's direction.

Ellie freezes as she sees Frae coming toward her.

Opal shrieks. "Did you hear something, Mr. Beadle?"

"I'll take a look around the grounds, Mrs. Crumm. No need to fret," he says, puffing up his chest. "Think I heard something over that way," he calls out, pointing toward the tree. Frae steps quietly across the yard, balling his fists. "Never know what may be lurking in those bushes. Could be one of those heathens trying to escape. Might even make their way over here."

Ellie can feel her skin prickle as he walks toward her, stopping just a few yards away. She feels as if she might faint, and struggles to stay calm as she sits unmoving, afraid to breathe. She wishes at this moment she could disappear.

Just then a couple raccoons bound across the yard, chasing each other up a tree.

Frae relaxes his fists, calling out, "Coons, ma'am. Careful they don't eat your corn. Picked my ears plum clean."

"Yes, I'll have the helper boy, Homer, chase them away tomorrow. Thank you for your concern, Mr. Beadle. Would dinner this Sunday be good? You could announce your plans at that time. I can tell you, Ellie's father will be most amenable. I spoke to him the other day about your interest in our daughter. He thought you to be a fine man whom he would gladly welcome into our family."

"Real pleased to hear he approves, ma'am," Frae says.

"You'll be calling me Mother Opal soon, Mr. Beadle."

Ellie thinks she might choke at those words, and forces back the bile that starts to rise in her throat. She swallows hard. Her entire body is on the verge of collapse.

As Frae rides away, Ellie slumps to the ground, trying to absorb what she just heard. After some time, her trembling eases. She moves from the tree and enters the house as quietly as possible, but the back door squeaks, betraying her.

When Opal hears the door open, she drops her knitting needles and bolts up from her chair. "Ellie, are you trying to sneak in here? Where on God's green earth have you been? It's late and you not only missed dinner but Mr. Beadle's visit, as well. I can tell you one thing—he was not very happy he missed you again."

Regaining her composure, Ellie replies, "I was busy at the school and I forgot the time." Then she looks at her mother in disbelief—suppressing her outrage as Opal sits in her chair, unconcerned about Chasing Rabbit. "You know a lot happened today, don't you? One of the little girls died."

Opal purses her lips into a thin line. "Of course, I know. The heathens caused quite a stir," she said. "Nasty business. Oh, and be home early tomorrow. Mr. Beadle is coming back. He has asked permission to court you. Your father and I feel he is a fine man and would make you an excellent suitor." Under her breath she said, "You're lucky he's interested."

Ellie responds with an icy stare. "I don't like that man, and you know it. His idea of courting would probably be a lecture from him on a woman's place in the home while staring at me. I want no part of him or his courting. Maybe Mrs. Coons' daughter would like to go out with him. She's been after him for a spell. I'm not interested!"

"Well, we'll see about that, Miss High-and-Mighty. Anyway, he's not interested in her, though I can't imagine why not. A fine girl, she is. Doesn't give her mother any sass like you do."

Ellie rolls her eyes, thinking it won't be soon enough for her to leave home.

"I want you to be nice to Mr. Beadle, young lady. He'd make a fine catch for the likes of you. You're getting a little too wild for your own good, and you're putting your father in a terrible position. Tongues are wagging all over town about you and the heathens. Mr. Beadle is shocked by your behavior, as well. We can't have this continue, or you'll be left with no suitors at all."

Opal goes back to her knitting, brows furrowed, as she plots how she might hasten this wedding between Frae and her errant daughter. She looks forward to the day when Ellie will be someone else's problem. "I do try my best to be a good mother to you—and this is the appreciation I get," she says, frowning. "Where is your respect, young lady?"

Ellie is in no mood to listen to her mother's lecture. She makes an excuse to leave and goes directly to her room, where she paces back and forth, trying to calm herself. "What am I going to do? I have to get away from here, somehow, someway, before they force me into a horrible marriage and ruin my life forever."

Climbing into bed, she resolves that, whatever it takes, she will run away. She loves to sew and she knows how to turn a drab calico dress into an elegant piece of finery. In the privacy of her room she often designs clothing inspired by photos from New York fashion magazines, which she hides from her mother in a latched box under her bed. Her friend, Rachael, ordered the magazines for her while living in Virginia and she poured over them every chance she got—copying the designs meticulously. She has just finished making some undergarments that are soft and silky, and she loves the feel of them against her skin. They make her seem elegant and feminine, maybe even a little sinful. She smiles at that notion and longs for the day when she can go to New York and work as a fashion designer, making beautiful dresses with calicos, velvets, taffetas, and silks. She refuses to be trapped here in Hickoryville with her parents' strict demands and with creepy Beadle, hot after her. The man makes her stomach lurch, and she cringes at the idea of him coming anywhere near her, or touching her.

There is also something sinister about him, even frightening—something in the way he looks at her with his cold pale eyes, cast in judgment. She can't imagine the depths to which he might go to control her. She thinks her mother is stupid to assume that Frae's willingness to dole out a free roast or a ham on occasion, means he is a good person. Worrying about the hold Frae has over her parents, she becomes increasingly anxious. Her mind reels as she hops out of bed and paces back and forth. She even ponders the notion of asking the Great Spirit for help, but dismisses it as a silly thought. The girls have talked about Him so much she can almost feel His kindness. But she isn't a Sioux. She isn't any kind of Indian. She's just a person trapped, with no way out.

Ellie feels a twinge of guilt, remembering how much sadness there is at the school, and yet, here she is, moaning about her own troubles. She thinks about sweet Otter and how awful it is that she had to die so young—*and now, Chasing Rabbit*. It all seems like a bad dream. She just saw her yesterday washing clothes, talking a mile a minute as she worked. She was so mischievous, and full of antics that made her laugh. Ellie will miss her terribly and thinks, *there must be something I can do, other than sit here and feel sorry for myself.*

Going to the window, she sits and stares out into the dark night and looks up at the expansive universe. There are thousands and thousands of stars blanketing the sky, each one filled with wonder. As she looks to the east she sees a particularly brilliant star on the horizon. *It's different from the others,* she thinks, hanging her head out the window to get a better look, and gasps, "It's enormous, and it sparkles like a glittering sapphire." Ellie hangs her head even further out the window, and waves at the brilliant star. "I hope you're up there, Chasing Rabbit," she says, as pain fills her heart. "I hope you'll race with the moon and dance on the breeze." Ellie blows a kiss in the wind. "This is for you, my little friend. My heart aches for all your suffering." Ellie sits for a long time staring at the sparkling shape. Finally, when the bright star makes its way across the sky, she closes the window and goes to bed.

Ellie lies awake thinking how unfair it is that the teachers and her father force their religion on the children. *Why can't they understand that the boys and girls are happy with their own beliefs, which sound a lot better to me, than the constant threats of "Hell and Damnation," to scare and control them.*

HEAVENLY STARS

A ROARING SOUND ECHOES throughout the heavens and the universe as Chasing Rabbit is whisked off to a distant, far-away place—into time immortal.

A luminous ray of light engulfs the young girl, as she lies motionless, suspended in air, wrapped in a cocoon of lavender and warmth.

After a moment—or perhaps eons, the lifeless body begins to stir. Chasing Rabbit sits up, looks around, flutters an eyelid, and wonders where she is. *It seems so tranquil*, she thinks, *like an ocean of silky blue water swaying gently.* She lifts her hands in front of her to examine them. They seem translucent and pale—she can see right through them. Slowly she looks around her. Everything sparkles and glows. Waves of brilliant colors billow in the air. In the distance a bright undulating light is floating toward her, dazzling and brimming with turquoise and shards of purple rays that flicker from within.

"It's so beautiful," she says, in awe. Taking another look around she tries to remember something—where she came from—how she got here. But everything is muddled. This place seems like a dream with its pulsating colors, swirling and shifting—as the hazy glow beckons her to follow. Curious to know more, she hops up, ready to follow the hazy glow. The undulating light wraps a flickering beam of turquoise around the girl, leading her to a serene meadow filled with a cornucopia of flowers—every kind and shade of colors imaginable—pale pinks, vibrant violets, iridescent indigos, magnetic magentas and on and on...

As the girl nears, each flower bows its fragile stem and smiles, as it sways peacefully in the current. Chasing Rabbit hears a faint chorus. "Hum-dee-dum... hum-dee-dum..."

"Are you talking to me? And if you are, I didn't quite understand what you were saying."

No answer.

"Did you say, 'welcome home'?" Chasing Rabbit asks, politely.

A slight lilt of laughter is heard.

"Well, if this is where I live—it's wonderful," she says, twirling in circles. *But still, nothing seems familiar* she thinks, and she wrinkles her brow in consternation. "I don't seem to have petals like all of you, and I certainly don't smell like tea roses or orange blossoms or lavender lilacs. Does anyone know how I got here, or where I came from?"

The flowers simply twitter—understanding her confusion. They gather the girl close into their silky blossoms and blooms, and let loose a heavenly fragrance. Chasing Rabbit feels divine in their presence, and lets the questions drift away. The aromas and sense of tranquility fill her. She marvels at a lovely purple blossom nearby, with its intricate bloom—curious about its beauty. Bending over it, she says, "My, you are a pretty flower. What is your name?" Not waiting for an answer, she takes a big sniff of the sticky center. A powder-like puff of pollen shoots up into her nostrils, making her sneeze. "*Ka-chew!*"

A lilting voice speaks up, dripping with pollen. "Excuse me, but you disturbed my cone," the flower says, brandishing her petals in annoyance. Then, it stops. "Oh dear..." The sneezeweed looks at the startled girl. "Pardon me. You must be our newest arrival." Then it reaches out to her playfully and pulls her hand inside its stem, where she feels the sticky pollen, and sneezes once again. A faint "Bless you!" follows. Chasing Rabbit licks her lips, tasting the sticky nectar. "This is delicious," she says, smacking her lips, eyeing the field of unusual flowers, thinking how silly everyone is. Then, suddenly, she catches a fleeting glimpse of a man with bushy eyebrows... bobbing. Backing away in fright, she loses her balance. A phantom ghost flower whizzes past, catches her mid-air, sits her upright, and disappears. Thousands of flowers gather around, enfolding her in their soft petals as they hum. "Ooooh... you need not worry. No one can hurt you here."

Grateful for their comfort, she gushes, "Thank goodness." Then she asks timidly, "Where did that man come from? He looks ever so frightful. Do I know him? And what a peculiar place this is! Can anyone tell me how I got here, and where I'm going?"

A tall lanky broomstick sweeps over and takes her hand, whisking her through the vast profusion of flowers. The soft petals tickle her feet and smile as she floats past. Forgetting the frightful image, she is delighted at how friendly and unusual everyone is. She is beginning to really like it here.

A bright orange thistle pops up and introduces himself. "I'm Hairy," he bubbles, graciously, extending his prickly orange tips to shake her hand. Chasing Rabbit winces as a thorn pierces her finger. "My! You are a bristly fellow!" she says, pulling her hand away, smiling at the pretty flower. Next, she comes upon some purple catmints, meowing and purring and rubbing their soft petals against her legs as she walks up—their way of bidding her welcome.

Skipping along through a maze of flowers, she shouts out at the top of her lungs, "Lemon Verbena!" A field of glossy tips appears, emitting a powerful, wondrous scent of lemon, and spritzing the air with its citrusy fragrance. Next, Chasing Rabbit thinks of the color green. And in a flash, everything turns a deep shade of emerald. "This is truly amazing!" she says, giggling in delight. Then she hollers. "Sapphire indigo!" A stunning array of sapphire blooms arch high, waving, as more flowers float by, infusing the air with their heady scents.

Next, she comes upon a cascade of yawning morning glories, stretching their luscious lavender-blue petals as the early morning sunlight glistens on their cups. Nearby, a halo of hollyhocks and blossoming bluebells are ringing and dinging their delicate bells—bidding the young girl welcome. Beside them, a bed of pink petunias blush and hum merrily while glorious gladiolas laugh gaily. Just down the path, a cloud of sugar sweet peas smile coyly, listening to the beguiling sounds of the angelic angel trumpet playing a captivating tune. Making an equally grand impression is the vanilla tuberose—its triumphant sounds blasting through the air.

Throngs of flowers cheer and whistle and sway as they start to move with the tempo. Lustrous blooms unfold in a whirl of colors as the music blares, exploding into riotous tunes. The buttery begonias and pink petunias swirl gracefully. Sidling up to the smiling Miss Sweet Pea, the young Mr. Hollyhock frolics gaily and swings her around and around, until she begs for a rest. At the same time, the stately foxglove sashays to the beat, grabbing Miss Daffodil by her long stem, and impressing her with his foxtrot. Miss Snapdragon twitters in circles, snapping her fingers to the melodic sounds.

Chasing Rabbit stares in amazement as the flowers waltz past—fluttering to the offbeat rhythms.

A thorny red rose approaches, with its reddish brown stem, bows deeply and asks, "Would you honor me with a dance, Miss Rabbit?"

"Sounds wonderful," she says, carefully avoiding his sharp thorns. She takes his prickly stem—and off they go, twirling gaily, shuffling to the beat of the intoxicating sounds. Chasing Rabbit dances with abandon, heels kicking, toes tapping, fingers popping. She bops about until she is out of breath. "How delightful, Mr. Rose!" she says, slightly winded. "Thank you ever so much for the dance."

By now, the music is slowly fading as all the flowers float to the ground—their thirsty roots sliding into the moist soil. A willowy wisteria glides next to her, panting. Its leggy roots grab her toe, pulling it with her into the soft mound. Nibbling at her toe is a bright green worm that pops his head up and winks at her with his violet eyes, then wiggles back into the ground and is gone.

Chasing Rabbit smiles as the flowers slurp noisily. After drinking their fill, they stretch their long willowy stems and wave goodbye—petals still dripping. Then, in a blink of glittering pollen, they simply vanish into thin air.

Alone now, she looks into the distance and sees the whirling light reappear, motioning for her to follow. This time she walks through a labyrinth of turns and twists, peaks and valleys, until she comes upon a winding path that shimmers and sparkles— blinding her each time she takes a step. Crossing over a moss-covered bridge, she stops to behold thousands of butterflies, their golden wings whirling over her head. Through the dense maze of wings, she sees an amazing sight—a forest of crystal trees with enormous trunks, silver branches, and leaves of spun gold. Each branch is dripping with glittering orbs and silvery stars. Chasing Rabbit twirls in circles around this extraordinary vision. "Everywhere I go, something even more unusual happens than before." Delighting in her extraordinary adventure, she still can't imagine where she is, or where she is going.

Continuing on, she follows the beckoning light, and comes upon a dazzling waterfall, flowing to the sound of beating drums. *Boom-ba-ba-boom!* The sound is so loud she covers her ears to block out the noise. Bending down, she looks into the water—to her amazement it stops flowing—and to her relief, the booming stops as well.

Curious what is in there, she nudges her way closer to the waterfall and peers into the stream. Splashing her hands in the water, laughing boisterously, she is taken off guard when the water rises up and sprays her in the face. *This doesn't feel like water, at all,* she thinks, giggling, as she examines the waxy droplets. Suddenly the waterfall reverses course and begins flowing backwards, chiming softly now, and turning iridescent in color. Mesmerized by the pulsating water, she watches it as it keeps changing course. *This place is magical,* she thinks, *but I wish I could remember how I got here.*

Something wispy touches her cheek and, when she looks up, she is staring into the eyes of a magnificent Indian, smiling at her. His baritone voice sounds like a well-tuned bass violin. "Welcome to the otherworld, my dear."

She looks into his face and thinks he seems vaguely familiar—as if from stories told long ago. But what did he mean by "otherworld"?

The man's eagle feathers frame his face, falling gracefully to his feet. Around his neck he wears a beautiful necklace made of bear claws. Chasing Rabbit stares at the bear claws for a moment, in wonder. Then her eyes fall to an elegant white buffalo, patterned with silk stitches on the front of his shirt. She swears she heard the animal snort as the handsome Indian gestures for her to follow. They walk down a path to a lush garden filled with giant stools, taller than she, where he motions for her to sit. She picks a particularly large, squishy mushroom, garnet in color, over five feet high, and scrambles up the velvety stool before sinking down in the middle. Aloft the strangely comfortable seat, Chasing Rabbit is enjoying herself as she waits for the man to speak.

"My name is Broken Feather. I am your grandfather from many moons past. I have lingered out here in the ethers to watch over you. I know you must be curious about why you are here, so let me show you your life that once was. Then you will know. Come."

Chasing Rabbit slips off the squishy mushroom and stands next to her grandfather. As he cups his hands together, she squints, looking carefully into the folds of his palms. At first, the images are a hazy blur. Then, everything clears. She is able to see a woman smiling and a man holding her. She cannot recall who those people are until Broken Feather taps her head and brings her memories flooding back.

Peering inside his hands again, she sees her short life pass before her eyes. She sees her mother and father, first as she was as a little girl happily playing with her friends, and now smiling no more. Next, she observes herself at the boarding school. She feels a shudder. Then, all too soon, she sees her life ending—and feels numb.

Remembering everything now, she asks sadly, "Why did this happen to me if you were watching over me? I was not ready to die."

Broken Feather says, "I cannot interfere with your destiny, my dear. Only you can choose which path to follow. The bear claw was your protection, but you let it go to help another. That was a courageous thing to do, but it also was your demise."

"What about Otter? Did you help her, as well? Did she come here, too?"

"Otter followed a different path, and has already departed to a place beyond. When the time is right you will be reunited."

Chasing Rabbit bends down and, peering closer, sees Little

Moon crying and feels a profound sadness for her friend. She pleads with Broken Feather to let her return so she can comfort her.

"I'm sorry," he says. "You are no longer of that world, and I cannot let you go."

"I beg you. Let me go for just a minute. Then I will return. I must help her. Please."

A second later, Chasing Rabbit glides next to Little Moon. She caresses her hair and says, "Do not mourn for me, Little Moon. I am with my grandfather, and the dancing flowers and the crystal trees." She kisses her head, but without response, so she blows as hard as she can on Little Moon's face. For a moment she sees her friend look in her direction, sensing her presence—if only for a fleeting second. Chasing Rabbit calls out and reaches her hand toward the girl—to touch her tear-streaked face. Then, just as quickly, Chasing Rabbit is drawn back to her ethereal place where Broken Feather awaits.

"We must go now," he says, taking her hand. "I have much to tell you."

Chasing Rabbit looks up, bewildered. "I still don't understand why this happened to me."

"In time, you will know more, my dear… in time. Look over there," he says, pointing toward the east. "A new star has appeared in the sky, glistening brightly. That star is special. I called it 'mastincala wichahpi'. The ancients sent this as a gift for you, and it twinkles as bright as your eyes. The color is sapphire. It will light up the horizon and shine on the earth for eons to come. You lived a life of bravery, and endured much for one so young. You will never be forgotten."

DARING RIDE

HIDDEN SPIRIT AND his wild mustang gallop into the night as heavy clouds bluster in the sky, teeming with bolts of lightning and thunder. Ferocious winds howl around them.

White Cloud had warned his son of many dangers awaiting him, but Hidden Spirit brushes away his concern saying, "I will be watchful, father. Please do not worry."

The ominous dark clouds race eastward in sync with rider and horse and the boy's cries mix with the thunder, reverberating across the desolate plain. Boy and horse—wild and free—flying with the wind, as hooves beat rhythmically across the rocky ground beneath them. A sheet of lightning cracks in the night, and Hidden Spirit spurs his horse even faster, on to breathtaking speeds. The moon hovers in between the clouds, and the valley is surrounded by glimmers of light casting mysterious shadows, as unearthly shapes float past. Boy and horse—earth and sky—meld into one.

Raising his arms upward, calling out to the spirits, Hidden Spirit lets off a searing cry—resounding deep across the ethers and into the night sky. On this magical night, a clap of thunder booms its commanding response to the boy's haunting cries.

Sensing his rider's urgency, the horse strives to go ever swiftly through the tree-lined shadows—hooves barely touching the ground as the rain pelts hard against his face.

The horse had appeared at his father's house a few days before Hidden Spirit was to leave for boarding school. People were in awe of the handsome gelding, and whispered excitedly that the horse was something truly special. They believed he carried a certain mystique and that he surely was a gift from the Great Spirit. Hidden Spirit knew the horse was special the moment he laid eyes on the animal, and he thanked the Great Spirit for his mysterious gift.

The painted mustang is a beauty—the color of warm autumn leaves spun with golden browns and bright patches of white on his back. His vivid blue, wide-set eyes express intelligence and his muscular body exudes stamina and durability. When Hidden Spirit looks into the horse's keen eyes, he sees answers indicative of one so wise. And when he whispers, "*hanblecheyapi*," the horse seems to understand and bobs his head in reply, making the boy laugh.

"You remind me of Crazy Horse, the one that goes into battle in a maze of bullets, and comes out unharmed. So, my sturdy horse, I will call you Ghost Dancer, the invisible one." He pats his long, sleek neck and the horse shakes his head and whinnies—then nibbles his hand. "Are you hungry, or is it that you like your new name?" The horse nudges him again. "Maybe it's both."

With the nights getting colder, Hidden Spirit pulls the thick buffalo robe his grandfather had given him tighter around himself, and clicks his tongue. Ghost Dancer takes off in a gallop.

Over the next few days, boy and horse skirt towns now dotted with new settlers, arriving by the hundreds. Whenever he hears a train roaring past, Hidden Spirit slides behind the trees and watches the belching smoke rise with plumes of black stench.

His fists tighten as he observes the railcars filled with hunters and armed soldiers on the lookout for any remaining buffalo and stray Indians. He reaches for his bow and arrow, wishing he could stop the invasion of these parasites. If he could, he would kill them all, but he has other concerns now—like his sister, Little Moon, and his beloved Morning Star. *Besides*, he thinks, *there are too many of these invaders, and I don't have enough arrows to kill them all.*

When evening comes, the boy and horse ride on through wooded areas filled with poplars, towering pines, and white birch. Occasionally they come across a grizzly or a mountain lion, making Ghost Dancer skittish. In the daytime, determined to make good time, and hide from the white eyes, they traverse the steep and windy hills filled with deep flowing rivers and meadows alive with brilliant fall colors.

A few weeks into the ride Hidden Spirit notices Ghost Dancer is starting to limp, but it is so slight and the boy is in such a hurry that he pays little mind and continues to ride on, tirelessly. He senses that the girls are in trouble and he has to reach them.

By the end of the next day, Ghost Dancer is limping more noticeably and Hidden Spirit stops to examine the injured leg. "I have ridden you too hard, my wild friend. I let carelessness get in the way of urgency." He rubs the horse's flank, damp with the ride. "I will make you a poultice, a special one," he says, gently patting the horse's head. "We will rest a couple of days so you can mend. I will find the powerful herbs to heal you quickly."

He takes Ghost Dancer further into the woods, far enough away from the main road, surrounded by dense shrubs and a cluster of oak trees. Glancing back warily, a stab of guilt fills him as he sees his horse hobbling badly now. Gazing appreciatively at Ghost Dancer, he asks, "Where did you come from, wild one?

Did the Great Spirit send you from the beyond, or maybe it was Broken Feather?" He stares at the horse a moment longer, brushing his nose, soft as velvet. "Well, wherever you came from, I need to get you well."

Bending over the horse, Hidden Spirit turns his attention to the injured leg and studies it for a few moments, touching the tendons. It concerns him greatly that the skin is hot. Closing his eyes, he prays in silence for his grandfather's guidance; asking him to reveal the secret herb to make his poultice. He sits in silence, waiting, and prays some more. Then he hears the sound of a muffled voice and feels something drop beside him—charged with mystical energy. Hidden Spirit smiles, and looks up to see a wavering shadow. He hears, "My son, inside this pouch is a berry filled with poison and power. The Great Spirit hides the berry well. You must use it with great caution, for it can kill as well as heal."

Holding the bag to the light, Hidden Spirit ponders the contents, then grasps the pouch tightly in his hands, praying a moment longer. Then, intuitively, he knows which of the berries to use, and unties it with great care. The bag is old and ancient—full of timeless remedies—along with assorted sweet grasses, salves, bark, roots, and berries. Hidden Spirit inhales their pungent odors, filling his nostrils with the powerful scent. He smiles with delight. Then he holds up the special berry to the light, and feels its power radiate up—grateful for the gift from the spirits. Carefully placing it on the ground, he takes another pouch from which he pours a small amount of its sticky contents onto the berries, and sings softly—mixing it until it bubbles. *It is indeed powerful*, he thinks and stirs some more.

Ghost Dancer seems anxious and paws the ground.

"Steady there," Hidden Spirit says, soothing the nervous

horse. "Is it a mountain lion out there that bothers you, or just the salve? It's not going to hurt, you know. It just smells awful."

Out of the corner of his eye, Hidden Spirit sees a movement in the brush and dismisses it, deep in thought about Ghost Dancer's injury and his poultice. Adding the last of the herbs, he smears the concoction onto the injury and wraps the horse's leg with strips of supple deerskin. He knows it will be dangerous to stay here too long, and he prays for Ghost Dancer to heal swiftly.

Suddenly, Ghost Dancer lets off a shrill whinny. From the cover of the trees, a nasally voice shouts out. "Stick 'em up real high, and don't move a twitch, or I'll shoot."

Hidden Spirit tenses, recognizing the voice. His mind reels, realizing his bow and arrow are lying by the tree. He glances out of the corner of his eyes, calculating his ability to reach for his bow. Then, without another thought, he lunges. His hand is just inches away from his arrows before an explosion of pain burst forth, sending him to his knees. Will kicks him in the ribs with the heel of his boot and Hidden Spirit reels over. A white burst of pain sears through his head before he blacks out.

A splash of water awakens him. He groans at the throbbing pain in his temple and he touches the back of his head where a huge bloodied lump surfaces, spewing blood. His face is bruised and swollen. As his vision wavers and his eyes slowly clear, he sees Will's face slip in and out of focus.

"Well, well, got ya, at last. You ain't gettin' away from me this time, and you ain't gonna try some kinda spell-like trickery either. I'm gonna give you a ride back to town you won't likely forget." Will gives Hidden Spirit a hard kick to his stomach, for emphasis, and then binds his hands and feet together in a slip knot, pulling the rope so tight it cuts off his blood flow—making his arms go numb.

A rustling in the bushes sends Will whirling around and

grabbing for his gun—then grins as he slides it back into his holster, and whistles. A handsome horse with startling blue eyes emerges from the bushes, nickering. Will and the horse stare at each other for a moment, then, limping slightly, Ghost Dancer walks up to Hidden Spirit. "Not only found a runaway Injun, but a fine piece of horseflesh, to boot," says Will with pride. He admires the muscular horse and its sturdy gait, and watches as it nuzzles the boy, nickering and clacking its teeth. "Damn well looks like he's talkin' Injun talk," Will says, raising his brows, still staring at the horse. "A bunch o' horseshit talk, for sure."

As Will nears, Ghost Dancer draws back his ears in warning.

"No need to be skittish, horsey," says Will, reaching out to grab the bridle. As Ghost Dancer backs away, Will tiptoes, inching his way closer, cajoling the horse. He grins nastily, "Come here, horsey. Wanna carrot?"

A trail of mist emits from Ghost Dancer's quivering nostrils as Will walks to his own horse, grabs a coil of rope and a whip from his saddle, and swings it around. "This is my lucky day, fer sure. Hot diggity dog." Easing his way toward the snorting horse, Will watches him warily as he slowly uncoils his rope, swinging the noose overhead. First to the left, then to the right, and high in the air—making larger loops at each pass. "Come on, horsey. Gonna getcha now." Will throws the rope, but it lands short and falls to the ground. "Damn."

Ghost Dancer is trotting in circles, nervously, as Will steps squarely in front of him. He whirls the rope high above his head, allowing the noose to widen, and—bam! The rope lands around the horse's neck. "Gotcha."

Screaming wildly, Ghost Dancer stands on his hind legs, pawing and kicking at the air.

"Settle down now, fella," says Will, shouting. "You ain't goin' nowhere." Will's breath comes in jagged gulps, as he fights like a madman to hold onto the bucking horse. Winded and aggravated, he hollers at him. "Settle down, or I'll bust you with my whip!"

There is no letting up with the horse, so Will struggles to grab his whip, hooks it around his shoulder, and snaps it back—filling the air with a sharp crack.

Ghost Dancer squeals and flails against the rope, his hoofs thrashing wildly. His left flank knocks into Will, sending his captor and hat flying across the ground.

Will rights himself and screams, yanking out his gun. "You're a stupid damn horse an' I oughta shoot ya right here an now. Saw you up fer a hunk a meat."

The horse shakes his flowing blond mane and paws the ground in defiance.

Having had enough of this nonsense, Will sees that the rope is still around Ghost Dancer's neck, so he grabs hard on it, pulling the fighting horse toward him. When the horse is close, he sticks his big revolver to the side of his face, and smirks. "Lucky I don't shoot ya." Then he shoves the gun between the horse's vivid blue eyes. "Ya better stand still now, cause yer makin' me boilin' mad." Will tightens the rope around Ghost Dancer's neck, wraps it around his hand and pulls hard, causing the horse's ears to go back and his nostrils to flare. Ghost Dancer stands erect, his long blond tail swishing softly back and forth. Then before Will can think or shoot, the horse starts to sway into a dance, all the while keeping his gaze locked on Will's, as his heels clomp on the ground.

Will stares wide-eyed at the horse in disbelief, and sputters. "What the devil?... Looks like the dang horse is dancing." He isn't sure if he should laugh or worry. *I must be drunker than I thought. Either that, or I'm seeing things.*

Ghost Dancer now moves in circles, hooves sending out a

sharp hollow sound while clopping on the ground—faster and faster. Then the mustang rotates, twists his long neck, and slides his wide sloping shoulders down. Before Will can react, the horse leaps free of the rope.

Rope still in hand, Will slaps it on the ground and watches incredulously as the horse prances off down the road. *Looks like that gol-dang horse is playing some sort of a game, tryin' to trick me, like his Injun buddy.* He opens his mouth to holler, and then shuts it, instead—his mind reeling with confusion. He looks down the road, and sees the horse click up its heels and buck a few times. Then he stops abruptly, turns around, and lets off a loud whinny. *That blasted horse is plum crazy.*

A shaken Will clears his eyes, then hollers at Hidden Spirit, kicking the dirt. "Yer gonna be mighty sorry... you and that damn stupid horse! He's nothin' but a crafty bag-o-bones." Will's hands shake as he coils his rope around Hidden Spirit, ties it to his saddle horn, and hops upon his mount. Looking back, he curses at Hidden Spirit. "Yer a sneaky son-a-bitch and yer horse is just as sneaky. No one makes a fool outta me... 'specially a lousy horse and a no-good Injun. You best hold on." Will slaps the reins, yelling, "Giddy-up." They take off like a rocket.

The momentum throws Hidden Spirit spiraling into the air and down again, landing him hard on his shoulder. It's as if Hidden Spirit is nothing more than a sack of potatoes as he skids across the arid plains, behind the horse. Before Hidden Spirit can catch his breath they hit another hole and he slams hard against the ground again.

Will kicks the side of his horse and urges it to speed up. The horse jumps across a log and Hidden Spirit feels his ribs crack. His buckskin shirt is torn into shreds and his back is a mass of bloodied raw flesh with a few shards of skin hanging loose. The punishing ride has taken its toll.

After going a few miles, Wigley slows his horse—his agitation dwindling. He is thinking that what he saw wasn't real. *It didn't really happen. Just crazy Indian shit, that's all. Plus, my nerves are shot.* To ease his troubling thoughts, he whistles out his frustration. "Gettin' a might thirsty, though." He pulls out a big jug of hooch, and takes a big, long drink. "Whoo-whee. That outta settle me down. Need it bad after this bat-shit crazy day." Holding onto the jug, Will looks back at Hidden Spirit, and hollers. "Say, ya wanna drink?" Smacking his hand on his leg, he says, "Heard tell whiskey makes you Injuns go plum crazy. Don't want no crazy Injun goin' loco while I'm around. Seen that before. Bet yer ass is sore, though." He let off a loud snort, and takes another gulp of his hooch.

Hidden Spirit lies behind Will's horse, barely able to open his eyes. He stifles his pain through gritted teeth as he passes in and out of darkness. Not sure he can make it, he steels himself to endure a little longer and prays through laborious gasps of breath. "Please help. I'm not ready to die," he whispers weakly. "Not like this." Blood drips from his mouth onto the ground, pooling bright red. "Don't let me die," he says, gasping. "Not now... I have..." His words trail off as Wigley kicks the side of his horse and starts running again. A moment later Hidden Spirit's head slams against a rock, sending a cry spiraling throughout the valley, into the wind and beyond. His eyes glaze over and then roll back.

A snap of lightning flares, awakening the ethers. Another bolt of lightning bursts forth, sending feathers flying out of the brilliant shards of lightning—along with a thump.

Oblivious, Will belches and takes another drink, swaying in the saddle. "How's it goin' back there, Injun? Yer kinda quiet." Will holds onto the saddle horn and, as his horse trots along, he belts out a song.

"Oh, pretty lady, would ya be my bride?

I'm a little tipsy, but I'll take ya fer a ride.

Ooohhh, sassy lady, would ya be my bride...?"

Smacking his leg to the tune, Will suddenly yanks back on the reins. "Whoa, Nellie. All that singin' makes me thirsty. An' I gotta take a leak."

Will staggers off his horse, hanging tight to the saddle horn. He rubs his eyes, looks curiously at the Indian boy, and slurs. "Say, cat got yer tongue?"

No answer.

Angry, Will walks over to Hidden Spirit and nudges him with the tip of his boot. Chortling, he bends down and peers at the boy through puffy red eyes. "Well, I'll be doggoned. Looks like yer a dead one. I'd leave ya fer the wolves, but they'd probably spit out your nasty tastin' red skin." He snickers at his remark. "Anyways, I'm gonna show Peale I finally gotcha. Show him I've..." Will stops mid-sentence, scrunching his eyes in disbelief, looking down the road. "There's that damn horse. I oughtta shoot him on account o' he tricked me." Trying to focus, he lets off a shrill whistle. "Here, horsey. How 'bout I shoot ya an' you can go with yer dead friend over there?" Will grins, sliding his .38 colt, out of his holster.

Ghost Dancer stops a few yards away, lifts his head high in the air, and nickers. Will steadies his hand, aims his gun, and cracks a laugh. "Guess yer gonna be a dead one, like yer Injun friend," he says irritably, and fires. The gun lets off a couple of blasts and the bullets whizz through the air. Ghost Dancer bobs his head to the left, then to the right, like he's dodging the bullets, then the horse curls his lips back showing his large teeth—grinning.

"How'd that happen?" Will wonders in alarm, looking at the horse who doesn't have a nick on him, then looks down at his gun, smoking.

Ears laid back, Ghost Dancer shakes his head wildly, sending his yellow mane fluttering in the breeze and paws the ground—huge blue eyes flaring, ready to charge.

Will backs up nervously, and stumbles. Sweat breaks out on his forehead and, before he gets a chance to aim his colt and fire another round, the animal lunges straight at Will—fast as a racehorse. Will scrambles to get out of the way, but not in time. The flailing hooves knock him on his backside—landing him in the scrub. Will groans and shouts at him, furiously, "Ya lousy bag o' bones. Yer worse than them Injuns! Ya need to be put out of your misery."

Ghost Dancer nickers at the raging Will—clacks his teeth together and lifts his forelegs like he prancing, and then starts pawing the ground.

Rubbing his rear, Will untangles himself and hobbles along, spluttering. "I don't care about that Injun' or you—you damn crazy horse. I'm gettin' the hell outta here." He scurries over to his mount. Just as he's ready to hop onto his back, he stops mid-stride, and watches in horror as a whirling mass of black feathers appear from out of nowhere, and linger near the boy. Hackles start to rise on the back of his neck. Will looks around, wondering what might happen next and cautiously slides his leg around the horse. "Gotta get outta here, and I mean pronto. Strange shit's goin' on." Then from the corner of his eye, he sees a stick hurtling through the air, like it's doing somersaults, coming straight at him. Will slams his body to the ground, covering his head. He yelps as the stick whizzes past, just inches from his face. In record time, Will hops onto his horse and races down the road, sending pebbles and dirt flying in his wake.

Ghost Dancer bobs his head, as if in satisfaction, nickers, and then trots over to Hidden Spirit and nudges the boy's arm. Whinnying softly, he circles around him and nudges him again.

The lifeless boy lies unresponsive in a tangled mass of blood and dirt. Letting off a shrill whinny, the horse hunkers down next to the boy, clacking his teeth, occasionally nudging his body.

All is silent now, except for the gentle nickering of the horse.

The sky in the west is growing dark, as heavy black clouds loom precariously in the distance. Within minutes the clouds race eastward, sending winds blustering and hailstones the size of small rocks. Out of the howling winds and clouds and hail, a noble figure emerges, drifting toward the ground. The face of a warrior appears. It's Broken Feather, draped head to toe in a brilliant mass of golden eagle feathers. He glides over, hovering above Hidden Spirit. Broken Feather, full of pain, laments. "Oh, my grandson! What have they done?" Stifling a sob, the warrior gathers Hidden Spirit gently in his arms, cradling him against his chest, crooning softly.

As Broken Feather holds the boy, a breeze begins to stir, ruffling the branches of an alder tree. A solemn murmur vibrates, and the sound floats around the figures, wrapping them in a gift from the ancients. They whisper about the spirit beings and their great mysteries to behold from the unknown and beyond—secrets only the ancients know. Then, Broken Feather sings for an hour his mournful melody, while holding tightly to his grandson. He pulls the sticky hair covering Hidden Spirit's face—matted with blood and dirt—and blows lightly onto his skin until the blood disappears. Then he sprinkles a fine misty powder. Crooning softly, he sings about the crows—about their magical powers, their uncanny wisdom. Then he moves his hands over the boy's face—first in a clockwise motion, then counter-clockwise. He sits there with his grandson until the sun starts to sink in the west, leaving a golden hue.

Then the crows begin to gather, clucking and chattering, filling the trees with their noise, while hopping from one leg to another. Pulling tufts of feathers from their wings and their backs, the crows send them soaring through the air. Other crows gather—fifty or more, then hundreds. They perch on a nearby bristlecone pine, their strong scaly feet wrapped around the thick branches. A bustle of feathers float by, wavering above the boy, while other feathers look to be dancing. One by one, the feathers glide near Hidden Spirit, lightly dusting the raw flesh with their smooth, silky tips to seal the cuts. One particularly long and fluffy feather with silvery black plumage sweeps a sprinkle of ash into the scrapes and the deep gashes that cover his back. After much kneading and pecking, the gashes close, leaving only a trail of bright red streaks where the open wounds had been. The crows start cawing—their triumph caws, echoes through the air.

A trembling of cries is heard through the mist as Chasing Rabbit looks down from the other world, and screams. "Hidden Spirit, my brother, who did this awful thing?" She zooms down and her cheeks brush against his, tears splash onto his face. "You are dead," she says in amazement. Touching his face gently with her translucent hand, she whispers, "I can hardly believe it. You were my hero. I thought you could never die."

Broken Feather looks at his granddaughter sadly and then softly scolds her. "My dear, please go back to where you belong. It is dangerous for you to be down here. I know you are anxious to see your brother, but the dark ones are gathering. I do not want you to get swept away by their tentacles and their malicious intent."

At the flick of his hand, he sends Chasing Rabbit soaring back into the other-world, her voice trailing through the clouds, calling out, "Hidden Spirit, I love you."

Gently touching the boy's forehead, Broken Feather says, "Mi-thakoza. It is between you and the Great Spirit—whether you are to stay or go the way of the light. I can do no more.

You are loved by the ancients in the hereafter and by the ones who walk the earth. Remember, my son, you were destined for greatness. The choice is yours to make. As darkness nears, Broken Feather wraps Hidden Spirit in a cloak of dusty hues, filled with musty sage and sweet grass to protect him.

In a nebulous cloud of smoldering mist, a shower of glowing sparkles appears. It emits a strange phenomenon, weird and wonderful—even peculiar, with its inexplicable beam filled with the most unusual colors of sapphire and crimson. The crimson mist hovers above Broken Feather, wavering and glowing. In an instant, he vanishes into the ebbing light.

Then the crows gather around the boy, their sharp beaks raised to the sky. Shrill caws reverberate upwards, catapulting the cries throughout the air until the sound reaches the misty clouds. Upon hearing the desperate cries of the crows, the clouds shudder and mourn, then lightly drift down and surround the boy— while the crows continue to croon and caw softly... waiting... wondering which path Hidden Spirit will choose—will he travel to the spirit world, or continue his quest in this world?

THE END—TOKSA AKHE

About the Author

This novel came to me in a flash and without warning. It was a vision so vivid that I had no choice but to succumb to its power. I quit my job, sold my worldly possessions, and bought a used motorhome. With my dog, Billy Bob, I traveled thousands of miles to Alaska. My characters came to life in the beauty and serenity of the remote wilderness and solitude.

This was my first venture into writing and took fifteen years to complete. It was a long and arduous journey. Thoughts of giving up, at times, entered my mind, but my characters would not let me go. As one re-write turned into another, the first book in the Keeper of the Souls series, is, at long last, finished.

I sincerely hope the story will touch your heart and resonate with you for years to come.

40063658R00133

Made in the USA
Lexington, KY
24 May 2019